Mine

MARY CALMES

Dreamspinner Press

Published by
Dreamspinner Press
382 NE 191st Street #88329
Miami, FL 33179-3899, USA
http://www.dreamspinnerpress.com/

Mine

Cover Art by Reese Dante http://www.reesedante.com

ISBN: 978-1-61372-425-5

Printed in the United States of America
First Edition
March 2012

eBook edition available
eBook ISBN: 978-1-61372-426-2

This is a thank you to Amy, who inspires me to write better; to Ariel, who is always there for me; for Lori, who says the best things when I really need to hear them; and Anastasia, who gets asked strange questions and just goes with it. I appreciate you all.

Chapter ONE

IT WAS way too early for him to have the TV up so loud.

"Landry!" I yelled. "Remember the neighbors, babe!"

The noise didn't stop, though, and since I didn't want to hear from Mrs. Chun again (she'd bitched me out in Mandarin six times in the last month because the love of my life was a screamer), I rolled out of bed and walked toward the French doors that separated our bedroom from the living room. Only halfway there I realized it was freezing in the apartment. I pulled sweats on over my sleep shorts and yanked on my gray fleece hoodie before I staggered toward the door and opened it.

"Fuck you, Chris, get out!"

Okay, not the TV.

My boyfriend, partner, the man who had been with me for the last two years, was in the living room with another guy I had never seen before. The stranger was maybe six two, my height, brown haired, blue eyed, and utterly forgettable except that he was in my apartment.

"What's going on?" I asked them both.

Both men turned to me.

"Hi," the one I didn't know said, crossing the room fast, his hand out in an obvious offer for me to take. "I'm Christian Carter—Chris—Landry's brother."

Brother?

"It's great to meet you," he said.

"Pleasure," I said, sounding dazed because I kind of was.

"Don't touch him," Landry growled, bolting over, yanking our hands apart, and shoving Chris backward. "Just get the fuck out!"

"Wait," I ordered, grabbing Landry's arm, because it was a lot of volume for first thing in the morning. "You're his brother?" I asked Chris.

"Yes," he answered and smiled at me. "And I came to see him because our mother is sick, and she wants to see him."

I turned slowly to Landry.

"No no no, you don't get to look at me like that. This is bullshit."

"Your mother?"

"Baby." His voice bottomed out as he took my face in his hands, stepping in front of me. "Please do not say the word *mother* and think of the wonderful woman who raised you and loves me and get confused. My mother is not like yours; she does not give a fuck about me."

"That's not true," Chris chimed in hotly, and when I looked at him, I couldn't help it. I softened because after studying him, I realized how much he resembled my boyfriend.

It wasn't something you noticed right away. It took a few minutes of scrutiny, because what struck you first were the differences.

Landry Carter was six feet tall and had wavy, dark-blond hair that never, ever, did what he wanted it to. He had, like, eight cowlicks in it, so it sort of kicked out in all different directions, and he had given up trying to tame the thick mop years ago. Now he just washed it, ran product through it, and let it fall where it wanted. It hardly mattered, though, because when you were looking at him, you were staring at his eyes. Big, dark, expressive blue-green orbs that always crinkled to half their normal size when he was happy. The laugh lines around them were already deep at twenty-six. They were wicked with mischief and humor and constantly sparkled like he had a secret, and men and women were drawn to him like flies to honey. The man was decadent and irresistible and lit up rooms simply with his presence. Being a big extrovert helped. Not that he had always been that way; I knew that it was me giving him confidence that made him sometimes savagely loud. But he could get away with being occasionally obnoxious since he was so pretty to look at. An artist friend of ours had called him luminous once, and I agreed.

In comparison to Landry's beauty, his brother was sort of plain, but I saw, on closer inspection, the similarity in their sharp, chiseled features, crooked smiles, and long curly lashes.

"Trev," Landry said and took a breath.

"Let's just sit down," I said, grabbing Landry's hand, lacing my fingers into his and tugging him after me to the couch. I flopped down hard, pulling him with me so we were both eyeing the man who had followed and taken a seat on the loveseat across from us.

"Can you catch me up?" I asked Chris.

"Sure." He leaned forward, giving me a trace of a smile. "I'm Chris, like I said, and you're Trevan Bean, right?"

"I am," I assured him, tightening my hold on Landry's hand because the slight tremble in him let me know he needed it. "So talk to me about your mother, Chris."

He took a breath. "I flew in last night from Las Vegas because my father told me where Landry was, and he thought that it was better I came instead of him. I mean, you know, I wasn't the one who cut him off when he was eighteen."

I knew that part. My boyfriend had come out the night he graduated from high school, and his parents had lost their minds. He had been disowned, given a day to get whatever things of his he wanted out of their house, and informed that of course they would not be paying for college, and he could not take his car.

Hurt, lost, and alone, he had packed and left. He went from one friend's house to another the whole summer until he figured things out with the help of his high school guidance counselor and the financial aid advisor at the school he had already been accepted to, the University of Michigan. He had always planned to run away to the opposite side of the country once he graduated, but he hadn't expected to have to leave without a safety net. Landry knew who he was when he was fifteen, and even though his friends had told him that it would be okay, that of course his parents would accept him and love him, that his brothers and sister would never turn their backs on him, in the back of his mind, he never actually believed it. So even though he was sad—devastated—he was also resigned to the betrayal of a lifetime of having been told he would always have his family. He was not an optimist, the man I loved; he was a realist, and he knew what was going to happen.

He bought a used Honda Civic hatchback, stuffed it full of everything that was priceless, and drove away without looking back. That was eight years ago, and now he was twenty-six and that time had blown by without a word. They had never checked on him, not once. He hadn't sent them an announcement when he got his bachelor's degree, opened his business, or launched his website. They were the past; I was his future. They were not important to him, as he obviously wasn't to them. His real family, he told people all the time, was mine.

My mother adored him and my sister wanted to marry him. We spent every holiday with my family, had friends that were originally mine that were now his, and between his business and my job, we had finally saved enough to buy a house in Berkley, which was a suburb of Detroit. We were supposed to meet with a Realtor the following week to start looking at candidates for home sweet home. Everything was on track, so I was not crazy about Chris, the long-lost brother, being there, but since everything happened for a reason, as my father had always said, I just needed to keep an open mind.

"My mother is sick, Trevan," Chris said to me. "And she wants to see her son."

I turned to look at my boyfriend.

"No," he said to me.

"Love," I said gently.

"Fuck no!" he yelled, getting up.

"Where are you—"

"I'm gonna go make you some coffee before you pass out," he grumbled. "You shouldn't even be awake yet."

And he was right: I did need coffee. Just to try to remain vertical after the night before, I needed vast quantities of caffeine. The guys I had collected from at two in the morning had been partying hard, and along with their payment of a grand each plus the *juice*, the 20 percent they owed the house when they lost, they had graciously offered me a line to help drive away the exhaustion. It was a nice gesture, but I had been too poor to ever pick up cocaine as a habit, and now, on the verge of having everything I wanted, the idea of even flirting with an addiction to a thousand dollar a week habit did not sound appealing. Plus, my boy didn't do drugs. He was a very good influence on me in more ways than one. I had plans to open up a restaurant, and nothing, especially a monkey on my back, was going to sidetrack me.

I looked back at Chris. "So talk to me."

"Look, I didn't come here to upset him, and I know he's still very angry, but I really need you to help me convince him to come to Las Vegas. He needs to see my mother, see my folks. She needs to talk to him and make amends and get our family reunited and back on track. It's what she wants, and we all want her to have it."

I rubbed the top of my head, which was a nervous habit of mine, before grinding the heel of my hand into my left eyebrow. I was tired, which wasn't helping me figure out what to do or say. "You have to think about it from his side, right? If your mother wasn't sick, would they be talking?"

He took a breath. "I understand, but she's in remission, so, you know, now's the time."

I looked at him. "Remission?"

"Yeah."

"What kind of cancer?"

"Leukemia."

I took a breath. "I'm so sorry."

There was only a quick nod in response.

"Here," Landry announced as he returned, passing me a steaming cup that smelled like a lot of things besides coffee. He had obviously already had it made, as we didn't have a time machine in our kitchen.

I looked up at him as he sank down onto the arm of my couch.

"There's cinnamon in it," he said, "and I used the vanilla creamer you like."

I nodded before I took a sip. "Thanks. Why don't you get your brother one, 'cause he looks like he could use it, while I go make a call."

His usually blue-green wonderland eyes flicked to Chris. To see them clouded and flat pained me. "Do you want coffee?"

"Please."

He got up again, his hand sliding over the top of my head. My hair was buzzed close to my skull and I knew he liked the feel of it under his fingers as many times as he'd told me. "Your phone is right there; you dumped it when you came in doing your shuffling zombie impression."

I smiled at him and reached for my iPhone on the coffee table.

"But don't call," he ordered. "Text. I don't want you to get stuck talking."

"Yessir."

"Knock it off," he snapped irritably. "And we're gonna talk about you smoking again."

"I wasn't smoking," I assured him. "I was just in and out of a lot of back rooms and clubs last night. I quit. I told you I would, and I did."

"Okay," he said as he went through the swinging door into the kitchen.

Watching him, I realized that he must have been in bed with me before he got up. He was still dressed in his flannel pajama bottoms, a long-sleeved T-shirt, and heavy wool socks. But this was November in Royal Oak, Michigan, so it was already cold. By December Landry would have the space heaters out of storage. The radiator was not enough to keep the apartment the toasty warm that he liked it to be.

"Sorry," I said to Chris as I punched in the security code on my phone. "I won't be long."

"Sure," he replied, smiling at me.

I just needed to send a message with my total for the night. I was carrying close to sixty grand, but I sent the message that I had thirty and knew that when they saw the net, somebody would call to arrange a pickup. Usually I never carried even thirty, much less double that, but more than one of my usual clients had finally paid what they owed me. I had been floating several guys for a couple of weeks, and it was nice that they had all come through as promised. I had never thought, as close to the holidays as we were now, that they would all make good on their debts. It was a testament to the relationship we had that no one had welshed. It wasn't my favorite thing to do, pay other guys' vouchers to the house, but I didn't like to be a hardass and collect with muscle unless I had to.

"Done," I told Chris, putting the phone face down on my right thigh.

"So, Trevan." He squinted at me. "What is it you do?"

What to say. "I'm in collections," I answered vaguely, so not wanting to get into it.

"Like, what kind?"

"He's a runner," Landry supplied as he walked back into the room with a cup of coffee for Chris and one for himself. He passed his brother a small mug and put his enormous café au lait cup down on the coffee table before leaning back beside me so his back was pressed into the left side of my chest.

I put my hand in his soft, silky mop of hair, pushing it back out of his face, pulling his head down into my shoulder. The sigh that came up out of him made me smile, and watching his eyes close was very satisfying.

"You collect for a bookie?" Chris asked me, dragging my attention away from my boyfriend, who was basically thrumming with need.

"Yes, that's what a runner is."

"Do you carry a gun?" Chris wanted to know, scrutinizing my face.

"No, that's asking for trouble." I shook my head. "And most of the time I don't get into any. I have regulars, and it's not a big deal. When I do need backup, I have a friend that comes with me. My boss is a businessman. He gets the line from Vegas; guys bet with me once they know what it is; some lose, some win; I collect what's owed."

"It's still illegal," Chris reminded me.

"True," I agreed, "but in all seriousness, with no record and the extent of my crime being the movement of money from point A to point B... what do you really think the cops would do to me if they caught me?"

"I guess not much."

"Not that I want to find out, but I also must point out that the number of cops I collect from is vast." I waggled my eyebrows at him.

"Is that how you met Landry?" he asked me with a trace of a smile. "Is he a closet gambling addict?"

"Hardly," I assured him. "No, we met the old-fashioned way, at a party, and I couldn't keep my eyes off him."

"Eyes," my boyfriend scoffed, nestling closer, turning his head to kiss my cheek.

"What?" I chuckled.

He turned to face me, his left hand reaching, fingers trailing over the right side of my face as he leaned forward so his lips could open on the side of my neck.

"I'm here," I soothed him, my voice soft, coaxing. "Baby, I'm here."

He nodded, and I heard him breathe. He had been holding his breath, seconds away from a full-blown panic attack that I had missed because I was tired. Normally, I would have been passed out in bed, and he would have gotten up and done his morning ritual and then kissed me before he left. As long as everything went along smoothly, nothing out of the ordinary, familiar sights and sounds, the normal pacing of his day, he was good, he was fine. But if there were changes, bumps, like a blast from the past, it was possible for him to combust. The breakdown I had just quelled was his typical reaction to glitches in his life, at least for as long as I'd known him. If I was there, he reached for me, I soothed him, and he took a breath and went on. It had been like that since we met.

I COULD remember the night he finally saw me like it was yesterday. He was waiting near the keg at a party we were both at, and I walked up beside him, grabbed a handful of his gorgeous ass, and when he turned to look at me, I asked him if he could see me.

"Yeah," he chuckled. "I can feel your fingers too."

"Are you sure you see me? I've been to a lot of parties you've been at, and it's like I'm invisible," I told him, not moving my hand, instead sliding my middle finger over the crease slowly, suggestively. "I wanna make sure to leave an impression this time."

His breath quavered, which made my mouth dry. "Consider it made."

"Lemme get this for you," I said, letting him go and bumping him gently with my shoulder. "I'll meet you outside on the balcony."

"It's cold out there."

"It's quiet. I'll keep you warm."

"You're fulla shit."

I tipped my head toward the sliding glass door anyway.

He left me then, heading for the patio. I got his beer and another Crown and Coke for me, grabbed my parka, and followed him out. He was shivering when I reached him, and when he exhaled, I could see it. I put my coat around him and stepped close so I could watch him drink.

"What?" He smiled at me, sniffling in the cold.

"You're beautiful."

He scoffed. "You don't hafta flatter me; I'll suck your cock for you." He looked over his shoulder. "There's a corner over—"

"Yeah, I saw you doin' that at Jimmy Drake's party," I cut him off, fisting a hand in his heavy wool sweater so he couldn't move. "You were on your knees all night, huh?"

His eyes were back, finally actually meeting mine instead of looking everywhere but. I lifted my hand to his cheek and dragged my thumb over his gorgeous mouth. He had full lips, plump and dark and made to be kissed.

"How 'bout I kiss you and after that you can put *your* dick in *my* mouth."

The huge eyes—blue-green, a color I remembered from a cup I had glazed in a ceramics class in high school, peacock blue, an absolute sum of the two—absorbed my face. "You don't have to work this hard," he told me. "I give it away."

I grunted as I leaned in and took possession of the lips that had haunted my dreams. And he tasted like beer and peanuts with a hint of cherry Life Savers. I pulled away fast, took his beer back, put my drink on the table beside his, turned, and rushed him. My hands were on his face as I kissed him the second time, pile driving him into the wall, taking it all, his breath, his saliva, his whimpers and sighs. My tongue pushed and shoved his, tangling and stroking, as I ravaged him and took what I wanted. My hands went under his sweater, burrowed down beneath the T-shirt and found skin that was sleek, warm, and silky. His smooth stomach trembled under my hand, and when I shoved my knee between his thighs, his hoarse groan made me hard. I kissed him until he had to shove me off to breathe.

"Come home with me and lemme talk to you, because you're confused about stuff."

"Not confused," he panted, long, feathery lashes fluttering. "Whore."

"Not anymore," I told him, and kissed him breathless again. I sucked his tongue into my mouth, loosened his belt, worked his jeans open, and got my hand down into his briefs.

His gasp as I unsealed my mouth from his made me smile.

"You're treating me like a whore."

"I'm treating you like you're mine," I corrected him. "'Cause from now on... this only gets done with me."

"No one keeps me," he groaned, pushing up into my hand, eyes closed, mouth open, head back against the wall.

"Until now," I said, reclaiming his mouth, chewing on his lip. I didn't let him pull away until, between me jerking him off, putting hickeys on his neck, shoving my left hand down the back of his jeans, and sliding my fingers over his crease, he came in my fist with a shuddering, muffled yell.

"Jesus, you made me come with just your voice telling me to."

That and a hand job with some frottage thrown in for good measure.

"Fuck."

I chuckled and licked a line up the side of his neck to behind his ear, sucking the sensitive skin before returning to his sweet mouth. The man took direction well, and I liked that. I wiped my hand on the T-shirt I was wearing under my own sweater.

"What are you doing?" he snapped at me, shoving me away from him so he could take a gulp of air. "If you do that, you'll have my cum on you."

"It'll just be the first of many times, right?"

He whimpered in the back of his throat. "Nobody wants me. I'm all used up and—"

"Nope." I refused to hear it. "You're a light, you're my light, gonna be just mine."

The tears came so fast. "Who the fuck are you?"

"I'm the guy you've been blowing off for the last three months," I told him, watching him tuck himself in, now that his brain was working again, and zip up. It was a shame not to be looking at his beautiful, long cut cock anymore, but I didn't want anyone else getting an eyeful. "I told you, I see you all the time, everywhere, and you never gimme the time of day. I just got sick of it, figured it was time to do something about it."

He lunged at me, arms wrapped tight around my neck, face in the side of my shoulder. "I'm sorry. I'm so sorry... forgive me."

"Nothing to forgive, you didn't see me. Now you do."

"Now I do," he agreed and shivered hard.

"Your name is Landry, right?"

He nodded, pulling back from me.

"My name's Trevan. Buckle your belt, 'cause we're out of here."

And he kissed me, laid one on me that was full of trembling hope and happiness that maybe he could rest and stop running and stop being alone unless he was on his knees.

I had been watching him for a while, stalking him when we showed up at the same places, and had tried to talk to him on a number of occasions. But he was so busy giving himself to anyone who asked that I, a good guy, a patient guy, a gentleman, never blipped on his radar. Because I liked what I saw outwardly—he was really just beautiful—I had to see if there was anything else there at all. Normally, no one caught my eye or kept my interest, so the fact that he had, had to mean something. Upon investigation, I discovered things about him.

The man was not a drug addict, but he did them to fit in. He didn't really like to drink, but he did that too. He had vices that he could give up in a heartbeat because they were never his, just convenient excuses for others to put aside their inhibitions and use him. I told him no one but me was ever putting their hands on him again. The smile as he cried was heartbreaking and dazzling all at the same time.

Since he was the only reason I had gone to the party, once I buckled his belt for him—he hadn't followed the last of my directions, too busy launching himself at me—I took his hand and led him back through the crowd. When I felt him stop, I turned and saw some guy with his hand on Landry's bicep. Landry squeezed my hand tight, and I saw it in his eyes, the pleading. This was the very first test: was he really leaving with me, or would I let him go? It was funny but I never once thought, why didn't he just tell the guy no. I understood, he had to see what I would say, what I would do. He couldn't stick up for something, for the idea of us together, if he didn't know he could count on it.

"You know me?" I asked the guy there, the stranger holding onto my new boyfriend.

"No."

I shrugged. "And you don't wanna. Let go." My voice was flat, my stare was level, and I stilled, waiting.

The stranger took my measure. "Whatever." The guy balked and then turned to look at Landry. "I'll catch you later. I'll bring the lube and condoms."

But he didn't, because I took Landry Carter home with me, to my apartment, to my kitchen table where I fed him, and then to my bed to sleep.

"I thought you wanted to fuck me?" he asked worriedly, standing in my bedroom freshly showered and dressed in a pair of my pajamas.

"I wanna hold you," I said with a smile, grabbing his hand, yanking him down on top of me. When I rolled him over on his side and spooned around him, brushing the hair away from the back of his neck before I kissed it, I thought he was going to fly apart with the trembling.

"Oh God." He was back to crying.

I chuckled, and he took a heaving breath before snuggling back against me. When I woke up in the night, he was wrapped around me, head in the hollow of my neck, arm over me and leg over mine. He was very cute, and when I bent and kissed his forehead, Landry's sigh was deep and long and content.

He needed me, and I needed him just as badly. No one ever let me just love them because I could. Men looked at me and saw a guy without a "real" job, a guy with only a high school education, a guy without a future or prospects. I looked scary, dangerous, and so they walked the other way. No one ever took the time to know me, to learn about my plans and what I wanted my life to be. They wanted a guarantee. No one wanted to build on me—no one but Landry.

I told him it was because he was hard up.

He told me he was definitely hard.

"Perv."

"You would know."

Most of our conversations degraded to name-calling, tickling, water fights, food fights, pillow fights, kissing, groping, rubbing, and then him held down and begging. It had been working seamlessly for two years.

The first thing I did was remove him from his circle and put him into mine. It wasn't that my friends were paragons of virtue. They were not perfect. But they were loyal and trustworthy and dependable and true. They were also, it turned out, really possessive, just like I was. So when some guy put his hands on Landry in a club, by the time I got back from the bathroom, the guy had already been run off, humiliated, jeered at, and one time, because the guy wasn't hearing the no, hit. The message was clear: Landry Carter was no longer available, and he would not be passing himself around like a party favor anymore. He belonged to me and me alone.

In the two years we had been together, the changes in the man were stunning. After six months, I helped him live out his dream of opening his own jewelry store, and in midtown Detroit, in the middle of a recession, he still did well. There was an online catalog and a website, and you could visit the showroom and order custom pieces once you got there. When people wondered why I was so beautifully accessorized, I always told them. My triple-wrap leather bracelets were always complimented, and he said the best thing he ever did was make me wear them. I saw so many people, and they all saw my bracelets and asked me where to get one. As far as I knew, I was the only runner who carried his boyfriend's business card.

He was doing well. Business was booming, his jewelry was in several upscale boutiques downtown, and he had just hired a public relations firm to help him launch a new line geared to the department store crowd. I was very proud of him, and between my savings and his being on the cusp of greatness, we were poised to move, buy a house, buy other property, and start to see a change in our lifestyle from living paycheck to paycheck to having some extra cash in the bank. I had done my days of peanut butter and ramen noodles before I met him, but when we first moved in together, before he knew what he wanted to do, it had been both of us on my single feast or famine money cycle. But things were looking way up for us, so the timing, with his family suddenly appearing, made me wary.

"So TELL me," Chris said, returning me to the present from my walk down memory lane. "How does it work?"

I was confused. Me and Landry? "What?"

"What you do for the bookie, how does that work?"

Bookie? Who even used that word anymore?

"I can tell you," Landry offered, sitting up, leaning forward out of my hold but still pressed against me, his leg sliding over mine.

"Okay," Chris agreed, and I could tell he was dying to get Landry to open up to him at all. And I understood; I was a slave to having the man's attention myself. "Guys call Trev and ask, like, hey, what's the line on whatever game, or gimme the line for half of the game or the over or the under, and then they place their bets. If they win, they get whatever they bet, but if they lose, they gotta pay what they bet plus the juice."

"Juice?" he asked.

"Yeah, that's the money the house makes if you lose, it's usually like 20 percent, but it could be more depending on the house. Trevan's takes twenty."

"Oh, okay."

"But there's all kinds of different bets," Landry continued, fiddling with the black leather wrap bracelet on my left wrist, hematite and turquoise, before touching the hammered silver ring that made me look like I was married. "There's teaser bets and parlay bets, but the more points you buy, the less your payout is."

His eyes flicked to Chris to check if he was listening. He shouldn't have worried.

"Let's say," he continued, "you have Green Bay and Indianapolis and the spread is ten points. Sometimes guys will say I want to teaser that bet by three points, so instead of the spread being ten points, it's seven. But the more points you buy, the less your payout is."

"Interesting," Chris said, not caring in the least about my business but able to talk to his brother because of it. He looked over at me then. "So Trevan, where do you come in?"

"He's the runner, like I said," Landry answered for me. "Trev collects what's owed and pays out winnings. On Monday and Tuesday he collects; on Wednesday he pays everybody."

"So you're popular on Wednesday." Chris smiled at me.

"Pretty much, yeah." I nodded.

"So what if guys don't have the money to pay you? Do you break their legs?"

"No." Landry grinned at him. "Trevan just cuts the guy off, and once the word's out that you're a welsher, you're pretty much done, ya know?"

There was more to it than that, but my boyfriend did not need to know all the ins and outs of my business. I answered to the house, and if the guys that I went to collect from didn't pay me, then the money had to come from somewhere. The house, or in this case, Adrian Eramo, didn't care who paid me, he only cared that *he* got paid. Period.

"You're not a cop now, are you?" Landry snapped suddenly, realizing everything he'd already said, his voice betraying him, the shiver in it. "You're not here to hurt Trev."

"No." Chris's voice nearly broke. "I'm here to get you to come home. That's all I want. I'm just a college student, Lan, I'm completely nonthreatening, I assure you."

Landry nodded, a quick shiver running through him as my phone rang. Normally I wouldn't have even bothered with it, but the number was my boss, so I turned it to Landry so he could see it. He moved his leg from where it was between mine, and I stood up to answer it.

"Trev," Landry said before I could walk away.

I looked at him but said nothing.

"Don't be long."

When I stroked my fingers through his hair, taking hold of a clump of it, he tipped his head back and closed his eyes. I bent and kissed his forehead, letting him go before I walked toward the living-room window that looked out on the park behind the apartment building. I answered by the eighth ring.

"What the fuck?"

"Gabe?"

Heavy sigh on the other end. "Yeah, sorry," he grumbled. "Where the fuck are you?"

"Home. Why, what's up?"

He cleared his throat. "Did Ellis Kady place any bets with you last week?"

"No, I cut him off."

Several ticks of silence went by. "Trevan, the man owns three nightclubs, a restaurant, and a car dealership. Why would you cut him off?"

He didn't sound mad; he sounded more like he was fishing. Sometimes when I refused to take bets from people, Gabriel Pike called to find out why. He never forced me to go against my gut feeling, but he liked an explanation. If he felt I was being unreasonable, he would take the bet from the player himself. Most of the time, Gabe took my advice and let the client walk, but every now and then, he overruled me and the little voice in my head.

"T?" he prompted.

"I cut him off because he didn't pay me two weeks in a row."

"But you weren't short."

"Have you ever known me to be?"

Heavy sigh. "No, Trev, you're the best goddamn runner I've ever had."

"Well, that's nice to hear, but I carry my friends, not assholes like Ellis Kady who think they're too fuckin' good to pay me."

"What does he owe you?"

"That's between me and Ellis," I told him. "I paid you, you paid Adrian—I'm square with the house, and that's how I like it. Whatever else is my problem."

"Normally I would agree, but a couple of his boys just did a number on Benji. The police found him in an alley, and he had to go to the hospital."

"Oh shit," I groaned. I liked Benji Matthews. He was a nice guy, sweet and even tempered. When our paths crossed, we always ended up eating together or having a cup of coffee before going our separate ways. "How bad was he hurt?"

"I dunno. Tony went to the hospital, and he says he's a mess, so now me and Ira and Pete are going back to see Kady and figure out what the fuck is going on."

"Just the three of you?"

"No." His voice dropped low.

I understood. I needed to stop asking questions about what they were going to do. "How do you know it was Kady?"

"He called Adrian and told him that any runners of his he found on the street were dead."

"That's pretty fuckin' clear."

He grunted.

"Okay." I took a breath.

"I'm sending Francesco to pick up your drop."

"If he's coming right now, I'll run down and give it to him, but if not, I'll just bring it by in a few hours."

"You sure? I know you, you hate carrying."

"I'll call Connie when I'm ready, and he can ride with me."

Deep chuckle from him.

"What?"

"Only you, Trev, I swear to God."

"I'm missing something."

"Jesus, T, Conrad Harris is a cold-blooded killer, but you're on a first-name basis with the sociopath—more than first name, nickname, which is even worse."

"He's a good guy," I defended my friend.

"He's a goddamn hitman is what he is," Gabe assured me.

"Never proven," I said, and I was right, even though I knew as well as anyone what the man did for a living.

"He's a contract killer, swear to God."

"Says you." Deny, deny, deny. Where Conrad was concerned, it was what I did. No one would ever catch me agreeing about what he was or wasn't, especially on the phone. I didn't care who was on the other end.

"Okay, T," he acceded, patronizing me. "We'll just pretend he ain't scary or nothin'."

"He's not." I sighed, because to me, he wasn't. I could not speak for others.

"Uh-huh," he grunted.

"Just… can we drop it?"

"Oh fuck yeah, let's drop it. Tell me about Kady. How many weeks did you carry him?"

"Just two, and then I stopped taking his calls."

"That's probably when he called Benji."

"I think he called Luis before that." I yawned again, rubbing my eyes; they felt like they had sand in them.

"Does he owe Luis too?"

"I dunno, but you know him. Luis doesn't let anybody chase their money. He'll beat the shit outta you if you don't pay up."

"Yeah, I know, so I wonder… hold on."

I stood there waiting while he turned our two-way call into a party line.

"Vargas, you there?"

Loud yawn. "Yeah, I'm here. What the fuck is going on? I just got in bed!"

At his best, Luis Vargas was an ass; tired and cranky just brought out more colorful and charming facets of his sparkling personality.

"Benji Matthews just got jumped by Ellis Kady and some of his guys. Talking to Trev," Gabe sighed, "he says that Kady owes him money. Does he owe you money too?"

"Yeah, he owes me. I took his bets after Trevan cut him off. I figured the action was too large and that's why the fairy didn't want it."

I loved being called a fairy just because I was gay. The fact that Vargas wouldn't think of saying that shit to my face made me think that much less of him.

"Nice."

"What? Just 'cause you and Adrian don't give a fuck that he takes it up the ass don't mean the rest of us are down with it."

"Can we get to the point?"

"Fine, I took the bets from Kady, but last week when I went to collect, he says he doesn't have the fifteen he owes me and that he ain't gonna have it this week either."

"And?"

"So I talked to him some and he basically told me that he needed me to carry him for another couple of weeks and then he'd have it."

"What'd you say?"

"What the hell do you think I said? I told him to go fuck himself and to pay me my goddamn money."

"Did he pay?"

"No, Benji paid me."

"What?"

"Yeah, he said that he'd get it from Kady, and he gave me what Kady owed."

"Oh shit."

"I dunno what's with your boy, Gabe, and when you tell me that Kady fucked up Benji's shit, I gotta wonder what the hell's with that, ya know?"

"Why didn't you hire some muscle and go get your money from Kady before Benji paid you? It's not like you to run scared."

"Fuck you, I wasn't scared," Luis assured him. "I just don't have the cash right now for enough guys."

"How many guys did you think you needed?"

"At least five," he grunted, "the way Kady's fortified at his big club at Jericho; I wouldn't wanna walk in there alone."

Long pause. "Adrian can't have people thinking they can fuck with his runners."

"Nope." Luis agreed.

"Does Kady have any backing?"

"You mean like muscle backing?"

"Yeah."

"I don't know."

"Do you want to come stay at the house?"

"We'll see."

"Should I ask Trevan?"

"Fuck no. He's got Harris watchin' his back and everybody knows it. Ain't nobody gonna fuck with him. Even if he sees Trevan walking down the street, Kady ain't stupid enough to fuck with him."

"Okay, I'll talk to you."

Luis was gone a second later.

"Sorry about all the faggot crap, T."

"Like I care," I said, letting out a deep breath. I had never cared what Luis Vargas thought about me, and I certainly wasn't going to start. "He's a dick, he's always been a dick, and he'll always be a dick. Vargas can kiss my ass, but what I care about right now is Benji and the fact that if you add it all up, I think Kady owes us, like, two."

"Are you shittin' me?" He breathed out because he knew when I said two, I meant two hundred thousand.

"No, 'cause he owes me thirty, he owes Benji more than that, and he owes what Benji paid Luis for him. That's bullshit that he doesn't hafta pay."

"Well, I think Adrian wants it, so just call Francesco for the next few days until you hear from me, all right?"

"Yep."

"Okay, so I'll tell Francesco that you'll be by to see him, when—around lunch or later?"

"Later. I gotta fuckin' sleep."

"Okay, I'll talk to you."

"Wait, which hospital is Benji at?"

"St. Vincent's."

"Okay."

"You gonna go?"

"Yeah."

"Before you sleep?"

"Have to, right? I mean, I gotta check on him, see what he needs."

"Get him whatever and just take it from petty cash when you get back."

"I'll take care of it."

"Just do what I tell you—anything you think he wants."

"All right."

When he hung up, I realized how much I wanted to go to bed. I wanted to lie down, do the deep stretch and the whole-body shudder before I let out all the air in my body. I wanted to deflate and close my eyes, but first I needed to go to the hospital and see Benji.

Walking back to the couch, I met Landry's eyes first.

"Everything all right, baby?"

"No, a friend of mine is in the hospital, so I should really go and check on him."

"Who?" he asked, reaching toward me.

I took the offer of comfort, slipping his hand into mine. "A friend. You met him that time. Benji, soft voice," I told him. "Sweet guy; you liked his accent, remember? He's from Georgia."

His fingers tightened. "I'm sorry. You want me to come with you?"

"Aww, no." I shook my head and turned to smile at his brother. "But Chris, buddy, you gotta go. I ain't leaving my boy here alone to deal with this shit, so we'll have to table it, and you can come back tomorrow morning."

"Why not tonight?"

"Tonight I have to sleep, and I'm not sure how long I'll be at the hospital. And Landry has to go to work, and Tuesday's his late night."

"But we could just talk some more and then maybe—"

"If you push, you won't be pleased that you did," I told him, sliding my hand over my hair that was shaved close to my scalp. "He ain't seein' you without me, and I won't let you see him at all if you don't back off."

"You don't decide things for him."

"Oh the fuck I don't," I told him, pointing. "There's the door."

He looked at Landry, but Landry was staring at me. Chris didn't get it, but there was no way he would have. Our relationship was a twisted, codependent mess, but it worked for us, and within the snarl that it was, we functioned pretty well.

My restrictions on Landry let him function. Perhaps there was a better way for him to live, a way that didn't factor belonging to me into the equation, but no one could argue with my results. The man had been on a downward spiral. I had seen his light going out, but now he was healthy and secure and successful, and between the two of us, me loving him, him letting me, we had done that. He was different now, but still, sometimes, he looked to me if things got dicey, if his space got too big, if he strayed too far from sight, from home. If he started to come undone, untethered, too buoyant, I yanked him back like a dog on a choke chain. It sounded bad, hard and brutal, but the domination soothed him.

When I said no, when I gave orders—come home, sit down, let me make dinner, eat, have a glass of wine, get in bed, kiss me—when I made him, he became grounded. At times his life snowballed, and that was when he needed me to make it stop. The minute he could take a breath and get himself centered, when he could feel the edge of where he belonged and what was his, everything was suddenly right again. Sometimes just seeing me did it, and other times he had to touch me, hold my hand, kiss me, fuck me; whatever he needed from me to show him where he was and that he was fine, I gave to him.

Of course, it was a fine line, and the reverse was true as well. At times Landry had to be managed, handled. There were, on occasion, times when I had to back off, let him make his own choices and let the man come to me. For the sake of his pride, every instance was not time for me to take charge. But I had to be attentive, to see when he was too angry or too fixated or too wound up to even respond to me. It was a dance and I knew the steps.

I had tried unsuccessfully on many occasions to get him to a doctor, a psychiatrist, a psychologist, or any of the number of nice people listed in his medical coverage brochure when he signed himself and his employees, all eight of them, up for insurance. He had been confused about why I wanted him to see a shrink. What, precisely, did I think was wrong with him?

Hard to articulate the way he came apart when it happened so fast. By the time I was squeezing him tight, he was over it and asking me what I wanted for dinner. The first six months we were together, I had thought maybe I was the one who went a little crazy sometimes; maybe I was imagining Landry coming apart so he would need me. But the fact that I questioned myself at all told me I was actually okay. The old catch-22 premise came in handy when figuring out who was really nuts. Not that I thought the man I loved was crazy, but I knew that he needed more than love and affection. I worried about me dying, not because of what that would mean for me, but more for what that would mean for Landry. His mental health was pinned to me and not himself, and while I didn't want it like that, it was a great big ego charge to know that he didn't just want me, he needed me, too. It was twisted and I needed to fix it. I just wasn't sure how.

"I guess I'll go," Chris said, looking at me warily as he stood up, returning my attention to him.

"Thanks," I said.

"I'll walk you to the door," Landry offered.

"I'm jumping in the shower," I told him.

I was surprised that he didn't bring his coffee into the bathroom and talk to me. He normally did that in the morning, but I was in a hurry, so it was fine. I shaved, looked at my eyes in the mirror, and saw how red and raw they looked. There was no amount of Visine that could fix it; I needed to sleep, and that was it.

I called for Landry once I was out and changed, and when I was at the hall closet putting my camel hair coat and cashmere scarf on, he came walking out of the kitchen.

"I made you breakfast," he told me as he crossed the room.

"Oh babe, I'm not awake enough to even eat yet. You have it, okay?" I smiled at him before checking in my shearling-lined denim jacket from the night before for my wallet.

I felt his hand on my shoulder. Turning, I was faced with the blue-green depths of his eyes. "What?"

"I'm worried about you."

"Baby, I'm okay, just go to work."

"You're tired," he said softly, his hand sliding around the side of my neck, stroking my nape. He leaned me forward so our foreheads touched, inhaling me.

"I'll be okay," I assured him, smiling as I drew back. "I just need my sunglasses."

"Maybe you shouldn't go, huh?"

"No, I have to go, and you need to go to work."

"Okay." His voice dropped low as he closed his eyes. "But please call me if you need anything, all right?"

"Yeah." I nodded. "You know I will."

"You'll come home for dinner."

"I'll try."

"Trev."

"I don't know what Benji's gonna need. I don't know if I have to go collect for him or pay people. I have to find out, and that could take time. I won't know anything until I get there."

"I can make pot roast. It's your favorite."

"You're not listening to me."

"Just come home."

He could get so fixated.

"Baby—"

"You worked all night," he cut me off sharply, his voice rising. "I hate it when I sleep alone, and I just… you need to not do that anymore. I hate it, I really hate it."

"I told you that you could invite any of your friends over to stay with you when I—"

"I need to feel you next to me when I wake up in the middle of the night, Trev. That's what I need."

"I know." And I did. Sometimes when he woke up alone in the dark, he would call for me, wanting to make sure it was me, in voice and body, there beside him. "I'm working on changing it."

"It's time," he insisted.

"Okay." I nodded, putting my hand on his smooth cheek. Seeing his eyes, the hunger in them, never failed to flip my stomach over. The man had no idea how sexy he was with his beautiful mouth that drove me right out of my mind. The way he kissed me; how expressive his lips were, and pliant; what they looked like when he smiled or laughed or smirked; and what they felt like stretched around my hard cock, gliding over skin he had made wet.

"You took that breath," he accused me, looking pained.

"I did not," I denied, even though I had.

"You want me on my knees."

"No," I lied.

"But I heard—"

"Hospital. I have to go."

"Trev?"

The idea of him sucking me off had me shivering with want. Whenever I got tired, I got horny, and I had no idea why.

"Trevan," he whined my name.

I groaned softly.

"Baby…."

I grabbed his face hard, stilling him completely, making him stop. "You think stupid shit sometimes. You think you have to do something for me to make me love you—like I could stop now even if I wanted to."

He caught his breath.

"Just stop. I gotta go." I sighed, dropping my hands off him, ready to leave.

He stilled my flight with hands clutched on my coat. "I'm gonna cook for you, so you need to come home, all right?"

"I'll try."

"Promise."

The breathless *promise*, combined with the narrowing of his eyes, was so hot it made my heart stop.

He chuckled. "I just saw your eyes glaze over. I've got you."

"Always," I said, my breath hitching.

His thumb traced the length of my jaw. "So, tonight."

I counted silently to ten. "Tonight."

The smile lit up his beautiful, sharp-angled face. "Good."

"Lemme go," I sighed. "I need to see Benji."

He suddenly leaned in and hugged me tight. "I love it when you give in, the noise you make... like you're just so disgusted with me."

I groaned as he laughed at me, certain that the only person in the world I would ever willingly give in to was standing right in front of me. And apparently he liked the noises I made when I did it.

Chapter
TWO

I GRABBED a cab to St. Vincent's Hospital and called Conrad on the way.

"You shouldn't be out by yourself, Trevan, especially if Kady's got somebody backing his play with Adrian alluva sudden."

"I'll be fine. I just don't wanna go see Francesco and drop the money by myself. I hate him and his bullshit."

"Yeah, I know. I'll pick you up at the hospital and we can go over together."

"Thanks, man, I'll give you your usual cut."

"For what, picking you up, driving you over there? Fuck you, Trev, you know you're my boy; don't be trippin'."

"I heard a little Philly in there," I teased him.

"I don't know how, since I'm from Santa Cruz."

I laughed at him.

"What hospital, asshole?"

I told him to meet me at St. Vincent's, and he said he would be there right behind me. It was nice to have someone I could count on.

I MET Conrad Harris at a private party I had been invited to where the host had mistaken me for a rent boy hired for the night. There was a poker game in a lavish suite, and when I slipped into the smoky room to collect bets from Gianni Shapiro, the guy who was hosting the party, Tyler Hawkins crooked a finger at me. Walking to his side, figuring he had a bet to place, I was surprised when his hand was suddenly on my ass, squeezing hard.

I was working and didn't want to make a scene, so there was no yelling or hitting. I just moved away fast, crossing the room to Mr. Shapiro to take his bet. As I was headed back down the hall to leave, I was grabbed roughly and thrown up against the wall.

"Who the hell do you think you are?" Mr. Hawkins said, twisting my arm up behind my back. "Piece of shit hustler, you think you can treat me like that? You think you can fuckin' ignore me, you little fuck?"

I might have been young, but I wasn't little. I reacted without thinking—not because he was hurting me, not because I was scared, but because he started groping me, and no one did that. I invited people to touch me; no one took liberties. I hated it. He had his hand on my belt buckle, and he was shoving his obvious erection against my ass. My mind shut down and a jolt of adrenaline tore through me.

I flung my head back and heard the crunch as it connected with bone. The instant release of pressure let me know he had moved, and I brought my left foot down hard on the top of his foot before twisting free of his loosened grip. I turned and kicked him in the right knee, and when he went down, I punched him hard in the side of the face. As he crumpled over, unconscious, someone yelled. Two men were standing there looking at me, both the size of linebackers.

I pointed at the prone figure at my feet, bloody and passed out. "He thought I was a hustler, but I'm not. I'm a runner for Adrian Eramo."

Both men looked at me for long minutes. It should have been funny that I was standing there trying to convince them that my ass was not for sale. I had met a lot of rent boys in my life, and the one thing they all had in common was that they were pretty. I was not, and never had been, pretty. "Handsome" could be applied to me, maybe, loosely, but maybe not. I had, my mother said, a good face, a strong face, a face that you remembered, with dark hair that was shaved close to my scalp and dark skin. My father was African American, my mother Cuban. I was not the boy next door; I was the other guy. Between my height of six two and my athletic, muscular build, how I was giving off the hustler vibe was beyond me. Maybe Mr. Hawkins liked *Jungle Fever* in his bedroom, but to cast me in that role was absurd. Never had I been mistaken for a prostitute. A gangbanger, unfortunately yes, but never a hustler.

"I'm here to collect cash," I told the two men, "not peddle my ass."

They moved toward me, and realizing that there was no way I could reach either the elevator or the stairs, I got ready to fight. But a door opened and a man stepped into the hall. He was more quarterback size—built leaner but still, even in the suit he was wearing, massive. I didn't want to mess with any of them.

"Who're you?" the bigger of the bodyguards asked the newcomer.

"Harris," he said softly.

Both the men were bigger than the third, and both of them took a step back at the same time, which I found very interesting and really intimidating. Just the new guy's name gave the other two pause? Jesus.

Several minutes ticked by. I had no idea how long the four of us would stand there, but I didn't want to move and bring everyone's attention back to me.

"I'm done," one of the two huge men muttered. "I didn't see anything. Fuck Hawkins, I work for Shapiro."

"Me too," the second guy agreed, and they both turned and headed back to the suite. They both had to step over the prone figure of Tyler Hawkins to do it, and it would have been funny if I weren't still freaked out. Seeing my chance to get out of there, I bolted toward the elevator.

"Wait."

At the tone of his voice, the command in it, I stopped, even though every part of my brain was screaming at me to run.

As my savior strode toward me, a sudden smile broke on his face, and the way he held out his hand, I found I could breathe again.

"You handled yourself nice," he complimented me, warm hand closing around mine as he stepped in front of me, staring down into my eyes.

The fact that I had to tilt my head back to keep the man's gaze told me that he was bigger and taller, and this close, I was dead if he decided he wanted to hurt me. "How do you know?"

"I watched."

"How?"

"Camera."

Asking more questions could be fatal, so I stopped and just held his hand.

"Conrad Harris," he said, and I noted his sparkling iridescent green eyes.

I caught my breath. I had not really seen him when I was in fear for my life, but I noticed then, when he smiled, that the man was gorgeous.

"Who are you?"

"Trevan Bean." I managed to get out my name.

He let go of my hand, put his on my shoulder, and steered me the rest of the way down the hall. At the elevator, he asked me where I was going.

"I dunno."

"So, you wanna eat?"

I looked up at him, thinking about what was smart and what was not. "Yeah, let's eat."

He nodded. "Cool."

And that I had not second-guessed his motives, I came to find out, was a very good thing. Because it was not that he was a bad man or a good man, he simply *was*. He was contracted to do a job, and that was all. He protected you, killed you, or left you alone based on who was paying him to make a choice on your behalf. The man was not particularly emotional, violent, or compulsive. He was just Conrad. Sometimes I woke up in the middle of the night and he was there in my bedroom, watching me and Landry sleep, he said, because it calmed him. By the same token, sometimes he simply disappeared in the middle of a conversation. I would turn around and he'd be walking away from me. He confessed to me "why?" when I was really drunk one time and he didn't think I'd remember.

"Sometimes just breathing the same air as you soothes me, and sometimes I get this overwhelming urge to snap your neck. When I want to see you, I see you; when I want to kill you, I walk away. Some people I don't walk away from, T, so never let anyone tell you that you're not special. You are very fuckin' special."

I always remembered that line of his, the fine line he walked that at any time, at any point, he could stumble over. He was very dangerous and very loyal, and I liked him more than he really knew. I realized, too, that everyone in my life was slightly insane.

"SIR?"

Looking up, realizing I had been daydreaming, I found a nurse squinting at me. "Sorry, um, Benji Matthews? He was brought in a couple hours ago, I think."

Her expression went from irritation to sympathy in seconds. She reached out, put her hand over my right one, which was sitting on the counter. "Let me get the doctor for you."

"Oh, no." I felt the air rush out of my body. "No no no."

She looked so sad.

I tried to breathe. We weren't even that close, Benji and I, not even what you would call friends, but I felt responsible. I had put him in Ellis Kady's sights.

"You did not," Conrad assured me half an hour later as we sat side by side in the chairs in the waiting room. I had my head in my hands after we spoke with the doctor, and he was gently rubbing between my shoulder blades. "You did your job, T. Kady wasn't paying you, so you didn't take his action. That's business, plain and simple. Luis did the same. Unfortunately, the one who was stupid is also the one who's dead. If Benji had been smart he'd still be alive." But I couldn't shake a feeling of responsibility. "Hey." I felt his hand squeezing the back of my neck. "Look."

Tipping my head up, I saw Gabriel, my boss, walking toward me. He had Ira Mann and Francesco Galan with him. I just watched as he and the others sat down in the chairs across from me and Conrad.

Gabriel exhaled after a few minutes. "You all right?"

I nodded.

His eyes flicked to Conrad and then returned to me before he reclined, arms on the backs of both chairs that the men with him were sitting in. Francesco leaned forward after a second.

"I don't like you, you don't like me; that ain't shit now."

I waited for what he was going to say.

"Everybody got hit today except you and Vargas. Adrian thinks Vargas was safe 'cause he wasn't on the street. Anybody who was where they usually are got wasted."

Jesus.

"And maybe they'll go after Vargas later, but not you, right? Never you."

What was I supposed to say? I knew why; everyone knew why. It was because of the man sitting on my right. Nobody in their right mind would mess with Conrad Harris. He'd kill you and anyone who was with you. He was not a man you messed with. Ever.

"Kady wants Adrian's businesses, all of them. It ain't just the house that he hit; he took care of other things, too, other places."

I understood. It was a clash above my pay grade.

"There's a lot to Adrian's business," he assured me. "But you know that."

"I do."

"Come here," Gabriel said, getting up and walking to the window that looked down on the parking lot.

When I joined him, his hand went to the back of my neck.

"So, Adrian wants you promoted. He likes you, admires your loyalty, and appreciates the fact that you're smart. Most of all he likes that you're calm and cool under pressure."

"Thanks. Tell him."

He nodded. "Listen, don't let Francesco or any of those other fucks tell you that you being a fag means shit to Adrian—he doesn't give a damn. He cares about money and results and that's it. I told you that you're the best runner I ever had, so in turn you're the best runner Adrian's ever had."

"Okay."

Long exhale from him before he turned his head to look at me.

My eyes were locked on his.

"Adrian wants you to learn other parts of the business, but I want you out."

I wasn't sure I heard him right. "What?"

"I know you heard me."

"No, I don't think I did. You want me to leave?"

"I do."

"Why?"

"I have a different future in mind for you."

I squinted at him.

"Right now… you could just step out of this, out of this life, and start what you want."

"That can wait."

"Maybe it shouldn't."

I shook my head. "I can't do that."

"What? Be out?"

"Yeah."

"But that's what I want."

"I can't," I assured him. "There's no way."

"Sure there is. You can walk away before people know your name."

"No."

"Why?"

"You know why."

"What's keeping you?"

My eyes locked on his.

"Shit." He shook his head because he knew. There was no way he didn't.

When there had been nothing and nowhere to turn, there had been Gabriel.

At the time I was working three jobs just to eat and pay rent and help my mother. But I knew I was coming to the end of what I could keep asking my body to do. A change was coming, and it would not be a good one.

Utterly exhausted, I had been running for days on no sleep and barely any food because I didn't even have a break long enough to allow me to run over to my mother's house and let her feed me. I had no time.

But my brain was still working, as was evident on the night a runner tried to shake down my boss. He came in with his collector, his muscle, and he wanted two grand. My boss said it was only one. After listening to the back-and-forth arguing for ten minutes, I couldn't stand it anymore. I cut everyone off, explained how my boss owed twelve hundred and not a penny more or a penny less, and told them all to shut the fuck up. The collector grabbed me for being a smartass, but I was not in the mood.

I wasn't proud of the beating I gave the guy, but he started it. I had my boss pay the runner, and then I threw both the runner and his bleeding knee-breaker out of the diner. I was next when my boss fired me. Later that night, I was on my way home when I saw the car out of the corner of my eye. They had followed me for two blocks, so, figuring it was payback time and not wanting to postpone getting jumped, I stopped, turned, and got ready to face whatever was going to come.

"You the wiseass from the diner?" the guy asked me from the lowered back window.

"Yeah. Who the fuck wants to know?"

"Me, you little shit," the man barked at me as he got out of the car. I noted the designer Italian suit, the Tiffany cufflinks I had seen in a magazine, and the glossy black dress shoes. He was wearing a wool and cashmere trench coat that cost more than my rent. I had never seen a more stunning man. "Come here."

I moved fast because whatever he wanted, I was down for. Though not handsome in the way that everyone agreed on, he exuded power. You could feel it rolling off of him. And I realized in that instant that I didn't want him, I wanted to *be* him.

His name was Gabriel Pike, and he had come to talk to me.

"Sure, man," I agreed and smiled at him.

"Get in the car."

He could have killed me—I was a lamb to the slaughter—but instead he took me to dinner. I couldn't remember the last time I'd had a steak.

The questions came fast when I was done wolfing down my food.

What was a teaser bet, a parlay bet, what were the odds on a three-team parlay? If it's Detroit and Atlanta and the spread is ten points....

I was stunned. We were talking about betting? Gambling? What the hell?

Did I know what the over was? The under? What was the payout on a two-bet parlay if the odds were three to one? What were the odds on a six-team parlay?

He didn't stop, just went on and on, and I answered just as fast as he questioned. Then he finally asked me the most basic thing of all: how did a house stay in business?

"Basically, the people who lose pay the people who win, and the house collects the juice," I told him.

"You gamble, huh?" He was grinning at me by then.

"When I have the money," I answered and shrugged. "Which is fuckin' never now."

He had scrutinized me and then offered me a job. They needed a new runner, since the last one had to be retired for skimming. I didn't ask him to define "retiring." I didn't care. I had his spot. It was my only interest. Gabriel knew what I could do based on my brain; it was all I needed to know.

"I WON'T leave you," I assured my boss, the man who had saved me from ruin and probably jail time, as I stood beside him at the window. My options had been limited when I turned twenty-one, and there had been no other avenues open to me but nefarious ones. But there was crime, which I did, and then there was stealing and hurting people. That was a road I had never taken, a corner I had not turned, all because Gabriel Pike had talked to me and given me a chance. "Tell Adrian, okay?"

He nodded slowly. "You don't give a shit about Adrian."

"No," I agreed.

"If you stay, it's done. You get that. There's no out once you say you're in unless Adrian says."

"I know that," I assured him. "I'm not some punk kid, Gabe. I know the fuckin' score."

The hand that was suddenly on my shoulder, squeezing tenderly, calmed my racing heart.

"What can I do?"

"I really need you to lay low, just stay away from me, from us, and—"

"We can't make money if we don't keep up business as usual."

"Adrian has it covered; I just need you to disappear for at least a week, all right? Really, I don't wanna see your face."

"I can help."

"And you will; you're gonna be doing a whole lot more. Adrian wants you at a new level, but for now, until we get things figured out, until we know who Kady reached out to… I want you gone."

I was going to argue, but he surprised the hell out of me when he grabbed me. Never, ever, had he hugged me—especially not me, the gay boy—in front of the others.

"You stay safe. Call me if you get in a bind, but otherwise, I want you invisible."

I nodded into his shoulder.

When he pulled back, I passed him the envelope with the thirty grand in it, and when he leaned close, he slipped one that he pulled from the breast pocket of his suit jacket into my jacket pocket. He had obviously come prepared.

"I don't need money, Gabe."

"I want you to have it. Adrian said make sure you have money, so there, just take it. There's five grand to tide you over in case we close up shop for a month."

I did not have the expenses they had, but I didn't argue. Any cash put me that much closer to my restaurant. "A month would be crazy."

He didn't argue the point. "Do you have a piece?"

I shook my head.

"Have Conrad get you one."

"Okay."

"Anything he has will be better, cleaner, than what I got."

"Yes."

"You have your knife, though."

I cracked a grin, teasing him. "I always have a knife; I'm Cuban, man."

He rolled his eyes at me. "Gimme a break, your last name is Bean."

"'Cause my father went for the Latinas even though he was a black man."

He chuckled. "And where's your father now?"

I tipped my head at him. "In heaven, watching over his boy."

His brows furrowed. "I didn't know. I'm sorry."

I shrugged. "Drunk drivers should just be taken out and shot."

"Agreed."

My eyes absorbed his face.

"I'll see ya," he said quickly, giving my shoulder a hard pat before he turned and walked away from me.

Ira, who never spoke, was suddenly in front of me, hand on my cheek for a minute before he followed after Gabe.

"Be careful, kid," Francesco said when he reached me, slapping my face gently. "And I never meant anything when I hassled you. It didn't mean shit."

I knew exactly what Francesco wanted from me—if he could be certain no one would ever find out, if I would allow it, if it would stay between us. The way his eyes always slid over me, the sound of his breath when he leaned close, how often he teased me about sucking his dick. I knew. I wasn't stupid.

"And if you need a piece, you call me. I'll get you something untraceable, like the others."

But Gabriel had already told me to ask Conrad, and I would have gone that route anyway. Francesco, regardless of what he said or tried to imply, was not my friend. He could not be counted on like the man who might one day, accidentally or purposely, kill me.

"I'm sorry Benji's dead. I'm sorry about all of them. Make sure you call his folks, okay?"

I was startled and watched him as he left, jogging down the hall after Gabe and Ira.

"Mr. Bean?"

When I turned, there was a doctor, and he wanted to know how to get in touch with Benji's family. I told him I needed my friend's phone.

"I better get you some coffee," Conrad said softly, appearing quietly at my shoulder, "'cause you're gonna be up for a while."

And of course he was right. He was always right.

Chapter THREE

I CALLED Landry and told him what had happened, and it took everything in me plus Conrad getting on the phone to keep him from coming to the hospital. Landry was scared that whoever had killed the other runners was coming after me, but I reminded him of who exactly my guardian angel was and that Gabriel had told me that as long as I stayed out of sight, all would be well. Kady and his guys weren't actively looking for me. They would just find me if I was hanging out in my usual haunts. No one was hunting me; it was more a question of opportunity, and even then, even if they found me, there was still Conrad to consider.

Landry didn't understand, but he had met Conrad, so when the man said I was safe, he believed him.

My friend had excused himself at the hospital for a while, and when he returned, he reiterated Gabriel's words to me and told me to lie low, steer clear of all the casinos and my regular clients. He promised that I would be fine as long as I didn't try to conduct business as usual. It was a clash beyond my scope; I did not need to be involved. They had killed the runners to interrupt Adrian's cash flow and that was it. As horrible as it was, if I stayed out of sight, no one was coming after me.

"Won't the cops be all over this?" I asked Conrad. "I mean, he was murdered. Won't there be an investigation?"

He shook his head. "You watch too much TV where everybody works and takes any death seriously. You have to realize, in the real world, with the way bodies pile up in any big city, no one is killing themselves to find out what happened to Benji."

I nodded.

"If anything, they might go question Adrian if they can make the connection, but he's careful, right? I mean, if anyone checks, you guys all work at his health club or some bullshit like that, right?"

"Yeah. Right."

"So," he shrugged. "Even if there is an investigation, you'll never know."

"I guess," I said, then dropped it.

Talking to Benji's father was exhausting, and when I finally got to put the nurse on the phone with him, I felt an overwhelming sense of relief. I did not want to be the one to coordinate with the morgue or to figure out how Benji's body would get back to Atlanta. It couldn't be me, and I was relieved that it didn't have to be.

"Kady should pay," I told Conrad in the car as he drove me to my mother's work later that day. I had to see her before she left for her trip; I wanted to give her some money. I had planned to stop at the bank, but Gabriel's gift made that unnecessary. I had all the cash I needed on me. "He shouldn't get away with torturing Benji."

"No, he shouldn't," Conrad agreed. "But from what you told me, Gabriel was on his way to see Kady already. My guess is that whatever revenge you're planning, Gabe's gonna try."

I looked out the window at the gray sky, the drizzle already beginning. "The doctor said he was stabbed and beaten, that it would have taken hours to inflict that kind of damage."

"Sure."

I turned to look at him. "If Gabriel can't get to Kady, can you?"

It took several minutes for him to answer me. "Yes."

"Okay."

He cleared his throat. "Just so you know, it's a big jump from defending yourself to killing someone. You're talking about premeditation, right? That's a whole other thing."

"Yeah," I agreed, taking a breath.

He cleared his throat. "Did Kady come on to you?"

"No." I shook my head. "I ain't pretty enough for Ellis Kady, or white enough."

He scoffed.

"What? I'm not," I said, holding up my arm, pushing the sweater up so he could see my dark-bronze skin. "I'm darker than you, man."

He grunted because that was a slight exaggeration.

"And you're prettier than me," I teased him. "And you've got the cool green eyes; mine are just boring-ass brown."

Deep annoyed sigh, and I smiled just a little.

"I wonder why that is; your eyes, I mean. I bet there's a white guy back in your family tree somewhere, huh?"

He was ignoring me.

"I should have the green eyes, since in with the Cuban, there's Spanish and some German and some French too."

"Are you still talking?"

"You know, if we were coffee, I'd be something with caramel in it and you'd be, like, a cafe mocha or some shit."

"Please stop talking."

I chuckled, turning back to my window, the raindrops hitting it hard now, blurring the world outside.

"Tell me the truth. Did Kady come on to you?"

I coughed softly. "Once."

"And?"

"He wanted to see what a guy from the hood was like in bed."

He scoffed.

I turned to look at his profile. "Why is that funny?"

"You? From the hood?" He snickered. "That's good."

I grunted because I knew it. My mother had married my father and they had moved to Troy, supposedly away from all the things that could hurt them. After my father was killed walking across the street on his way home, my mother went to work as an office manager for a man who owned a string of dry cleaning stores. She liked it, but it wasn't enough to take care of her and my sister. So I helped out, putting my sister through college, helping my mother pay the mortgage and her bills, making sure that I stepped in where my father, Donald Bean, would have. I missed the man a lot.

Even after ten years, I still could have used his advice. Mostly I missed that he had never met Landry. I would have liked to see them sit together and talk. I had told him I was gay, and my dad had given me the nod and said okay. He wasn't sure that I knew everything at fourteen, but he agreed that my sexual orientation was one of those things I could be sure of. He had been surprised but never judgmental or angry or anything. He was the sort of father every kid should have: kind, supportive, and loving.

"Are you listening to me?"

I hadn't been, I realized. My mind was drifting instead of listening to Conrad. "No, man, I'm sorry."

"It's all right, but look, now, I need you to go into that glove compartment and get the gun there."

I didn't really want to, but what was I going to do if somebody broke in during the night? The bat I kept under my bed wouldn't help if the guys invading my home were armed, and I had to be really close to use my butterfly knife.

"You need a gun." Conrad shrugged. "The life you have, the life I can't convince you to leave… you need one."

"What's with you and Gabe wanting me to open my restaurant now? You both know I don't have enough, and I ain't ready to go yet anyway. I figure three more years, maybe two, I'll be done, but not right now. I only got sixty saved, man; I need more."

"Landry can't—"

"Landry's money and mine don't mix for dreams."

"You used your money to get him started, and then he took out a loan for the rest."

"Which he's still paying off," I told him. "Until what he sells completely covers his costs, all his profit has to go right back into his business. I mean, he's close, you know. We go see the accountant together and I see his books, but there's still a way to go."

"It's up to you." He shrugged. "I just need you to understand that I don't want to see you hurt. Gabe's trying to get you out; that's his idea of protection. Mine is a gun."

"Okay."

He nodded and tipped his head at the glove compartment. "Go ahead."

I was expecting something out of *The Matrix*, of course, but what I got was a Glock 22. It was what most policemen carried, and basically once the safety was off, you aimed and pulled the trigger. Conrad promised to take me to his gun club on the weekend to show me how to shoot it properly, but until then, he wanted me to have it.

"Is it registered to you?" I asked him.

The look I got, like I was just so stupid, was one I actually deserved.

"Sorry. Do you have any guns that are actually registered to you?"

"Of course, just not one I would give you."

"So what do I do if I'm being chased by a policeman?"

"Why are you suddenly contemplating a scenario where you would be chased by law enforcement?"

"It's just a question."

"Jesus," he groaned.

"C?"

He growled at me. "If you're being chased by cops, ditch the gun. If you're being chased by some guys from the neighborhood or someone from Kady's crew, shoot at them."

"Cop, ditch; bad guy, shoot," I teased him. "Leave the gun, take the cannoli."

"I will shoot you myself."

I started laughing even though I shouldn't have. He was very dangerous.

"You're really a wiseass, you know that?"

I did know that, I thought, as some of the tension in my shoulders and neck finally started to dissipate.

"When we get out of the car, I'll help you with the holster."

And then it wasn't funny anymore. "I wish Benji had had a gun."

"Me too," Conrad agreed. "At least that way it would've been over faster."

"Why?"

"He would have shot at them, and they would have killed him right then."

I shouldn't have asked the question.

MY MOTHER was happy to see me. It was her last day of work, since she had asked off starting the following day, Wednesday, to go to Dallas to visit her sister, my Aunt Janet, who just had a baby. It was strange. Her sister was forty-three and having her first child, and my mother at just forty-six had been finished bearing children years ago. I was twenty-four and my sister was twenty-three. She'd had me at twenty-two, when she met and fell in love with my father. Everyone had said she was too young, but now, when she was still really young with no children in her house, she was free to do whatever she wanted.

"When are you going to take a real vacation?" I smiled at her from where I was leaning on the counter above her.

"After the first of the year," she said softly, her eyes flicking up to me and then away. "Marissa and Clover and Patrice and Judy and I are going to Jamaica."

I chuckled, and when she looked up, she was scowling.

"What?"

"You know what," I teased her.

"No I do not, or I would not be asking."

"It's like that movie, *How Stella Got Her Groove Back*."

She growled at me. "I'm gonna hit you."

I smiled bigger and braced for the smack with her pen.

"You and I both know that a man for me is out of the question," she assured me, making my knuckles sting where she hit them with the pen. "I won't be—"

"Don't say that," I told her, reaching into the breast pocket of my coat. Gabriel had given me money, which had shortened the number of places I'd had to go. Not having to stop at the bank had been nice. I had separated the cash out in the car on my way over. "Here, this is for your trip and for the mortgage payment this month."

She took the envelope and looked inside. "Trevan." Her head snapped up, her dark brown eyes on mine. "There's twenty-five hundred dollars here."

"I know, but you might need to get Aunt Janet stuff, and you need to pay the mortgage, like I said. I was gonna come see you tonight, but my plans changed, so this is better. I wanted to hit you up before you left."

"Honey, you have a restaurant to save up for and—"

"I know, Mom, but you need things too."

She nodded. "Thank you, baby, this helps, and now I don't have to owe Aunt Janet for the plane ticket. I felt bad about that."

"There, see."

She stood up, leaned forward, and kissed my cheek. "How's Landry?"

"He's fine," I lied, realizing that I was more than tired and really not able to hold onto my good mood or my fake smile much longer. I loved her and I'd wanted to see her before she left, but I was beat. "I gotta go, though; he's expecting me for dinner."

"Of course, you go ahead and go."

I smiled at her, my mother, Serena Bean. "You're so beautiful."

"You're full of crap, but I love you." She beamed at me. "Come around here and hug me proper and then get out."

I did as she said, very careful not to let her put her arms anywhere but around my neck. All I needed was her bumping the gun. I would never hear the end of it, and the questions about the true nature of my business would be interminable. I was in no way prepared to get into that with her, and I didn't want her getting on the plane tomorrow pissed off at me.

"When I get home, I want you and Landry to come for dinner. He wants to learn to make bouillabaisse, and I promised I'd teach him."

"Okay," I agreed. I smiled at her, squeezing her tight, unable to help myself.

"I love you," she sighed, letting me go. "But these barrels in your ears are just—"

"Plugs, Mom," I teased her. "Rico has barrels—they're hollow—but I have plugs."

She made a face. "Why you have to put those in your ears? You and your cousin? Why?"

"'Cause I like it," I teased her. "Just like I like the huge-ass tattoo on my back and shoulders and arms that you hate."

She had never wanted me to have the tattoo, but it had been for my father, to honor him and his belief in the afterlife, the wings around the cross to represent heaven, my testament on my flesh for him. It was enormous, covering my back, shoulders, biceps, and triceps, the lines tribal but intricate, done lovingly by my cousin Manuel, scrolling and delicate and thick and heavy, all of it flowing beautifully, seamlessly. It had taken a year for him to finish it all the way he wanted, his masterpiece. He appreciated me letting him take pictures of it to put in his book at his shop. When he had had to add onto it for Landry, finally putting color to my skin as well, he had been thrilled. I had never told him how necessary it was.

Outside on the street, I was surprised to see Conrad parked at the corner. When I reached the black SUV, the tinted black passenger-side window rolled down slowly.

"Why are you still here?"

"Because I want to drive you to Landry's gallery, and then I won't worry."

I sighed heavily. "So can I go out? Can I go to a club, see a movie— I mean, seriously, how fucked am I?"

"You're not. You don't go near any casinos, any of your regulars, and if you see anyone out and they ask you anything, you say you ain't working. But you do need to get out of town for maybe a week. Can Landry do that?"

I suddenly thought of his brother Chris. "Maybe. You wanna hear something funny?"

"Yeah, funny would be good. Get in the car."

As he drove me to Landry's gallery, Asil, I explained about Landry's brother showing up out of the blue.

"That's fucked up."

And I agreed that it was.

"You're doing it again."

I was snapped from my explanation. "Doing what?"

He smiled at me. "Whenever you're worried, you either rub the top of your head or over your heart with your right hand."

"I knew about rubbing my head, but I rub my chest?"

"Yeah."

"Huh, I wonder why."

"'Cause that's where the *L* is." He assured me.

ALONG with my entire back and shoulders being covered in a heavy black tribal tattoo, another design had been added above the cross: a ribbon that looked like it was laid over my skin. It spilled over my left shoulder, thickening and thinning down over my left pectoral and branching out, becoming roots over my heart where the Old English *L* was, entwined with roses and thorns. That was Landry, a rose with horrible, deadly, wicked, sharp thorns. He had nearly fainted when he saw it; he had needed it there, so ready to mark me himself if I had not asked Manuel to do it for me.

I never told anyone about waking in the night to him standing over me with a knife. It was small, one of my switchblades, chosen for carving, not stabbing, but still sharp, still able to kill me. He was breathing hard, stroking himself and looking at me with glazed eyes.

"Whatcha doin', babe?" I asked him, voice calm, swallowing down my fear, reaching for him.

He didn't even see me, intent on my chest, tugging and pulling on his hard, heavy cock, his breath catching, his body trembling.

I waited and he let go. His seeping dick twitched as he bent toward me, his slick left hand went down on my sternum, the other holding the knife like a scalpel.

"What're you gonna do?" I asked, reaching for him, my fingers closing around his hard, wet length.

"Carve my name in your skin so everyone knows you're mine."

I squeezed and he hissed out his pleasure, head back, eyes closed, his intent to cut me forgotten as he moaned my name. Rolling out of bed, I went to my knees and took his cock down the back of my throat fast and hard, sucking violently so he could feel it even through the haze of whatever had come over him.

He palmed the back of my head, as there was no hair to grab hold of, and tried to push his way in even deeper. When I brushed his hand off and pulled back, he whimpered loudly.

"Are you awake?" I asked, licking from the base of his long, beautiful cock to the tip and back again, too turned on to worry about the fact that he still had a switchblade in his right hand. I fondled his heavy balls, loving the feel of them. "Baby?"

There was only gibberish coming from him, only sounds, no words, as I licked the glistening head before stretching my lips around it, taking the length of his thick, leaking erection back into my mouth.

"Trev," he managed to get out as I sucked and nibbled and stroked, my cheeks hollowed out with the force, my tongue creating swirling pressure. "Gonna come… swallow it all… drink me."

I moaned and he exploded in my mouth, hot semen hitting the back of my throat as I swallowed frantically, gulping, hearing him yell, one of his hands digging painfully into my shoulder as he fucked my mouth.

Knowing that he loved to see his spunk on my skin, I shoved him off me. He froze, standing there, letting cum spurt from the flared head as he shuddered through his climax. I watched and waited, and when he was done, still frozen, I watched thick wet semen slide back down his shaft to his balls. I saw some of it drip to the floor, and some of it was on me, on my collarbone, cooling on my skin. Only then, when he was shuddering with aftershocks, did his eyes flutter as he suddenly saw me.

"Trev?"

I squinted at him as I stood up, the two inches of height I had on him still enough to make his head tip back.

"Oh shit," he gasped, realizing he had a knife in his hand, letting it drop open to the floor.

"Jesus, Landry," I griped, jumping back. "You never drop an open knife."

"What the fuck?"

I picked up the weapon, retracted the blade, and placed it on the nightstand.

"Trevan?"

"Were you sleepwalking?" I asked gently, turning back to him, putting my hands on his face. I knew he did that sometimes, having had entire conversations with him when he was not awake.

"No, I…." He shivered and moved closer to me, his hands sliding over my hips. "Your dick is hard."

Of course it was. I had just given my boyfriend a blowjob. "Never mind, what were you doing?"

"I fell asleep on the couch," he said, fingers sliding around my painfully hard erection, "and I had a dream that you… this is like velvet in my hand."

I couldn't help pushing in and out of his fist; it felt too good.

"I was thinking that if I just put my name on you, marked you… branded you… that no one would ever be confused about who you belonged to."

Instantly, I had understood.

We had been at a party earlier in the night. There was a girl who had asked me to dance and she was cute and funny. She had a snake tattoo on her upper arm, and I told her how much I liked it. She wanted to know if I had any tats, and when I said I did, she wanted to see. It was just conversation to me, forgettable. I had obliged her interest because it meant nothing, but it had meant something to Landry. It had, in fact, meant a great deal to Landry.

Later, the same girl had been cold outside where we were all hanging out on the patio. I had pulled the heavy wool sweater over my head and given it to her. She had put her hand on my back, tracing my tattoo the second time before she helped me pull my T-shirt down.

When I had gotten up and gone to look for my boy, as he had not returned from the bathroom, I found him in the hall, hugging himself tight, shivering hard.

"What's wrong?" I asked, hands on him, leaning our foreheads together as I inhaled.

"Oh, now you love me?"

"What?" I chuckled, leaning back to look at him. "Are you all right?"

His eyes were dead.

"Landry?"

There were sudden tears.

"Oh baby, what's wrong?"

And he had breathed suddenly, it seemed, like he hadn't been but now could. I had pushed him up against the wall, shoved my tongue down his throat, and mauled him. I pressed into him, broke the kiss and bit down on the soft flesh between his neck and shoulder. He arched up into me, his now familiar chant beginning again.

Need me… over and over.

Always the same, like I didn't already or could stop. And as I stood before him in our apartment later that same night, staring down into his hooded eyes, feeling the clench of his fingers on my hard, hot shaft as precum dribbled from the tip and he smeared it with this thumb, I understood. He didn't just want to have his mark on me; it was a necessity for his continued sanity.

"Tomorrow," I managed to get out. "Gonna go put you over my heart forever."

The eyes were so lost and so hopeful, all at the same time.

"I swear," I said, hand over my left pectoral. "Gonna have an *L* right here so everyone can see. An *L* for Landry."

"On your body."

"Yes."

"Like a brand."

I nodded.

He sucked in his breath. "Fuck me before I die."

"You're not gonna die."

"I could. I thought I was. It felt like it before."

Jesus. "I'll get in bed, and you ride me."

"No," he whispered. "Wanna be fucked."

I moved fast, grabbing the back of his neck, hurling him face down on the bed, landing on top of him, stretching for the lube from our nightstand even as I pinned him in place.

"You can't do it," he taunted me, and this too was his way. "You can't fuck me, you don't even want to. You want that girl that you gave your fuckin' sweater to."

The thoughts that consumed him were so stupid sometimes.

"We left without it, you know, and fuck her if she brings it back. Fuck her! I'll burn it, I swear to God, and if you even try to—"

"Shut up," I ordered him, spreading his legs, feeling the tension in his shoulders, the fatigue from where he had been clenched earlier, frozen in pleasure.

His hands were fisted in the blankets, still warm from where I had been sleeping. I dribbled lube over the cleft of his ass, more than I needed but wanting to make a mess. Gently, even though he was verging on madness, I slid my fingers inside of him, scissoring, stroking, slow but steady, relentless as I curled them over his gland, feeling him jolt under me, twist and squirm with shallow breaths.

"Can't make me yours; I won't be. I'll find someone that won't pay attention to stupid girls who say they're cold."

"Idiot," I told him, adding a third finger, pushing deep, circling wide, adding my thumb from my left hand. He was whining, the words incoherent but pleading, writhing under me, and the mantra of my name became demanding. I didn't slide my fingers free. I yanked back, and he gasped in outrage before I grabbed his tight, firm ass, spread the cheeks open, and thrust hard and deep in one long, smooth glide.

He howled his rage and drowning, devouring pleasure.

"Oh fuck!"

His muscles were like a fist closing around me, holding tight, rippling and hot. My whole body tingled as I eased back and thrust in again, deeper, shifting my angle, finding the spot that made him scream. There was the first thump of poor Mrs. Chun's broom against our floor. We had woken our neighbor yet again.

I smiled as I pumped in and out of my boyfriend's ass, pounding him down into our bed, bucking as hard as I could so he'd know it was only him I wanted to fuck.

"Trev!"

I knew.

I pushed my fingers through his hair, made a fist, and jerked up, arching his back, lifting his ass, putting him into a position of submission, taking away all his power. He was there only for me to use.

He was sobbing, I could hear it, and I wasn't sure what was most needed.

"Shall I come on you or in you," I asked, my mouth next to his ear as I reached under him and squeezed his rock-hard shaft.

Between the panting and gasping and crying, I understood that I needed to fill him up; he wanted it to leak out of him for hours.

I was too close, my control was gone, so I grabbed his shaft, stroked and pulled, and when I felt his muscles clamp down, I plunged into him, lifting him with the force.

We were a bad porn movie together—not pretty, not gorgeous, but loud and messy and sticky with fluid and awash in tears.

My orgasm was endless, and I held him tight until it was done, until the flood receded and I could realize where I was again and care. We were covered in lube and cum and sweat, and I wiped my hands on the comforter and laughed huskily in his ear.

"Jesus, Trev, I think I'm dead."

"You're not dead," I told him, chuckling, kissing his ear, his cheek, licking the salt from his skin, dabbing at the blood on his lip. "But you're gonna feel like shit in the morning when all this nice euphoria bails and all you've got are bruises and laundry to do."

He shivered hard.

"Hold on, lemme move so you can—"

"No," he stopped me, reaching back, fingers grazing over my ass. "Stay there. I can still feel your dick pulsing inside. It hurts."

"Well if it hurts, idiot, lemme pull—"

"I'm stretched and full and fuckin' sore, but ohmygod how bad did I need that? How bad did I want it? Jesus."

I was basically lying on top of him; I needed to move. "Baby, I have to be crushing you, and your ass needs a break."

But he clenched his muscles just to make sure I didn't move, which almost killed me, my skin overly sensitized, my penis slowly softening inside of him.

"I'm sorry I gave that girl my sweater. I'll never do it again."

"I wouldn't have cared about the sweater if she knew you were fuckin' mine."

"Honey," I soothed him, my voice hoarse and low, freeing myself from his still clenching channel, the tightness and heat too much to bear. "Everybody knows I'm yours."

"They will once I carve my name into you."

He sounded crazy again, but I was beyond being scared because I knew what needed to be done. Rolling over on my back, I patted my chest as he rose over me. "Come here."

He was on me fast, wrapped so tight I barely managed to get the blankets up over us before we froze. Snuggled close, his mouth open on the side of my neck, I slowly traced my fingers up and down his spine, over and over, like he loved. The man craved me petting him like nothing I had ever seen. Putty in my hands.

"Right where my heart is, right there. Gonna have the *L* for Landry so everyone will know that it's you it beats for. Only for you."

His skin sliding over mine was sleek and smooth as he lifted and plastered his mouth to mine, the kiss to taste me and suck and nibble and build heat all over again. He felt so good twining around me, and I felt the roll deep inside of me and the desire rise and slowly ripple.

"Fuck, Landry." My voice gave out on me. "What will make it better?" I had not realized that what I thought had been nothing, talking to the girl, had filleted him open and exposed all his vulnerability and insecurity, his bleeding, oozing heart.

"Inside you," he said simply. "Now."

Whatever he needed.

He flung the covers away and grabbed the bottle, which was still on the bed beside my leg. His hand was on his cock, slicking it, lube running through his fingers as he coated it, brushing some over my entrance although what he had on his shaft was more than enough.

I planted my feet and lifted and he got to his knees, lined up his cock, and plunged inside of me hard and fast, burying himself deep.

The pain was jarring, instant and overwhelming because there had been no prep, nothing, and I was still recovering from my own orgasm. For a second, I thought I would throw up. I hardly ever bottomed because he loved to and told me often. But there were times when he needed to let me know that not only did he belong to me, but I belonged to him. And it was never good because he was a poor top, erratic and rushed. Angles were lost on him. As far as I knew, he couldn't even come when he was inside me. It was instead an exercise purely in power.

"Hey," I breathed through the pain, reaching for him, determined to try and enjoy it this time. "Stop, look at me."

His eyes slowly lifted and I saw them swimming with fresh tears.

"It's okay."

"No, I'm fuckin' hurting you for no reason."

"No," I lied, my voice coaxing, kind. "Do this, slow down, lemme put my legs on your shoulders, okay? Roll forward and see how deep you can go."

His eyes never left mine as he followed directions, the angle making me gasp as the long, thick length of him grazed over my prostate.

Different, better. Just with small changes, his speed and his descent, I felt an electric shock run through me.

I moaned loudly.

"I should do that again?" He sounded so hopeful.

"Fuck, Landry," I panted, my back bowing up off the bed. "I gotta grab my… I gotta get myself off. Just hammer me right there, okay? Don't fuckin' stop."

"Yeah?"

"Oh baby could ya please…. Fuck!"

The sizzle was there, the heat, the bubbling, verging, consuming rush that I had never felt on my back before except when he was riding my cock.

"Does it feel good?" he asked, his voice guttural as he bucked into me—harder, faster, deeper with every stroke. "Because your whole body is shaking; you feel fuckin' amazing. You've never felt…. Jesus, Trev, your ass is so tight and so hot. I'm gonna come! I'm gonna fuckin' come!"

I came, spurting over my stomach, my fingers, my hand, my wrist, making everything slick and wet. And then he pulled out and added to it, splattering over my abdomen and on my chest, watching, staring, and missing nothing.

We were both heaving for breath, panting and exhausted, but the way he was looking at me, the predatory gleam, had not left.

"Am I marked enough now? Have you done enough to me or does there actually need to be blood? Tell me."

The look in his eyes terrified me for a second before he bent and lapped at my stomach. Our seed, together, mixed, that apparently was finally enough. He slurped and sucked and swallowed, and when I dragged a finger through it and licked it clean, he shuddered. When I did it again, moving my finger toward my mouth, he leaned forward, lips parted.

I should have been freaked out, grossed out, anything, but all that mattered was bringing him back from the dark place he had gone to. So I touched my fingertip to his tongue and watched him lave at it, suck and taste, then move downward to my wrist and elbow. He licked and nibbled to my shoulder and then beneath, his face in my armpit, still licking before he moved across my chest, his mouth opening to suck my nipple, tug it, pull and finally bite down hard.

I gasped but he didn't care, and it hurt and didn't, everything blurring together, becoming the same.

"Your skin is driving me fuckin' crazy."

He was manic and he had to sleep, but he was still in a frenzy of need. And it was my fault. I knew better. When we were out, especially when we were out, he needed to be in my lap, holding my hand, close to me. I had forgotten that if we were home, had people at our place, it didn't matter; a woman could use me like a pole and wrap herself all over me and it was fine because he knew where he was, knew I was his. But out, when he couldn't look around and get his bearings, there was only me, and if I didn't keep tabs… then it was on me.

"I need water," I said suddenly because it was my last gambit.

"You do?"

I nodded.

He left and I could hear the ice trays in the kitchen being cracked, dumped into the tray in the freezer, and then the water running as he refilled them. When he came back, I saw the splotches of dried cum all over him and how he shivered. I thanked him and drained the glass. I saw it then; saw Landry back behind his eyes. That I had needed a favor, small, simple, and domestic, that had grounded him, reminded him of who he was, who I was, and about the two of us together.

"Let's strip the bed and take a shower, okay?"

He nodded because he was coming down—quiet, contained, and worried suddenly about what he had done.

I ran the shower and put him under the warm spray before I went back to take care of the sheets. We had two sets of linens for the bed and that was it. Lucky for us, the apartment had come with a washer and dryer, so that was really all we needed.

By the time he padded into the bedroom, a towel wrapped around his waist, I was done.

"Okay, I'm gonna go jump in the shower. I'll be right back."

He nodded, but I heard the stilted breath so I stepped in front of him on my way out of the room.

"Are you mad at me?"

I put my hands on his face. "Hell no, why would I be mad? You fucked me good."

He didn't like the answer, too glib, so I bent and kissed him, softly, tenderly, my tongue tracing over his bottom lip until he whimpered in the back of his throat. When I lifted away, he leaned with me.

"I love you, I will always love you, everything's fine and I'm not mad. I just need to sleep. You wore me out."

Lots of nodding, lots of smiling, and he let me go. By the time I was done with my shower, he was passed out in the bed. He didn't even move when I slid under the covers with him and turned off the light. That night we had both learned something, I understood my absolute place in his life and what he needed, and my boy learned how to top. It had been win-win in my mind from something that had started out very scary.

"TREV?"

I looked over at Conrad, the spell of my memories broken.

"Listen, you're not in any danger if you just are smart. Stay away from places you do business, simple as that."

I nodded. "Okay."

"Okay? What were you thinking about?"

"Nothing."

"Can you focus, please?"

"Sure."

"About the gun. If you go out of town, put the gun in the lockbox I gave you, and it goes in the hamper with the dirty clothes."

"Got it."

"Good."

My eyes flicked to his. "You know I appreciate it, right? Everything you do for me. I don't know how to show it without giving you money so you know I'm sincere."

"I know you're sincere, it's why I give a shit."

I nodded and then yawned, my eyes watering.

"You're so fuckin' tired."

"I am, shit."

"Just get Landry and the two of you go home and go to bed."

I grunted as he patted my knee.

Chapter
FOUR

CONRAD had to shake me awake when we reached Asil, and once I was there at the door, in the dark, I realized that I really needed to go home and get in bed. It was a little after six on a Tuesday night, and I saw at least five couples milling around. Landry's small boutique gallery, only a thousand square feet, was open Monday through Friday from nine in the morning to eight at night and on the weekends from eleven to four. It had simple cream-colored walls with a single orange-red accent color used once behind the cash register with the logo and again on the outside of the door. He had wanted a location with a window, and I said no, not downtown where he was thinking, not right there on the street. I had the door custom made so the glass was protected. Even if you broke it, you still couldn't get in. The alarm was set for the sound of breaking glass as well, either from the cases inside or the door. I was taking no chances with his safety or his livelihood.

We had picked a place with a wall of ivy beside the front door, which made graffiti impossible. On the other side of the gallery was an alley that cars drove through, so as far as trash and vandalism went, Asil was in good shape. The lady who owned the shop above sold shoes, which was why, as I came into the sandalwood-scented showroom, my boyfriend was walking—or rather, strutting—for his two salesgirls in four-inch patent leather platform boots. It was hot. He looked good in them, and they were doing something amazing to his ass, but the man was enormous. Normally six feet, he was now six four and all legs.

I flopped down on the riveted leather bench by the door.

"Hey, Trev," Chantal called over to me, her eyes sparkling in the light. "Check out Landry. He looks like a model."

"He's so gorgeous," Megan agreed, her eyes full of adoration for her boss.

"Oh, hi," the man himself greeted me coolly, pivoting around to face me like he was on the runway. "Aren't these fabulous?"

They were something.

"I'm so impressed you can walk in those," I told him. Then I realized that his hair, which had been dirty-blond in the morning, was now streaked with several different colors: chestnut, bronze, copper, and a bright red that was not a naturally occurring shade. Whoever had done it, the job was masterful, the highlights and lowlights blending well, but it was still a lot of colors on one head of hair. "I thought you weren't gonna mess with it anymore."

He shrugged. "I lied. It had to be done."

I realized instantly that he was furious. Not just annoyed, not just mad, but seething with anger at me. And I was tired, but now I had a fight on my hands.

"I like the round toe on the boots," I offered, trying to make peace for whatever I had done. Looking at the boots, seeing that the front was built up at least an inch and a half, maybe two inches, I was even more impressed that he could do the pivot walk and be so steady; my sister would have killed herself.

"They were only two hundred."

I nodded. We were supposed to be saving for my dream now, and a house and a car. We had expenses, and two-hundred-dollar shoes, though nothing for a lot of people, were a big deal for us.

"And my hair was a lot too."

Pushing, testing… seeing how far my patience would stretch. Would I yell? Could he actually, finally, get me to hit him? So many of the guys he let fuck him had hit him, too, got him drunk, drugged him up, and passed him around. One of his exes used to get off on watching him get gangbanged, and Landry had let it happen, not caring, just wanting to be loved. His self-esteem where his business was concerned was built up now, strong, fortified, but personally, he still craved constant validation.

"Well, you look amazing, and those are hot." I smiled at him, getting up. "But I'm beat and starving, and since you're not ready to go, I'm thinking pot roast isn't happening, right?"

"Nope."

"Okay, so I'm gonna head out and you come home when you're done, okay? I'm just gonna grab a sandwich at Antonia's and—"

"Fine, I don't need the play by play."

"Okay," I said, leaning sideways, smiling at the girls. "I'll see you guys."

I opened the door more slowly than I normally did, giving him ample time to stop me, giving him his out, making it easy for him to ask to speak to me outside without losing face in front of his staff. I knew his pride was important to him, mine not as much. But he didn't stop me, didn't call out, instead letting me leave. At the curb, I flagged down a cab and was gone seconds later.

My phone rang and I let it go to voicemail, which was childish, when I saw it was him. I was tired, though, and a little hurt that he had considered me so very little. When I saw a new number, I picked up.

"Hello?"

"Uhm, Trev?"

"Chantal," I replied with a smile while the driver took a left where I had told him.

"Landry's kind of upset."

"Well then Landry shouldn't be such a prick after the day I had."

"Okay."

I let out a deep, weary sigh. "I'm sorry. Is he there?"

"No, he just left, and he said he was going out to get laid."

I grunted.

"You're not—"

"He told you to call me."

"Yes, he did."

I shook my head. It was so like him, this drama. "It's fine, don't worry about it, okay? He'll be in tomorrow morning. Don't forget to set the alarm."

"Sure, but… can I ask you something?"

"G'head."

"I only deal with his shit at the most seven hours a day. You deal with it every day all the time… how do you do it?"

The man was more high maintenance than she knew, but that was between him and me. Those were secrets never to be shared. "The business is a big deal for him, that's why he's intense when he's there. He just wants everything to be perfect, that's all."

"That's what you're going with?"

"What do you mean?" I played dumb.

"Okay, Trevan, you're a really good guy. You don't even dish the dirt when you totally could. It's impressive. I hope I find one just like you."

"Awww, thanks, Chan," I teased her.

"Goodbye." She chuckled and hung up.

The cab driver let me out at the corner across the street from Antonia's Italian Bistro, a place I loved. I darted across the street in the now-driving rain, and when I walked in with a jingle of bells, I was greeted warmly, as I was every time I stopped to get food.

"Food or sandwiches?" Mrs. Mancini called out to me from behind the deli counter.

"Sandwiches."

"Two or one, Trev?"

"Two," I answered her, smiling big. "And his cannoli, two cream sodas, and my tiramisu, okay?"

"'Course." She beamed at me before turning and yelling the order back as I paid her daughter, Angela.

My phone rang as I waited, and I saw my friend Tommy's number. "Hey." I smiled into my phone, yawning at the same time.

"Hey, where the fuck are you?"

"Why?"

"Well, Landry just walked in here, and I don't know what the fuck he's wearing, but he's, like, eight feet tall, and he's sittin' at the bar lettin' some dickwad buy him a drink."

I snorted out a laugh, because how transparent could the man get? If he wanted to get a drink and get laid and cheat on me, why go to where he knew my friend Tommy tended bar and not any of the other places closer to his gallery?

"You guys fighting?"

"He's fighting alone." I sighed. "I think he's mad because he thinks I didn't need him earlier today, which isn't the case, but you know."

"No, I don't know, and I don't wanna know 'cause it's none of my fuckin' business. But what I do want is for him not to get drunk at my goddamn bar. And I can't watch him all night so—oh, never mind."

"What?"

"I see Skyler and Nate; they'll babysit him."

"Do me a favor."

"What?"

"Water down his drinks, okay?"

"Will do. See ya."

Normally I would go to wherever he was, take a seat on the other side of the bar from him, and keep an eye out, making sure that everyone understood that if they touched him, got too close, or even breathed on him, I'd remove their lungs. It was one of his favorite games, and my friends asked me how come I never went, sat across from him, and flirted with other people. Why didn't I ever give him a dose of what he gave me? Turnabout was fair play, wasn't it? Why not let some guy, or some girl, put their hands all over me?

The answer was simple: it would kill him, and I liked him alive and breathing. If the man ever saw me allowing someone else to touch me, it would break his fragile heart into a million, trillion pieces. We existed on the premise that he was the only one for me; he could never be shown any different.

After I got my order, tied up in a plastic bag to keep it dry, I walked home as fast as I could. I was still drenched by the time I got to our building and went up the stoop and through the outer door, where I stopped to check the mail before continuing through the inner door toward the elevator. It was a converted freight elevator, but I liked it.

Once inside the apartment, I checked the radiator, realized it hadn't kicked on yet, dumped the food in the kitchen, and went to stash the gun and take a shower. I was starting a fire when the front door flew open with a bang, slammed closed just as loudly, and Landry stormed in, boots loud and clomping on the varnished wood floor.

"I just came home to change," he announced haughtily.

"Sure," I said softly, returning to the task at hand.

He disappeared into the bedroom through the double French doors.

I got the fire crackling nicely as I turned on the stereo and got Melody Gardot, one of my favorites, crooning softly in the background. I sat at the small butcher block kitchen table, unwrapped his meatball sub and the horrible deep-fried pickles he liked, and poured his cream soda. He came out a few minutes later, all in black, the boots still on, jeans and a turtleneck sweater now making up the outfit. I was struck by how beautiful he looked, but I swallowed down the compliment as I ate my food.

"What is that?"

"You should eat," I told him, my voice husky and soft. "Don't wanna drink on an empty stomach."

"I've already been drinking."

"Dancing, then."

"I guess," he snapped at me.

He took his usual seat beside me instead of across from me, which was more telling than he realized even though we ate in silence. When I was done, I got up and went to the refrigerator to get my tiramisu but then thought better of it. My plan was simply to pass out; I'd save it until I could enjoy it.

"Your cannoli's in here," I told him. "You want it now or later?"

"Later," he said, and I saw the muscles in his jaw clenching, the way he was chewing on his bottom lip, and how crumpled his napkin was from being crushed in his hand.

I cleared the table and wiped it, and still he sat there.

"Thank you for remembering the pickle chips," he said softly.

"You're welcome."

I did the dishes, the two plates and two glasses, and put them in the dish rack to air dry.

"Where ya gonna go?" I asked, leaving the light on above the sink but flipping the kitchen one off, only the fireplace illuminating the apartment.

"To Spin, I think."

"Okay." I yawned and stretched, yanking my T-shirt off over my head and flipping it over my shoulder as I crossed back to where he was and leaned on the chair. "I just wanna tell you that talking to you earlier helped me a lot. Just knowing that you're here every night to come home to, it's a big deal."

He nodded fast.

"Oh, and I had to drop off money to my mom today, and she said that when she gets back from visiting my Aunt Janet, she'll teach you how to make the bouillabaisse."

"Good."

"All right, then, make sure you take your key." I smiled at him, then turned around, heading for the bedroom.

"I might not come home."

"Whatever you think is best," I said from the entrance to our room, opening one side of the French doors.

"You don't care if I don't come home?"

I turned and looked back at him, and he was still at the table, his eyes welling with tears that I ignored. "I just want you to be happy."

He sucked in a breath.

"Are you happy?"

His brows furrowed.

"'Cause you don't look happy," I growled at him. "Beautiful, but not happy."

His eyes went to the fire, the couch, the kitchen sink, and back on his restless hands. He was trying so hard not to look at me. "I'm sorry about the boots. I was upset."

"Sure."

"I won't do it again."

"It's okay, I know you won't."

"And I used the last of my tax money to get my hair done; I didn't touch our checking account."

"Again, it's fine."

His eyes were landing everywhere but on me.

"You didn't answer... are you happy?"

Finally, the blue-green pools came to rest, meeting mine. "Are you?"

"I would be happy if you came to bed with me, but it's too early, and you have dancing and drinking to do. I don't wanna make you just lie there and watch TV while I go comatose next to you."

He was trembling, and I narrowed my eyes as I looked at him.

"Those boots make your legs look amazing… and your ass."

He was biting the inside of his cheek, I could tell. "You like the ankle boots?"

"Love them."

He sucked in his breath. "I thought you didn't need me."

"I always need you, but your routine is very important, and when I upset that, you don't do well. So it was better for you to go to work and stay there and for me to just handle my day, deal with having a gun—"

"A gun?"

I grunted. "I don't want anyone to hurt you, so I have to be ready. You're my baby; I have to protect you."

He rose then and walked to the front door, locked it and the deadbolt, and turned and looked at me. "I thought you could handle things on your own, that I wasn't important."

"But you know better than that," I muttered, turning and walking away.

"What?" he called after me. "I didn't hear you."

I knew he hadn't, and I walked deeper into our bedroom and climbed into bed. I didn't stretch out, though, didn't sink down into the pillow. He needed me; I couldn't sleep yet.

"What did you say?" I heard his voice following behind me.

I rolled over on my back and looked at him, my eyes tracing over the lines of him, his flushed skin, wet lips, long eyelashes, and legs that went on forever.

"Come here for a second before you go," I said, pretending that I had not seen him lock us in for the night.

He walked to the side of the bed.

I reached under the elastic waistband of my sweats and stroked my cock, feeling it harden with anticipation, the slither of arousal moving through me.

"What do you want?"

"I want you to take off all your clothes and get in bed with me."

He gasped. "I thought you liked the boots."

I grinned at him. Only Landry would get hung up on that. "Baby, I love the boots and I can't wait to lick them some night when I'm remotely coherent, but right now I would give anything for a kiss."

"You would?"

"I would."

He stripped fast, pulling, yanking, and then he was straddling my thighs, knees on either side of my waist.

His shaft was hard, bumping against mine as I reached up with both hands for his face.

"I'm sorry," he whimpered, the tears slipping down his cheeks. "I'm such an idiot and you must hate me and—"

"Never hate you."

"Forgive me."

"Forgiven," I promised, easing him down, my lips parting to receive him.

He twitched and jolted like he did sometimes when he was really wound up, and slanted his mouth down roughly over mine, bumping me with his teeth, in a hurry, grinding into me. That fast there was blood, his teeth cutting my lip.

"Oh God, I'm—"

"It's okay, baby," I sighed, my voice sultry, his shallow breaths letting me know the effect I was having on him. "Just slow down and come here."

The kiss I gave him was languid, drugging and deep. His lips fit mine perfectly, and when he moaned softly, hoarse and needy, I rolled him gently to his back, parted his legs, and slid my freed cock against his.

"Here." He was breathless as he slipped the lube he had pulled from beneath his pillow into my hand.

I flipped the cap open, dribbled some on the ends of my fingers, and tenderly began making small circles at his entrance as I continued to make love to his mouth.

"Trevan," he breathed out, bending his knees, giving me better access as I slowly breached him, my fingers pushing inside the tight ring of muscle, pressing, sliding. I was careful not to plunge them deep until I knew he was ready. He was always so tight, which was a continual source of pleasure for me.

When he lifted his hips, I added two fingers, three now plunging steadily inside, massaging, opening him up and making him slick, relaxed.

"Please."

I folded his legs in half so his thighs were pressed to his chest as I slid the head of my cock inside of him, moving so slowly, stretching him, filling him, letting him feel every inch of me.

"You're so hard." He sucked in his breath.

"And you're so hot," I growled, pushing deeper, my hips snapping forward, plunging in to the hilt, needing to be fully sheathed.

His head was thrown back, eyes closed, and as I shifted my angle, driving forward, hammering inside of him, he begged me.

"No," I said flatly, stopping, rolling over at the same time, bringing him with me, my hands digging into his thighs to keep his ass plastered to my groin, our new position impaling him on my shaft.

He gasped, hands on my chest, levering up only to sink back down seconds later. As he lifted again, I fisted his cock, milking it slowly as his inner walls rippled around me, the spasms of heat and pressure making me spear up into him even as he pushed down.

"Why did—why do that?"

"Because I should have left you up here," I groaned hoarsely, having trouble speaking. "You're so beautiful when you're riding my cock, and I get to hold you in my hand and feel your heartbeat right here."

"Oh," he whimpered.

He felt so good and I needed him so badly. "Landry," I whispered.

His head fell back as he gave in, his muscles clenching all at once as he came over my fingers, cum dribbling down over my wrist, coating my abdomen.

I pounded him from the bottom, fucking him though his climax as I reached mine, filling him up and making him pant with the sensation.

"I love you… God, I love you," he told me.

I reached for him with my left hand, with the one not covered in spunk, and grabbed him hard around the back of the neck, wrenching him down so I could devour his mouth. He fell into the kiss, and it went on, our mouths mashed together, lips stretched almost painfully as he lay against me, semen pressed between us, sticky and slick.

When he finally lifted up off me, it was like glue coming apart, stretched thread-thin. I started laughing and he joined me, and then we were both gone, the relief, the joy, all of it mixed up together.

In the eventual silence, Landry sighed deeply. "I'm sorry about Benji."

"Me too."

"I don't want you to get hurt."

"I won't. Conrad says I won't, and so does Gabe. I just gotta lay low for like a week."

He nodded.

"So maybe we could go see your folks. What do you think?"

"Okay," he agreed after a moment of thought.

"And if it's bad, we'll leave and just go get a hotel room on the strip and order room service and watch porn."

He rolled his head to look at me, reaching out, hand over my heart, over the L for his name. "I'm sorry, okay?"

"Nothing to be sorry for; I knew you weren't going anywhere," I assured him, brushing the hair out of his eyes. "You threaten me, but you'd never fuck around on me."

"No."

"I know." I smiled at him, my eyes fluttering, so tired I was barely conscious.

"I shouldn't threaten you, though. It's stupid."

"It's human," I told him, admiring his cute little upturned nose and his long gold eyelashes even as I fought to stay awake.

He sighed deeply. "I'm okay. Go to sleep. I'll clean you up, tuck you under the covers, and lie down beside you and watch TV. I won't leave—why would I want to?"

"You promise?"

"I promise," he said breathlessly. "I'll never leave you. Without you I don't even know who the fuck I am."

"Yes, you do. You're okay."

"Only because you say so."

I really need to think about fixing that, I thought before my eyes fluttered closed.

I WOKE in the night to fingertips being trailed slowly, sensuously, up and then down my spine from the nape of my neck, following the groove that ran the length of my back, to the divots above the swell of my ass. The motion was delicate, reverent, the touch enjoyed, savored, and when lips made the same journey, I sighed deeply.

"Don't wake up," he whispered, fingers back, stroking so light, so infinitely gentle. "I just need to say that I'm sorry, so sorry. I was selfish today, and I didn't mean to be. It's just sometimes I think something, something bad, and then I get stuck there, in that place, and I can't get out. I want to, but I just can't."

I knew that.

He pressed his lips to the small of my back before he turned his head, and I felt his weight settle over me as he used my ass for a pillow.

My sigh was deep.

"I love you," he said, his voice trembling.

"Me too," I whispered back.

The kiss on my right cheek made me smile. The bite made me giggle.

"Go to sleep," he chided me.

I whined under him. "Maybe I could get laid first?"

He grunted like it was a hardship. "Roll over."

"Not if you're gonna be like—"

"Now."

I rolled over.

Chapter
FIVE

WE WERE sitting in the boarding area, and I was looking across the terminal at Landry as he stood in line at Starbuck's. When Chris had appeared the following morning, Landry had given him the good news that we would go to Vegas with him. He had grabbed his brother and then me, repeating over and over how much he appreciated it. I told him that touching me a lot was not the way to endear himself to Landry. When Chris saw his face, the glare, the clenched jaw, the corded muscles in his neck, he understood. "Possessive" was an understatement where Landry was concerned.

I had called my friend Donna, who was a travel agent, and she did some wheeling and dealing and got the three of us coach seats together on the left side of a 747.

Landry packed because as OCD as he was, you could not ask for better. He never forgot anything. We could be lost at sea and be okay the way the man accounted for every possibility.

So early the following morning, right around five thirty, I was sitting in the chairs watching him stand in line to get drinks for the flight and fiddle with his iPod at the same time. As usual, Landry had surprised me. I had thought he'd be a mess, be scared or worried, but he wasn't. He was a rock. His voice had changed to matter-of-fact, and he had politely refused his brother's offer to buy our plane tickets, busting out his American Express and telling him that we would take care of it. And that was Landry. He could be a complete and utter basket case and then flip and become the epitome of a cool, calm yuppie businessman. Chris kept looking at him, waiting for some kind of psychotic break.

On the plane, I got the window because that was where Landry wanted me. He took the middle seat, and Chris got the aisle. Once we were in the air, Landry lifted the armrest between us and snuggled into my side, head on my shoulder, thigh wedged next to mine. I was still tired, so I succumbed fast, military cap down over my eyes, my fingers buried in Landry's thick hair, massaging his head as I listened to his breath even out. I woke up two hours later when we hit some choppy air and the flight attendant wanted to check if Landry was buckled in. I moved the blanket so she could see and then showed her mine.

"Thank you so much," she whispered to me, smiling. "Some people get so annoyed."

"My Aunt Anita." I smiled at her. "She's a flight attendant at Continental. She tells me great stories all the time."

She nodded. "Well thank you for understanding. Go back to sleep."

I nodded.

"Your boyfriend?"

"Yes."

"He's very handsome," she told me.

And I agreed. I realized, after a minute, that Chris was gone, probably in the bathroom or something, but since I didn't really care where he was, I went back to sleep.

The rest of the flight passed unnoticed, and I woke back up around nine thirty in the morning Detroit time, which meant that it was six thirty in the morning in Vegas. We had just another half an hour to go so I got up; since most everyone else was asleep, there was no wait to get into the bathroom. When I got back, I climbed over Chris, and when I sat down, Landry sat up, bleary, hair sticking up, looking confused.

"Morning, baby." I smiled at him.

He squinted at me and tried to push Chris off of his shoulder.

"Quit that," I chided, chuckling. "He's asleep; that's mean."

"I don't care. He has to get up anyway, and he's fuckin' drooling on me." He squinted and put his finger on Chris's forehead, pushing him away, moving as far into me as possible.

"You're such an ass."

He turned to look at me, and the smile was the one I really liked, wicked and confident, eyes glittering. He was beautiful.

"Leave him alone," I said, taking my cap off, rubbing my buzzed to the scalp hair that I never let grow out, and smiling at him. "Gimme a kiss."

"All these orders this morning." He sighed and leaned in, his lips sliding over mine, fitting, as always, like they had been custom made for me.

"God, I gotta pee," he said when he leaned back.

"By all means," I teased him.

"Get up," he snapped at his brother as he climbed over him.

Chris straightened in his seat, looking worse than both Landry and me. "Did you get up?"

"Yeah."

"So I guess you weren't, like, a total shit like he just was."

I squinted at him.

After a few minutes he took a breath. "Sorry. I just... you can't possibly understand, but this is huge for me, for my whole family. We've all been living without Landry for the past eight years, and every time we get happy or take a family picture or spend a holiday, it's always not what it could be because he's not there."

I nodded.

"I was fourteen when he left," he said, eyes on me, "and I missed him."

It hit me then, what Chris was seeing when he looked at my boyfriend—a piece of his past.

"He was my older brother, and he was there my whole life, and then suddenly he wasn't, and I remember asking my folks, 'Where is he? When's he coming back?' And you know—" He swallowed hard. "—at first it was, 'he'll be back at the end of the summer', and then when he wasn't, they were certain they'd hear from him once school started."

I stared at him, into his eyes, which were a piercing blue, pretty in their own right but not heart-stopping because they were missing the green that made me go weak in the knees.

"I guess my parents hired a private detective when he first left, so they knew where he was," he told me. "They've always known, and they could have reached out, but they were mad, I guess, and so was he, and all this time, no one wrote or sent a Christmas card or anything. It's just nuts, you know, and what started as, like, this small hurdle or whatever has become this fortified fuckin' wall, and when I found out what really happened I—"

"What do you mean?"

He squinted at me. "What do you mean what do I mean?"

I leaned back in my seat, not sure what we were talking about. "Your folks threw Landry out because he was gay," I told him.

"No," he told me, "they didn't."

"What do you mean they didn't?"

"They threw him out because of the drugs, because of the stealing and the lies. They threw him out because he was diagnosed as having a severe bipolar disorder, where he's manic one day and severely depressed the next. He takes medicine, doesn't he?"

And that fast my whole world flipped upside down, because somebody was lying.

"Trevan?"

I leaned back in my seat and just stared at him.

"What's wrong?"

"Your folks hate Landry because he's gay."

"No. They've known he was gay since he was, like, sixteen, maybe fifteen, why would they care if he was gay?"

Shit.

"Wait." He was processing. "Is that why he—I mean, the other day when he said that my mother hated him I thought he just meant 'cause they've had no contact for the last eight years, but he doesn't actually think that… he hasn't actually convinced himself that they threw him out because he was gay, has he? That's not what he really believes, is it?"

"That's exactly what he believes."

He exhaled fast, looking like I'd hit him. "No no no…." He put up a hand. "That… Trevan, he was supposed to go into this really good program and this private clinic in New York, and my mother rented this apartment in town so she could be close to him and… ohmygod…." He closed his eyes, face in his hands, just reeling. "Jesus Christ, he's completely delusional."

My eyes narrowed as I looked at him.

"Trevan," he gasped, swallowing hard, his fingers raking through his hair. "You gotta believe me. My folks didn't give a shit about Landry being gay. I mean, they found him in the stables with their best friend's son, you know, and he, Will, got sent to some conversion therapy, reparative therapy, reorientation whatever place, and his parents made him go, but my folks, they never even considered that for Landry because who were they to tell him how to live his life. His orientation had nothing to do with them, but his illness… that was the problem, nothing else."

There was nothing that led me to believe that he was lying to me. He seemed completely and utterly stunned.

"Ohmygod, I thought he was… I thought how he was acting, how angry he seems at me… I thought that was because I didn't have the balls to look for him. I mean…." His eyes lifted to mine. "I've missed him…. I… my mother's expecting him to be mad, but she's not thinking that he didn't get help. She figured he—"

"Not much of a detective your parents hired if they never knew that he never got help."

"No. All they heard was where he was, that he was alive and well."

Remembering two years ago, when he and I had just begun, I wondered what the private detective's idea of "well" was. "So your folks just let Landry walk out of their lives even though he was sick?"

He cleared his throat. "You don't know how it was. Just to have him gone for a while, it was such a relief. He stole from them—money, my mother's jewelry, my father's old coins. Did he tell you about his cocaine habit? Do you know about that?"

But how could that be? When I met him, there had been vices, addictions, but they had all been abandoned so quickly, so completely, so thoroughly, and never seen again. The man only drank socially, sometimes had wine or beer at home with me, but that was it. He never hid anything from me. I saw him every day, knew where he went and who he saw. There was more reason to doubt *me*.

"My folks think… I mean, I told them how good he looks, how amazing his business is, and all about you. They're dying to meet you."

I had not anticipated that.

"How is he?" he asked, and his breath was shaky. "I mean, how does he function?"

"What are you talking about?"

"I mean, he used to go into these rages and just... he came at me with a knife once. We were in the kitchen and I said something, and our maid was cooking, and he grabbed the chef's knife, and if my father hadn't been there... I mean, he came at me, do you understand?"

I understood what he was saying, but Landry's intent was lost to me since I hadn't been there.

"I went into his room one time and he was slicing up his arm, and I remember screaming for my mother, and everyone came running and they took away the knife and held him down and just.... Trevan, if he's never gotten any help, then you're living on borrowed time." He said it earnestly, willing me to believe him. "I swear to God he could hurt you... more than hurt you."

The concern was there, real, on his face.

Yes, Landry could be volatile, but so was I. And Landry was the guy with the balanced life now; mine was the scary one.

"Hey."

We both looked up, and there he was, yawning, eyes watering as he looked down at me and Chris.

"Can you move so I can sit?" he asked his brother.

"Sure," Chris said, getting up so Landry could push by him to retake his seat next to me.

Once he was down, Landry put on his seatbelt and offered me either the chocolate chip granola bar or the Power Bar from where he had stuffed them into the pocket in front of his seat.

"I'm not hungry," I assured him.

"You sure?"

I nodded, and he reached up and touched the ten gauge hammered steel plug in my right ear. "What?"

"I got those red jade ones for you for Valentine's Day, but you never wear them."

"That's because they're red." I smiled at him. "What do I own that goes with red?"

He smiled at me. "You need to try something new."

I closed my eyes. "I don't like change."

"I know," he said, and I felt his fingers tracing over my eyebrow.

"I like all those bracelets you make," Chris told Landry.

"I have one for you, but I don't know if you want it."

Silence.

"You made me one?"

"I picked you one. I didn't have time to make one from scratch, but I have one that I think fits with your vibe."

"Really?"

"Yes."

"Can I have it? I mean… I'd love it." Chris was breathless, and no matter what he thought of his brother, about his brother, Landry doing anything for him flipped him inside out.

"Here," he said, and I didn't open my eyes to see. It wasn't that important to me. What was important was that Landry had done something for his brother.

"Oh shit, Lan, this is awesome," he breathed out. He was in awe, and it was good to hear.

"You like it?"

"I love it."

"Good. Now the amber is supposed to ground you so you don't go crazy," he told him. "Trev always tells me that I should be draped in it."

Chris sucked in his breath, and I started chuckling.

Landry let out a snort of laughter before his lips pressed to my jaw, his fingers grazing my throat. "Let's get drunk tonight, okay?"

"Whatever you want."

"Whatever I want?" he asked, his voice almost a growl. "If I beg down on my knees, will you please tie me up?"

Sometimes Landry needed to be rendered completely helpless to allow his brain to just shut off. In the following moment of vulnerability, when there was no choice but to surrender to me and trust in me, everything could just stop. He was asking me now for the peace that only I could provide for him even as I recognized his desire for the reset even sooner.

"Yes," I assured him.

He was instantly breathless. "Thank you."

I could tell from the way his hands were clutching at me that he needed something else. The problem was that I had no idea what it was.

The landing, getting off the plane, getting our luggage, all of that was easy. It was when I told Chris that we were going to rent a car that he balked.

"My father sent our driver to pick us up; he'll be at your disposal when we get home. You don't need to get a car, Trevan."

I cleared my throat. "We do."

"I just—"

"If we need to leave, we need a car," Landry said flatly, eyes leveled on his brother. "So let us rent the car or we'll just get back on the plane. Your choice."

Chris wasn't happy. He told me, leaning in, whispering harshly over my shoulder, that he felt I was adding tension that had not even been necessary. I wasn't going to argue; it was how I needed it to be. I had to have an escape route, and I was much too independent to ask for permission. If I wanted to go, I would go, and that was it.

"I'm starving," Landry told me minutes later.

"I called Mom last night and told her when we would be in; she's having breakfast catered this morning."

I looked at Landry, surprised and a little intimidated. How rich was his family? Catered.

He shook his head, disgusted.

"What?"

"Typical."

Typical?

Once we were in the silver Dodge Charger following the black Audi sedan, I asked what he meant.

"It's just like I told you they were. They're not like your mom or your aunts or your sister. Breakfast for me for the first time in eight years—catered."

"It's nice." I shrugged. "I mean, this way no one has to get up. It's like being at a restaurant, you can all just talk."

He was quiet, and I reached out and took his hand, lacing my fingers into his.

"You know what I'd like?" he said.

"What's that?"

"I'd like you to pull over so I can give you a blow job."

I rolled my eyes. "Or, you can think about what you're gonna say in the next half an hour."

He sighed deeply and looked away from me.

I so wanted to ask him about what Chris had told me, but I really didn't want to sound like I doubted his word. We would go with his recollection of the events until it was proven that he was wrong. If he was.

It took a lot longer than half an hour to get to Landry's childhood home. We passed the strip and just kept going. I had never seen so many mansions, golf courses, and long private drives. The one that led to the Carter home was a mile in and tree lined, so it was like driving under an arbor the whole way. The grounds looked like a botanical garden. There was a man-made lake, and when we were almost to the house, we were suddenly driving over cobblestones. The house was huge—I couldn't see anything else—and it looked like a giant white Spanish-tiled movie set.

"Holy fuck" was all I could think of to say as I leaned forward over the steering wheel and laughed. "Are you shitting me?"

"What?"

I turned and looked at him, chuckling.

"What?" He was starting to smile.

"Oh, c'mon," I teased him, waggling my eyebrows at him. "Hey mister, can you keep me? Can I have a diamond car?"

"Ass," he groused at me, smacking my shoulder.

I turned off the car and got out, closing the door gently, turning around, absolutely blown away by the display of wealth and privilege just from the damn driveway and what else I could see. The front door was under an archway, and the ground was covered in what looked like hand-painted tile. There were walls of water on both sides of the entranceway, all blue with mosaic tiles. I had never seen such opulence in my life. To say I was overwhelmed was an understatement.

"Fuck." I shook my head, turning to look at my boyfriend over the roof of the car. "What are you doing hanging out with me?"

His eyes were locked on mine. "The only thing I see that's real here is you."

"That's a good fuckin' answer." I smiled, waving him over.

He was pretty happy with himself and strutted around the car for good measure, diving at me when he was close, arms around my neck, kissing me happily, hungrily. I grabbed him tight, kissed him back, and when we parted he looked good, solid, content.

"Come on, you guys," Chris called over to us, gesturing at his driver. "Juan will bring in the luggage, don't worry."

"Juan," I called over to the driver, "we'll get our own stuff, man, no worries."

He nodded as I walked around to the trunk of the car.

Landry got his garment bag and his rolling suitcase—the man had brought enough clothes to stay for a week—and I grabbed my bag, whipped it over my back, and followed after him.

Once we went through the outer door, we entered a courtyard with a tile sort of path and a garden on each side, patio furniture, an outdoor fireplace, and what could only be called a grotto, complete with frescoes. Following Chris, we walked over a stone footbridge that crossed over water, and on the other side, there were wide steps covered in grass and wildflowers, and then it looked like you entered a cabana. The porch was huge, all wooden planked and carved and solid. There were chairs every five feet or so, and tables. You could have a party just on the front deck.

It was all windows, floor to ceiling, like the house was just made of them, and we walked into a huge space that was a living room, I guessed, but the doors were open on the other side, and there was the biggest pool I had ever seen in my life, a back deck, and stairs.

I trailed after Landry and Chris. Outside, the stairs descended to a bigger deck where there was a Jacuzzi and a covered area. Down those stairs was another pool, long and skinny, that emptied into a backyard that was lush green grass and tennis courts—two of them—and buildings that were probably for the servants. All I noticed, everywhere I looked, were huge trees. It was like a movie set; I expected dinosaurs at any second.

I did not belong there. I was uncomfortable, so far out of my comfort zone that I was seriously ready to bolt, and every drop of confidence I had just shriveled up and died. It was like a siren blaring in my brain. I was in way over my head.

"Landry!"

I looked, and there was an older woman, and you knew as soon as you looked at her that this was Landry's mother.

Cece, short for Cecilia, Carter. Landry looked just like her. They had the same delicate, fragile features, same short little upturned nose, and the same dimples when they smiled. They also shared wide, symmetrical almond-shaped eyes that were almost but not quite the same color. Her hair was blonde; he had inherited the color from her, but the thickness and the waviness, he got from his father. Neil Carter had also gifted him with the breadth and strength of his shoulders, long legs, and a square jaw. His parents were both gorgeous, but that followed, since their son could stop traffic. Landry was like a perfect melding of both of them.

Other people hovered around, a couple and two men. As I followed after Landry, I wasn't sure what to do with my hands. I really wished I was still carrying my duffel, but Chris had had us leave the luggage beside the couch in the big room that we had walked through.

"Landry!" She bolted for him, the mother flying to her son, and he let out a breath and opened his arms to receive her.

I thought she was going to knock him down with how hard she hit him, but he absorbed it, holding her tight as her arms wrapped around his neck and she hugged the life out of him.

"My baby," she chanted, kissing his cheek, hugging him, so happy, whimpering and whining, more kissing, squeezing him as tight as she could.

He patted her back, stroked her hair, told her he'd missed her, offered condolences on her illness and hoped she was better. And all the time he did, none of the kindness of his words or the smiling he was doing touched his eyes. They didn't change. They didn't soften. They didn't warm. So I knew—and maybe I was the only one—that he wasn't feeling any part of what he was showing them.

That was not to say that he was not genuinely sorry that his mother was ill. He was, but sorry in the same way he would feel if a coworker was sick, or a neighbor—it wasn't special because it was her. If my mother was sick, God forbid, he would have been devastated and been her new shadow. This was different, and I saw the distance on him, all over him, from his posture to the furrowing of his brows to the smile that did nothing for his face. He didn't light up, he didn't glow—there was nothing. I was stunned, and even more so that I was the only one who even noticed.

"Yes, I am better," his mother breathed out finally, bringing my attention from my boy back to her. I saw her hands on his shoulders, her eyes everywhere, absorbing his face, his clothes, his shoes, his hands—she missed nothing. "I'm in remission right now, but we just don't know how long it will last. That's why I reached out to you. I won't miss this, I won't miss reconnecting with you... I won't."

He nodded, forced another smile before turning to look at me. "I'd like you to meet Trevan."

She turned her deep blue eyes to me.

I took off my cap and smiled. "Pleasure to meet you, ma'am."

Her breath caught as she let go of her son and walked over to me, her arms open as she moved. "Trevan," she gasped. "Please, call me Cece."

Whatever I had expected, the reception she gave me was not it. The woman was on me, arms around my neck, kissing my cheek, pressed tight to me, thanking me over and over for coming because she knew sure as she was standing there that without me there was no hope.

"He would have never come without you," she told me, her breath shaky as I heard the tears. "Oh darling, thank you... thank you so much."

My eyes flicked to Landry as he walked over to us, putting his hand on the back of my neck, squeezing, massaging.

She let me go, stepping back to look at us, taking us in. "Well, don't you two make a beautiful pair."

Landry's smile was instantly brilliant, all there, animating his features. She gasped, the understanding hitting her. Compliment me, make her son deliciously happy. She was observant, and that lesson was an easy one to learn.

"Come see everybody," she commanded, taking Landry's hand, tugging him after her.

He let go of my neck and grabbed my hand, and I took hold of it and held on so his mother ended up pulling a chain, first him, then me.

"Landry."

His father, Neil Carter, held out his arms, and it was obvious that Landry was supposed to go to him, not the other way around. He moved after a second and they did the guy clench, but that was it. I was surprised at his father's lack of emotion and warmth, but at least it was real. The handshake the man gave me, with the added squeeze of my bicep, seemed friendlier. At least it wasn't just pleasant. He was really very pleased to meet me.

Landry's brother Scott stepped in beside his father and gave Landry the same greeting, but the handshake I got could barely be called one. He didn't want to touch me at all.

Jocelyn, Landry's sister, was next, a female version of him, but smaller boned, like a bird, with flawless skin and sharp-angled model features. Her husband, Hugh, looked like he belonged in a magazine with her with his perfect smile, perfect hair, and perfect suit. She hugged her brother tight, leaned on him, and told him how much he'd been missed. Hugh shook his hand and told him how pleased he was to finally meet him. It didn't feel real to me, but I was used to my loud "grab you tight and steal your breath" family.

When my father passed away, at the funeral, his parents, my grandparents, walked right up to my mother and begged her not to disappear from their lives. They wanted to make sure, even though my father was the youngest of six and they had plenty of other grandkids, that my sister and I would still be around. They didn't want to miss out on seeing us grow up. My mother started bawling, and my grandfather wrapped her up in his strong arms. I wasn't sure, but I thought maybe some of my mother's hesitancy about waiting so long to date stemmed from how close she still was to my father's family. It had been a blessing for me and my sister having so much family, so many people who kept tabs on us and cared. And we knew we were loved.

Either side you chose, my mom's Cuban contingent or my dad's African American camp, everybody hugged and kissed and force-fed you and held your hand and got up in your face if they had a question. I was loved, I knew I was, and there was no way to miss it. Seeing how quiet everyone was at Landry's home, how subdued, I didn't wonder why he so adored my family. The level of "showing" that Landry required, the physical demonstration, the verbal assurances, the ordering for him to come and sit his ass down and eat and talk—he knew he was loved to pieces in my world; he had to have floundered in his.

"I'd like you to meet my boyfriend," he told his sister.

I leaned forward and shook her hand, shook Hugh's, and smiled.

"Will," Landry said then, and I realized that he was talking to the guy standing behind his sister.

"Your folks thought it would be nice for you to see an old friend," he told him, walking forward, arms out. "And I was thrilled to hear that you were finally coming home."

Landry took a step back and offered Will his hand instead of the hug the other man had obviously been expecting. "Thank you."

Will was hurt; it was in his eyes even as he tried to smile and shook the hand that had been thrust at him. "I can't wait for you to meet my family; I'm bringing them with me tonight to your welcome home party."

Landry withdrew his hand. "Your family?"

"Yes, my wife and children."

"You're married?"

"Of course, why wouldn't I be?"

Landry nodded and reached for me.

I took the questing hand in mine and squeezed tight.

"This is my boyfriend, Trevan Bean. Trev, this is my old friend Will."

"Oh." He was very surprised, downright stunned to be looking at me. "Your boyfriend?"

"Yes," was all Landry said.

"But I thought you—"

"What did you think?" Landry asked quietly. "That I did what you did?"

He was staring at Landry, trying to understand something.

"We were never the same," my boyfriend said icily.

"No," Will agreed, and I saw all the pain and all the longing on his face.

It made me uncomfortable, seeing another man utterly grieving for a lost love who was standing right in front of him. I offered him my hand to break the spell.

He didn't take it; he just looked at me. He didn't even lift his hand. It was very obvious that he had no intention of touching me at all.

"You must be starved," Cece announced into the awkward silence as she walked back over to us, taking Landry's hand, patting it. "Come sit down and eat. I want you to tell me everything."

The table was big and round, so nobody was stuck sitting at one end or the other. It was also lavishly set like nothing I had ever seen. There were water goblets already filled and an orchard of fruit on each place setting. My mother would have loved it. Our idea of Sunday morning breakfast was a serve-yourself line in the kitchen where everyone piled on their own food and you got utensils and a napkin at the end. At my apartment, there was a paper towel roll instead.

There was a choice: strawberry crepes, eggs Benedict, or something else I couldn't pronounce. I went with the crepes, wishing we had stopped somewhere. What I really wanted was steak and eggs and lots of salsa and pancakes and… just more.

I had never seen a waiter in a house, but there were two, bringing us a hot washcloth to wipe our hands on and then juice and coffee.

"Landry, darling, what do you do?"

As I sat there and listened and ate and drank the coffee that I would have died without, I realized again how different it was from what I had imagined. There was no tearful emotional scene. Landry did not attack his parents; they didn't tell him how sorry they were. It was all so civil, so *"Are the crepes to your liking?" "Oh yes, they're lovely, thank you."* My stomach started to flutter with how fake it all was.

Landry explained about his business, and his sister, who was in pharmaceutical sales but had just launched her own Christmas ornament line on Etsy, was very interested to hear how he was doing. He gave her the web address so she could look him up and then passed her his phone so she could see the pictures of his gallery.

"Ohmygod, Lan." She beamed over at him. "It's beautiful, and your pieces are just gorgeous. I, uhm—" She cleared her throat. "—couldn't get you to—"

"I brought something for you and Mom," he told her, turning to get into his messenger bag, which was hanging on the back of his chair.

"You did?" Cece lit up, excited.

"Yeah, Chris already got his."

"Let me see," Jocelyn demanded.

Chris rolled up the sleeve of his cardigan and showed them all the triple-wrap amber bracelet. Jocelyn leaned over to examine it.

"You sew each one of these beads in. That's amazing," she told him.

"And his has a piece of carnelian beside the toggle clasp to ward off the evil eye."

"I love this; where's mine?"

He chuckled, turned, and passed his mother her gift bag, and then he stood to lean across the table to offer another to Jocelyn. They were drawstring bags, lightly beaded, a navy one for his sister and a maroon one for his mother. The velvet bags he put his jewelry in all had his logo and "Asil" in Parchment font stamped into a leather piece on one side.

"I love this bag." Jocelyn smiled at him as she touched it. "It reminds me of a Middle Eastern bazaar or something."

"Exactly," he agreed and grinned at her.

"What does 'Asil' mean?" she asked him.

"It means pure in Arabic."

"Oh, I just love stuff like this."

He seemed very pleased at the compliment, but again, as he would be from a stranger in his store. When my aunts complimented him, he puddled into goo.

She leaned forward, still not even opening it. "Lan, your packaging is stunning and your place is just... your sense of style.... I'm so impressed and so happy for you."

"Thanks." He sighed. "I wanted to go green, you know, but the recycled boxes and bags just didn't go, and so the brilliant man sitting at my right suggested we have bags that people can bring back or trade up— we have lined and unlined—and keep forever and use as jewelry bags."

Her eyes flicked to me. "Brilliant."

"I have my moments," I told her.

"We have small sandalwood satchels with the Asil logo on it that we sell too."

"To go with the idea of jewelry bag, scent a drawer or a box." She nodded. "Of course."

He shrugged in agreement that it was a no-brainer.

"I love everything about this."

His hand went to my thigh and squeezed. He was nervous, and I had no idea why.

"Look at this," his mother gasped.

All eyes were on her as she held up the hammered gold chain with green jade accents. It looked like it was five necklaces because the beads were different sizes and the chain itself was thick and thin in places. It looked rustic, and I knew it was one of his biggest sellers. He'd made many, but each one was breathtaking.

His mother was overwhelmed. "Oh, Landry, I adore it."

"Ohmygod!" Jocelyn almost shrieked.

Hers was blue quartz and Tahitian freshwater pearl, and because it was a long piece, it could be worn either draped to her stomach or double-wrapped around her neck. Again, it was one of his best. It had been thoughtful, and his mother and sister were gushing. I was reminded of Christmas every year.

Family, friends, all the women who knew Landry waited in breathless anticipation for his gifts. My sister would scream and squeal and take pictures of herself and post them on Facebook and link them to his website the day after her birthday or Christmas. She loved his jewelry—everyone we knew did—and once I started sporting the wrap bracelets, my male cousins and even some of my uncles started wearing them. The difference was that Landry never handed out pre-made things to my family or to me. Every piece he made was lovingly crafted with us in mind. All my mother's jewelry had some shade of purple in it because he knew it was her favorite. Everything I owned had a ruby on it somewhere because, supposedly, a ruby symbolized love. I had teased him once because my green jade leather wrap bracelet had no ruby on it and he had shown me the small, inconspicuous stone under the clasp.

"What are you thinking about?"

I came out of my thoughts to find him looking at me, his eyes worried for whatever reason. "You. I was thinking about you and how nuts the women in my family go every Christmas."

He cackled evilly, waggling his eyebrows at me. "They do, don't they?"

"Yeah." I leaned sideways and kissed him because he was too cute, and the worry that had been behind his eyes poofed away, and he was oozing happy all of a sudden.

"So Landry, where did you go to school?" his father asked him.

"University of Michigan," he explained. "I have a marketing degree, obviously."

There were lots of questions after that, and I sat and listened, watching everyone, seeing Chris's eyes flick over to me worriedly. He was concerned, I was sure, about what he'd said to me on the plane.

Jocelyn was really interested in Landry's answers and pressed him for more and more. I could tell that she had really missed him. Her husband Hugh was very interested as well. I noticed Landry's father watching him, studying him, and I wasn't quite sure what he was looking for.

Landry's mother explained about the leukemia and the hard road it had been and how the remission was a blessing.

"The party tonight," she said, smiling at all of us, "is to welcome you home, Landry, and to celebrate my new lease on life."

Everyone clapped, and he leaned against me.

"We have the rooftop of one of the best hotels rented out for the party," his father explained. "And tomorrow we'll have brunch here for us and a couple of close friends."

I heard Landry catch his breath.

"Once you're settled into the guest house, you'll have to come back up and sit with us. We have over eight years to catch up on."

Landry made a strangled noise in the back of his throat, and I understood that he needed to be alone with me to decompress, to breathe, maybe even to scream. "Okay," he told them, and then he turned his head and caught me in his blue-green gaze, willing me to fix it, to make it stop.

"And where is the guest house?" I asked, standing, putting my leather bomber jacket back on. It was cut long, and I liked that. I pulled my scarf back on as well, concerned about leaving anything behind.

"There's more than one but I know where they are," Landry told me, standing up beside me. "We'll be back."

No one said anything, and it was just weird. If I hadn't seen someone I loved for eight years, I would have been sitting on top of them until I got every one of my questions answered in rapid succession. At gunpoint, if necessary.

We walked first back up to the living room—showroom—retrieved our luggage, and then we went down another set of stairs and came out on the side by the trees. There was a cobblestone path that led to a small gate opening onto a huge rose garden. It looked like something out of *Alice in Wonderland*.

"Jesus."

"Come on."

"I need the tour map," I said snidely. "Can I get one at the gift shop on our way back?"

He snorted out a laugh. "You're funny."

I grunted, but I was watching him. "Why wouldn't you just lie to them, let them pay for school and be gay thousands of miles away?"

"Because I didn't feel like lying about who I wanted to love for the rest of my life. It seemed counterproductive. My father said I could go to the same retreat as Will and he would still send me to school. I told him no."

The blanks were starting to fill in.

"I thought you came out to your folks the night you graduated from high school?"

"No, my father found out the day he caught me—well, whatever, that's a whole other story—but no, the day he and Will's dad found us, that was the day my father found out."

"And what happened to Will?" I asked, even though Chris had told me already.

"Will went into one of those programs where they un-gay you after we graduated, and I left for college."

"Did your mother know what happened?"

"Of course."

He was so calm.

I realized that I didn't want to have the floodgate-opening talk right there in the open. I cleared my throat. "I had no idea you came from this kind of money."

"It's shit."

"Spoken like a man who never had to go without anything."

"Oh, fuck you," he growled at me, stopping, rounding on me as I tilted my head and appraised him. "I've gone without quite a bit in my life."

"But you didn't have to; that was your choice."

"And so that makes me what, spoiled? Stupid? What?"

I stared at him, at his clothes. He bought things cheap at consignment stores and Target and then paired them with extravagant pieces like the ankle boots he'd bought or his cashmere peacoat. He had scarves that looked like they came off the pages of *GQ* that in reality came from small ethnic stores in our neighborhood. He had a flare for fashion, for accessorizing, so he always looked like a million dollars walking down the street. But I knew, the platform boots from the night before notwithstanding, that normally, frugal was his middle name.

"Trev?"

I squinted at him. "You live on my bullshit budget and you don't have to."

He spun around and started stalking away from me.

I followed, trying to think of what I meant.

The guesthouse, and the walk down to it, reminded me of Greece when I had seen it on the Travel Channel. How white it was, the walls—all that was missing was the azure Aegean and we would have had a damn postcard. I needed to hurry up and get used to the luxury, because it was screwing with me.

The entrance was a sliding glass door, and the back opened out onto a little pier that had five steps down to the water. In the summer, it had to be beautiful, but now that it was slightly chilly, I had no desire to dive in.

He flung his luggage down in the living room and pivoted around to face me. I walked by him into the bedroom, put my duffel on the wingback chair, took off my jacket and scarf, draped both over that, and then dived into the bed.

"What are you doing?"

I lifted my leg. "Take off my shoe."

"What?"

I grunted, letting it fall. "I'm being an idiot because this is fucking with me. I'm sorry, I know you're on a budget because it's not mine, it's ours. We're working on building our life together, and this belongs to your parents, not you. So we'll visit for the next week, and then we'll go back to our shitty little apartment until we can buy our tiny dream house and live happily ever after."

He was shaking.

"Oh." I grinned at him, sitting up to unlace my wingtips, ready to put my Nikes back on because my dress shoes scrunched my feet. "You wanna fight instead?"

"No." He rushed over to the bed, swatting my hands away, sitting with my feet in his lap, working the laces himself. I noticed that he had dumped his scarf and peacoat in the outer room.

I cleared my throat. "Your brother says you didn't leave because you were gay but because your parents thought you were crazy."

He continued what he was doing, dropping first one shoe and then the other to the floor before he finally turned and looked at me. "And you think what about that, since you wanted me to see a shrink a while back?"

"I was going with you; I'm just as fucked up as you are."

He went to move, but I pressed my legs down, making them heavy, trapping him beneath them.

"Lemme go." He sounded disgusted.

"Uh-uh," I said, moving fast, flipping around and putting him on his back under me on the bed. "I need to get laid."

"Well I don't need—oh." He gasped as I bent and licked a long wet line up the side of his throat before biting his neck. It tasted and smelled so good, like Landry. When I inhaled deeply, he jolted under me.

"You need me," I said flatly, noting the goose bumps, the flutter of his lashes, his hands fisted in my jacket.

"Yes," he hissed, bowing up off the bed, trying to get closer.

I yanked his hands off me, which made his eyes spring open wide, all big and beautiful, and I attacked him, his belt, his zipper, rough with him because I was frantic to connect, to be reminded of who I was.

He whimpered and whined, and when I yanked down the thong he was wearing and his cock sprang free, I deep throated him in one decisive movement.

"Oh fuck!" he shouted, hands on my head, gripping my skull hard since there was no hair to pull and fist.

I held him tight with one hand on his hip, the other squeezing his ass as I sucked and stroked with my tongue and mouth, swallowing down precum, making him wet.

"I can't... I'm too...," he rasped, pumping in and out of my mouth, holding me tight against him, knowing that I had no gag reflex at all.

I took him down the back of my throat and swallowed around his engorged shaft as he babbled and made a litany of my name. "Trev! I don't wanna come, I want you to fuck me!"

No. He wanted to come.

"Trevan!"

I made the suction too good, too strong, and he came hard, yelling my name, filling my mouth before I drank him down, gulping the hot, salty fluid.

He clutched at me, my shoulders, tried to move, but caught between me holding him down, his dress shoes, and his pants, he was at my mercy. I held him as his orgasm consumed him and he moaned loud and long. His convulsions made him buck against me and slam his spewing cock against the back of my throat.

Sometimes Landry needed to be reminded that I owned him body and soul.

"You're an idiot!" he yelled at me.

I lifted up, allowing the spent, flaccid cock to slip from between my lips. Landry, seeing the long strand of saliva that connected my bottom lip to the flared head of his cock, groaned deep and hoarse. When I licked my lips, he shuddered.

"Jesus, you're so fuckin' hot," he stammered. "But you don't have to blow me for me to feel it—to know that I belong to you, for me to know that you're all there is."

Our eyes locked together. "Maybe I needed to be reminded of who I am. You ever think of that?"

He reached down and put his hands on my face. "Take everything off; take your damn clothes off. I wanna see you… your skin."

I rose up over him, not listening to him at all, still fully clothed as I loomed above him, over my man who was now a study in debauched beauty.

His eyes were glazed, his hair was tousled, he was flushed and panting, and his stomach was covered in a fine sheen of sweat. The dress pants were shoved down to his knees, and his sweater was pushed up to his hard pecs. He was less muscular than I was, but his body was toned and hard. I bent to taste him.

"I want your clothes off." His voice rose, commanding.

"No," I told him, turning away, getting up off the bed so he couldn't see my smile, just hear the tone of my voice. "We need to go back up and talk to your folks."

"Trevan!" he yelled at me as I grinned and left the room.

"Better hurry up," I called back over my shoulder.

"One!"

He was counting?

"Two!"

Oh, shit! I bolted back into the room to find the man I loved standing beside the bed completely naked, hands on his hips in such a stance of indignation that I burst out laughing.

"I am going to murder you if you do not get your ass in this bed!"

But it wasn't necessary anymore. I was real and he was real, and the love between us was vibrant and alive and sometimes ugly, sometimes even mean, but it was there, and I could see it all over him. His eyes couldn't lie, and they were full of me.

I darted around the bed and grabbed him, and after a whimper in the back of his throat, he wrapped his arms around me and molded his beautiful body to mine.

"I want to make you feel as good as you made me feel."

"Oh, but I feel good." I smiled into his hair, pulling back to brush my nose along his and close my eyes with the surge of feeling that swamped me. "I'm perfect."

He grunted.

"I meant I feel perfect, ass, I didn't mean I am perfect."

His head turned, and he kissed a wet line up the side of my neck as I leaned my head over so he could reach all my skin.

"I love you," he told me, nibbling under my chin as I let my head loll back on my shoulders. His lips were so soft, and between the pressure and the nibbling, I felt my body heat.

"Trev." His breath was hot on my face.

"I love you, Landry Carter," I said, smiling as I bent forward and nuzzled his adorable little nose before zeroing in on his mouth. "How 'bout I kiss you until you come again."

"Oh God."

I chuckled before I slanted my mouth down over his.

"Not fair," he whispered even as he returned each kiss.

WE MADE the mistake of getting back on the bed, and when I saw his eyes fluttering, I pressed my advantage, grabbed him, and lay down with him in my arms. Head on my chest, listening to my heartbeat, the man passed out minutes later. I followed him into sleep and smiled when I thought how weird it would be if anyone walked in on us. I was still completely dressed except for my shoes, and he was naked. I patted his ass as I smiled.

The nap was good, and when we woke up, we headed up to see his parents. They sent us right back to the guest house to shower and change for dinner. We never ate at six, but since it was supposed to be a whole night of fun and partying, we did as we were asked.

I was done fast—showered and shaved, the cologne Landry had bought me for Christmas clinging to me as I waited for him in the living room. I had one suit and I was in it, my beige Armani that I was wearing with a white dress shirt underneath.

When Landry emerged, I almost swallowed my tongue he looked so good. The black Prada suit fit tight, and the red dress shirt underneath was very sexy.

"No velvet?" I teased him. "No leather?"

"It's my parents," he said flatly, and there was a shadow in his eyes. "They don't find my eccentricity the lyrical thing that you do."

"I find you lyrical?" I teased him.

"Yeah, you do."

I chuckled, holding out my hand.

"You're breathtaking, by the way," he assured me as he laced his fingers with mine and we headed for the door.

"And you're the only one who thinks that." I grinned, kissing his ear loudly, wetly, making him giggle.

"Knock it off, I can't wrinkle."

I shook my head and he laughed, deep and loud. I liked it.

"Well don't you two clean up well." Cece beamed at Landry and me when we met them in the driveway. The limousine was there to take us to the party.

The two of us had neglected to wear ties, but when I asked Cece if we needed them, she said no. But all the other men had them on.

"It doesn't matter," she assured us.

"Of course it doesn't," Landry said under his breath so only I could hear. "Because she's already stunned that we even had suits. You heard her: we clean up nice."

"Which was a nice thing to say," I assured him, pulling him closer to me so that his head leaned against mine.

"It was a backhanded compliment at best, and I hated it."

"You're overthinking, maybe?" I offered.

"No," he said, hand on my thigh.

I hated ties, and it had never even crossed my mind to put one on. Neil, Chris, Scott, and Hugh did all look very polished, but it was a party in a hotel on the Vegas strip. Was it necessary?

"The necklace looks gorgeous on you," I told Jocelyn, who had chosen a crushed silk, low neckline wrap dress to show off her gift from Landry. I loved that the first opportunity she had, she wore it. Landry's mother had chosen a diamond necklace, like a long tennis bracelet that laid flat. I understood—it was stunning—but it was not Landry's piece. And no, he had not made it specifically for her, but he had still chosen two of the best pieces from his collection and gifted them to his mother and sister. My opinion of his mother dropped quite a bit, while his sister's stock rose.

"Oh I just love it," she cooed, hand on the necklace, smiling at Landry.

He nodded and nestled closer to me.

As we neared the strip, Cece turned to Landry and asked how he and I had met.

"We met at a party," he told her.

"Yes, but how? Did you walk over to him? Did he walk over to you?"

"He walked over to me," he told her. "And that was it. I knew he'd never lie to me and I knew he'd keep me safe and I knew everything would be okay."

"Safe?" She looked concerned.

He shook his head. "It's old news."

Her brows furrowed. "I have so many questions."

"That are better left for tomorrow," he told her. "Not for a fun night of celebration."

"Exactly," she agreed and smiled at him. "I planned the party early so everyone could walk the strip later, and I figured after your plane ride that breakfast and a nap and then dinner was the best bet."

"Excellent plan," Chris assured her.

She patted Landry's hand happily.

The strip was clogged with people, and the limousine had a slow slog down the street to the front of Caesar's Palace. A staff member met us out front and led us to the penthouse elevator. We then went up to the roof nightclub's lounge, which, along with the terrace, had been rented out for the party. There were already people there, drinking, milling around, when we walked in.

It was gorgeous up there, the entire strip laid out. The nightclub was done in white, the warmth and luxury on display. For the second time that day, I was overwhelmed, and as I was passed a glass of Cristal champagne, Neil called for the first of many toasts of the night.

"To my beautiful wife, we are blessed with your presence, and to my dear son, welcome home."

There was clapping and the clinking of glasses, and then Landry was basically rushed. I had to move out of the way; there were just too many people who wanted to get to him, talk to him. And he was smiling his dazzler, eyes glittering, face animated, hands going wild, as he was an expressive talker. It was fun to watch him hold court, and I moved to the edge of the terrace so I could see the world below me.

"Would you care to dance?"

I turned and Jocelyn was there, grinning at me.

"Are you sure?" I teased her. "I didn't wear a tie."

She rolled her eyes and grabbed my hand.

We had a good time, and after a while, some of her friends joined us, and it was me and all the beautiful women. I had to take my jacket off because I got hot, and because Jocelyn's best friend, Daria, got cold, I gave it to her to wear. I led four women to the bar, and Jocelyn was surprised when she ordered a Midori sour and two cosmopolitans for her friends and I had bottled water.

"Not drinking?"

"Gotta be clearheaded," I told her, inhaling.

"Hungry?"

"God yes, the food smells amazing."

She was laughing as she took my hand and tugged me after her toward the buffet. I was watching for Landry, and every now and then when he looked up to scan the room, I waved so he'd see me. And I got the nod; he could see Jocelyn as well, and everything was fine.

"Boy, he keeps a close eye on you," she remarked and smiled at me.

"It goes both ways," I said, grabbing a napkin, turning to go.

"I thought you were going to sit with the girls," she said, actually sounding sad.

"I am," I smiled at her. "I just need to make sure he eats. If his blood sugar dips, he gets frantic, and he'll start bouncing off the walls."

She nodded, touched by that.

I carried the plate across the room and leaned into the circle, which included Landry's brothers, Will, and others.

"Eat," I ordered him, passing Chris a bottle of water. "Hold this for him."

Chris nodded. "Yessir."

Landry's smile was huge. "Yes, dear."

I grunted and left them and returned to the girls.

"Daria will be back," Jocelyn said as I took a seat beside her. "I made her promise not to disappear with your suit jacket."

"Thank you."

"It's a patented move, you know," she said with a chuckle, arching an eyebrow for me. "Steal a guy's jacket and when the guy comes to get it, go home with the guy."

"Huh."

"I explained that she had the wrong equipment."

"And the wrong face."

"Mostly that."

I nodded. "Most of all that."

She cleared her throat. "So tell me, what kind of meds does Landry take now?"

It was meant to be just conversation, but it nearly killed me. "He doesn't take anything."

She scowled at me. "How is that possible?"

"Could you please just tell me the whole story, from the beginning?" I asked her. "I'm getting bits and pieces, and I don't want to ask Landry for the whole explanation right now because I know he's not ready."

Her breath was shaky. "Trevan, I—"

"Please," I pressed her.

"I'll do my best, but you'd be better off to ask Mom or Dad."

"I'd rather hear it from you."

"Okay, well, as you know, Landry's the son of a very rich man. We were all exposed to drugs very early, but in high school, Landry, with his crappy self-esteem and his need to fit in at any cost, he let it run right over him. I mean, we knew he was manic and then depressed, but until Mom and Dad gave us the diagnosis, that he was bipolar, we had no idea it was anything more than just the way he was."

"And the drugs did what, made it worse?"

"Of course." She sighed. "My parents were all freaked when they found cocaine, but really, that was the tip of the iceberg stuff; the meth was the real problem."

But there was just no way.

He had quit the social drug use right after we met. I had told him I was clean and had to have a partner who was going to be the same way. He had told me it was no problem, it was only recreational so could be easily terminated. And it had been. He quit the day we had the talk. I had never known an addict who could do that without a relapse or withdrawal or anything. He could not have been a drug addict; there had to be another explanation.

"He stole money from my parents, took some of my mother's jewelry for drugs, and all of it while they were trying, along with the doctors, to get his meds worked out—ohmygod, Trevan, you have no idea the horror it was. He became a completely different person."

The question of why remained, however, and the only person who had answers was Landry himself.

"I don't—oh." She blanched.

"Jocelyn?" I questioned her because I had never seen anyone go completely white and their eyes get quite that big.

"Oh God... oh God...." She was starting to hyperventilate.

I took hold of her arms. "Honey?"

Her head snapped up, and I was faced with huge scared eyes as a woman stepped up beside us. She was tall and tan and stunning. She looked like a Barbie doll come to life.

"Who's this, Jo, your next conquest? My husband not good enough?"

I noted her heavy-lidded eyes, the martini glass, and the combative stance. She was ready to fight, wanted it.

"He's a little rough, isn't he? This one might actually be too much man for you." She was immaculately dressed.

"Who are you?" I snapped at her, annoyed over the change she was causing in Jocelyn.

Her eyes moved slowly over my body as she looked me up and down. "You first. Where did you come from?"

I squinted at her as a man joined us.

"Evie, please. Don't make a scene."

"Fuck you, Marc," she told the man behind her, tipping her head sideways. "I'm talking to the boy toy here."

"Who the fuck are you?" I demanded.

"Oh," she said with a low chuckle, hand over her heart. "I'm Evelyn Tate, sweetheart, and this is my husband, Marc Tate, and this"—she pointed at Jocelyn—"is the woman he fucks around on me with, one of his reps, Jocelyn Collins. And you are?"

I squinted at her. "You should leave."

"I was invited."

"This is a party for Jocelyn's mother and her brother. Do not drag your bullshit in here. This isn't the time or the place." I tipped my head at her husband. "Take your wife home."

"I don't know who the hell you think you are, but—"

"Please," I asked her nicely.

"I—"

"Take her out of here," I ordered Marc.

"Evie, please."

"What the hell is going on?" Hugh shouted, charging up beside me, grabbing Jocelyn and whirling her around. "You couldn't even deal with this shit for one fucking night?"

"Don't manhandle her," Marc barked at him, wrenching Hugh's hand away from Jocelyn.

"Oh God." Evelyn broke down, and I got why; it had to be hard to watch your husband defend his mistress right there in front of you.

Jocelyn's friends came back, and I could tell right then and there that I was smack dab in the middle of a situation that had been simmering for God knew how long. Tempers flared. Words were spoken under breath and then erupted.

Evelyn started crying, Daria started yelling, Jocelyn tried to get everyone to calm down, and one of Evelyn's friends called Jocelyn a whore. And then it got loud, at which point Hugh balled up his fist and hit Marc in the face really hard. I had to reassess my first impression of the man. He had looked like a *GQ* model to me, vapid, dull, with only plastic pretty going for him. But he was certainly possessive of his wife, as was evident from the way he picked Marc up off the floor and started pounding on him.

I had no idea rich people had *Jerry Springer* moments. It was illuminating.

No one was coming to break it up since it was supposed to be a very exclusive and elegant affair, so I ended up having to separate the two men. Getting in the middle of any fight is painful, so I was not surprised when Marc caught me in the face and split my lip. It was an accident. Hugh got me in the ribs, but that, too, was unintentional. It stung for a minute, but I'd been hit much harder before. What was problematic was the beer that got spilled on me, on my shirt, soaking through to my skin with all the jostling. I got pissed and grabbed Marc's bicep and shoved him down into the closest chair.

"Do not get up," I warned him.

He glowered at me but stayed there, and I shoved Hugh toward the cabanas and ordered Jocelyn to go with him.

"Who do you—"

"Shut up," I told Evelyn, yanking her forward, my finger in her face. "I told you this was neither the time nor the place. So sit the fuck down and don't move."

She sat, silently.

I sent Daria to the bar for ice, sent another of the women for bottled water, and used one of the dinner napkins to stem the blood flowing from my lip. When Daria returned with an icepack and a bucket of ice, I sent her with the latter to Jocelyn and Hugh, and I made Marc lean back as I placed the pack on his face.

"Shit," he groaned.

"Just don't move," I grumbled at him.

I went to check on Hugh, put some of the ice cubes in a napkin, and had him press it to his knuckles. Pushing back his head, I checked his eyes and his nose.

"Thank you, Trevan," he said, his left hand closing on my wrist. "What you must think of me."

"You?" I shook my head, untucking my shirt and unbuttoning it, not wanting to reek of alcohol anymore, yanking it off. "Who did you cheat on?"

He smiled sheepishly. "No one."

"Well then." I smiled at him, satisfied that he was fine. "You're not in the wrong here."

He cleared his throat. "We should run downstairs and get you another shirt."

"I'll run down myself. You and Jo need to get out of here before anyone sees you."

"Nobody saw that?" He was astounded.

I shook my head.

"Are you sure?" Jocelyn finally found her voice.

"No, I think you're good. Everyone else is way on the other side. Just leave now. You guys need to talk anyway."

"Yes." Jocelyn began weeping.

"Finally, yes." Hugh sighed heavily, hand tightening on my forearm just for a moment. "Thank you."

I nodded and walked back over to Evelyn and Marc. "You guys ready to go?"

"Yes." He cleared his throat. "Who the hell are you, anyway?"

"Just go home." I was annoyed and certain it was in my voice as I walked over to Daria. "Sorry." I smiled at her. "I need my jacket to go downstairs."

Her eyes were all over me. "I'll go with you."

"I don't need company. I just need my jacket."

She drew closer, hand going to my chest. "I have a room; come with me."

I moved her hand and reached for my jacket.

Quickly, she stepped away. "Baby, I can't tell you the last time I saw a carved eight-pack... and all tatted up." She bit her bottom lip. "Very nice."

"Please," I asked nicely. "Just—"

"Hey!" she yelled as the jacket was ripped from her hands as she clutched it around her.

"Oh back off, Daria," a voice said, full of disgust, and we both turned to Landry's friend William. "He doesn't even like girls."

"You're fulla shit, Will," she told him. "Run on back to your beard now before she realizes that you slipped and fell on another dick. How much gay porn does she have to find on your hard drive before she gets a clue that her marriage is all for show?"

"Fuck you, D," he spat at her.

"No, fuck you, Will," she hissed back, pointing. "You may have fooled your family with that bullshit conversion therapy, but your friends... we know you're still fuckin' rent boys because you didn't have the balls to tell the whole wide world that you're gay."

"Go to hell."

She made a show of looking around. "And where is the little woman tonight, Will? Did you even bring her? Where are the kiddies?"

"Since this is an adult party and Rose felt that—"

"Rose didn't feel shit," she scoffed at him. "You didn't want her to meet Landry. She'd know her life is a fuckin' sham if she saw you look at him just once."

"You're so full of—"

"I hope you're not still pining for Lan," she cackled. "I mean, I really hope not, 'cause it looks like someone got past white bread, huh? Someone goes for the dark meat now."

I jerked my jacket from Will's hands, leaving them to have their bitchfest alone as I pulled it on, wadded up my dress shirt, and fisted it in one hand as I headed for the elevator. Once I was in the lobby, I went directly to the John Varvatos store I had seen earlier, walked in, and told the sales clerk I needed a shirt.

He eyed me coolly, and I groaned. I got a smile after a second and a sarcastic, "Oh yeah?"

I appreciated sarcasm in all its many forms, and when I threw up my hands in defeat, he put out his hand for my soggy, beer-soaked shirt.

"It's marinated in Heineken," he observed. "I think it's done."

"I agree."

"Let's do a lightweight crew sweater at this point, huh?"

I nodded, let him pick what I needed, paid him, put it on, and then headed back to the elevator to return to the nightclub and the party. Maybe if I stretched it, my elapsed turnaround time was twenty minutes. When I got back up to the nightclub, though, as soon as I walked back in, I had a hand grabbing hold of my bicep.

"Where were you?" Chris gasped, looking terrified.

"What's wrong?" I asked, looking around instantly for Landry.

"He's looking for you," Chris told me. "He's upset and he's getting loud and scaring my folks."

"Where is he?"

"Someone thought they saw you toward the back, I think that's where he went."

I made my way across the enormous rooftop, and as soon as the crowd shifted and parted, I saw William. He moved fast to reach me.

"Where were you? Landry's freaking out!"

But I doubted that. I was already getting the impression from his friends and family that what was huge to them was sort of a minor irritation for me and mine. What they considered a freak-out in their polite, everyone-is-civil world might simply be Landry being annoyed. My family, our friends, when Landry had a snit, we all just dealt with it. But if when Landry was growing up, they had responded to him with panic instead of calm…. I was starting to get the idea of what had gone on. "Where is he?"

"Daria told him you were over by the cabanas, so he's looking there."

"Thanks," I said, turning to leave.

"So," he said, keeping pace with me. "I'm the one Landry was caught with all those years ago in the stable."

"I know," I grunted, looking for my boyfriend.

"Did he tell you?"

"Chris did, he did, so yeah, I've been informed."

"I went to a reparative therapy camp and he left home."

"Maybe he got the better end of the deal, huh?"

"What do you mean by that?"

"Nothing."

He stopped me with a hand on my bicep, and I turned to face him.

"I love my wife and I love my children."

"And I don't doubt that, but you also cheat on your wife and your children," I told him. "Right?"

He said nothing.

I waited.

"I cheat on my wife, yes," he acquiesced.

I scowled at him. "Make no mistake, you cheat on your kids too."

"You don't know what you're talking about."

I arched an eyebrow at him. "One day they'll learn the truth, and they'll know the whole damn thing was a lie."

"What are you—"

"The marriage," I told him. "One day your kids will find out it was bullshit, and then they'll wonder, was anything he ever said real? If he didn't really love her, does he really love me?"

"That's ridic—"

"I know about lying. I've met a lot of liars, seen them doing their thing. You need to fix it now, make it right for everyone, plus you, and give your wife a shot at the happiness she deserves."

"She's happy!" he shouted at me, upset and defensive. "She has everything. Cars, a house—a mansion—jewelry. She's not an idiot. She likes her life, and she'll play along until the kids are grown, and then as long as I'm always discreet, she'll give me my divorce and take the settlement I give her."

I stared at his eyes and could see what Landry had found alluring. The man was blond and handsome, and his eyes were soft, and so was his mouth. "That's so fuckin' sad."

"You're not listening. You—"

"I'm listening," I assured him. "But you're talking out of your ass."

"I—"

"No doubt you'll be able to keep a boy who will be discreet, but what I'm saying is that you won't be able to have a partner because no out and proud gay man will live his life in a closet. You will always have a boy who belongs to you but never a man who walks beside you and holds your hand."

He took a shuddering breath. "And Landry's life is, what, so much better than mine because of that?"

I shrugged. "Yeah."

"Because you're such a fuckin' catch," he scoffed.

"No, man, it has nothing to do with me and everything to do with how he is. He's true to who he is, and he doesn't hide, and he can walk in here and be gay and not give a damn if people care about that fact. He's real."

"I'm real too, and so is my family."

"Listen, I have a lot of friends in the closet for one reason or another, but don't stand there and tell me that you or them are living a real life. How can you be?"

"I will not stand here and defend my life to you!"

But he was standing there doing that exact thing.

"I'm happy!"

"Yeah, you look it."

"You're just trash, and that's all that comes out of your mouth."

I smiled slowly. "You're gonna be dreaming about my mouth tonight, thinking of it sliding over your ex-boyfriend's beautiful cock and what his face is gonna look like when I do it." I sighed deeply because suddenly I felt really bad for him. He was obviously still very much in love with Landry Carter. "I feel so fuckin' sorry for you."

He backhanded me hard, and I took it because I'd pushed him and my last comment had been totally shitty and rude. Unfortunately, two things happened at the same time. First, my lip started bleeding again, and second, Landry saw him hit me.

"What the fuck are you doing?" he roared, outraged and furious, coming fast.

I stepped around Will to intercept him.

"How dare you touch—what the fuck!"

"Baby," I soothed him, hands on his face even as he tried to lunge by me at Will. "I'm fine. Come here."

"You're bleeding!" His face crumpled, but his eyes, his eyes were murderous.

"Not because of him," I said softly, taking his hand, leading him away fast, down to the last cabana where it was quiet, pulling him after me inside.

"Who hurt...? Trevan, what the hell is going on? Where were you? What're you wearing? Why...?" He swallowed hard. "Where did you go?"

I fell back on the chaise lounge, pulling him down on top of me to straddle my hips. His moan was loud as his hands went to my chest and he pushed forward over my groin.

"So these people are all nuts," I told him flatly.

His eyes were all over my face as he winced. "Oh baby, I need to get you some ice. Jesus... who else hit you?"

"Why?"

"Because I'm going to kill them," he said evenly.

I chuckled, pushing up against him, and smiled as he narrowed his eyes and bit his bottom lip. "It's okay; this is me we're talking about. And a split lip ain't shit."

He bent close, hands fisted back in my new pale blue sweater as he traced the tip of his tongue over the wound, tasting my blood so gently. My skin heated and I felt the tingly, prickly sensation wash over me as my cock twitched under my lover's firm, round ass.

"I like the feel of this sweater," he told me, bunching it in his hands, pushing it up so he had access to my torso. "But your skin is better."

I arched up against him, and his fingers traced over the deep groove in my abdomen and then back up to the L over my heart. Slowly, he rocked down over my now-swollen groin, sliding his crease back and forth.

"Stop."

He bent forward and sucked my nipple into his mouth, tongue swirling over the pebbled nub, biting gently.

"Landry," I breathed his name into his hair.

He got up fast, walked to the covering, and yanked it down, grabbing the zipper pull, closing it fast, letting anyone who came near it know that we were not to be disturbed. But I would not let him be that guy in front of his parents.

And it hurt to move: I was hard and my body ached to be buried in his, but I got up and stood on the other side.

"Lay down," he commanded me, taking off his jacket and tossing a packet of lube onto the chaise. He draped the jacket over the back of the small chair and started on his belt buckle.

"No, let's go home."

He shook his head. "I saw you dancing with those girls, their hands all over you."

"No one had their hands on me," I assured him, because I was very particular about my personal space, half because of me and half because I knew Landry hated it.

"Daria was wearing your jacket, and you smell like cheap perfume."

There was nothing cheap about that girl. I might have smelled like *expensive* perfume, but not like low-priced anything. "So we'll go back to the house and I'll take a shower."

"No." He pointed at the end of the chaise. "Sit, put that lube on your cock. I wanna see you stroke yourself, and then I'm gonna ride you."

"Lan—"

"Do what I say," he snarled at me, and I saw it then, the fury, the jealous rage simmering right there below his satin-smooth surface.

I had been careful, but the dancing I thought had been benign had caused a rise in him, my disappearance had added fuel to the fire, and when he saw me get hit, the truth was that he wanted to be the one smacking me around.

"I deserve to be hit, don't I?"

He nodded.

It was inevitable and I wanted it, so I tore my jacket off, threw it down behind me, and yanked the sweater off over my head. I unbuckled fast, unsnapped, unzipped, dragging my dress pants to my knees before I sat down and tore the lube packet open. It was warm from being in his pocket, so I squeezed the packet into my palm and grabbed my own cock tight and hard, pulling, twisting, tugging.

My head fell back and my breath caught.

"Stop," he growled, smacking my hand away, grabbing my face, tilting it up, and bending at the same time to take raw possession of my mouth. The mauling hurt; I tasted blood, and then it didn't matter, nothing mattered but his legs on either side of my waist.

I grabbed hold of his firm, tight ass, spread his cheeks, and tried not to come as he sank, slowly but without pause, down over my shaft, taking me all in, deep inside his body until he was fully, completely impaled.

"Jesus, Landry, you're so fuckin' hot."

He lifted and drove back down, seating himself even deeper, pushing forward so I could feel the muscles clenching tight around me, rippling, the spasm milking my entire length.

"I love this."

"I know," he rasped. "Me too."

My head, which had lolled back, came forward and my eyes met his. Normally they were glazed, clouded with passion, but that was not what I was seeing. There was dark, deadly intent there, and I should have been frightened.

"Mine," he told me as I felt his hands dig into my chest and saw him lean forward, felt his teeth in my shoulder.

"What do you need?"

"I want you to throw up the covering, put me over the chaise, and I want you to fuck me while they all watch. I want them all to see your big fat cock sliding in and out of my ass."

Why? Why would he need that? Why…?

Sometimes it took a minute. He felt like he was floating away. He needed grounding, to know where he belonged. He was terrified that I would leave him here with his family. That I would go home without him, cast him aside without care.

He felt so good, and as I grabbed hold of his hair, yanking his head back with a sharp jerk, the choked sob confirmed everything.

"Get up."

No question. He rose fast, and I shoved him forward, standing and then dragging him by his hair to the back of the chaise, bending him over it as I smacked his ass hard enough to leave a handprint on his pale, smooth skin.

"Oh Trevan, please," he whined, the ache, the wanting, all of it in the plea.

I grabbed his hips hard—my fingers would leave bruises—and slid my slick cock between the round cheeks at the same time he arched his back. I drove forward as he yelled my name.

"Don't leave me here."

Stupid man. Like that could ever happen.

I pounded into him steady and hard, watching my cock plunge deep, feeling the slippery heat and the suction, the velvet vise fist around me.

"Trevan!"

"Never fuckin' leaving you… never!"

"Swear!"

"Baby, I fuckin' swear," I said, hammering into him as he frantically jerked himself off.

"Gonna come." His voice cracked. "I need to come!"

"Now," I ordered him.

His muscles clamped down on me, spasmed and clenched with the violent force of his orgasm. He was loud, my boy, a screamer, and this time was no exception. The volume combined with the pressure and the suction wrung my own climax from me. I emptied into him, deep inside, pumping him full until semen was rolling down the inside of his thighs and dripping off his balls to the floor.

I leaned forward and buried my face in his hair, pressing my nose to the nape of his neck, ready to pull out.

"Don't." He stopped me, one hand reaching behind him, grabbing at my hip. "I'm not ready yet."

I never rushed him.

Chapter SIX

LANDRY used the T-shirt he was wearing under his dress shirt to clean us both up and then wadded it up and stuffed it into the garbage can beside the chaise. When we went back out to find his parents, I heard a song I loved and told him I wanted to dance.

"Whatever you want." He smiled at me with his narrowed bedroom eyes.

I dumped both our jackets on the chair beside his mother and led him to the dance floor. Once we were there, my hands went to his hips and his arms locked behind my head. We swayed together to "Can't Take My Eyes Off of You," the version I liked, the Lauryn Hill one. Staring into his eyes, I saw how they glowed and was certain that I looked the same way.

He stepped closer, pressing tight, and I put my hands up under the untucked dress shirt and slid them over his warm, sleek skin. His head went down on my shoulder, and he pushed his face against my neck as I began to sing softly under my breath.

"I love when you sing to me," he whispered.

Sometimes, when he couldn't sleep, I sang oldies to him, or stupid songs where "Landry" replaced some key repeated word. It was his favorite thing.

"And I love you." He breathed the words over my face.

I squeezed him tight and then moved with him as Sade's "Please Send Me Someone To Love" came on next. It was nice that no one cared that we were the only two men out there among the other couples. When Landry's parents moved by us, I looked up and got a luminous smile from Cece and a nod from Neil. It was very nice.

When Janet Jackson was next with "That's The Way Love Goes"—it was kind of an odd mix—Landry and I put space between us as we danced. I put it on for him, exaggerating my movements, and he started laughing, the deep, throaty sound coming up out of him. I sang Janet's part and he did the chorus, and his face, the seven layers of happy that it was, made my whole night.

Landry's parents had sat down, and we walked over after picking up bottles of water from the bar and joined them at their table.

"Oh," Cece sighed, smiling at us. "You two are so adorable together."

I turned and looked at Landry and then lifted my hand and pushed his hair out of his face. "Aww, your mama thinks you're cute."

He laughed, moved over into my lap, and drank his water as he grinned at his mother.

She could not stop sighing.

The Carter party concluded at eleven since the lounge was needed for other guests with parties that could ensure copious amounts of alcohol would be ingested well into the early morning. Everyone drifted down the elevators to the casino and to other clubs. Landry's parents went home, but his brothers and their dates and their friends wanted to dance. Since Landry wanted to as well, I followed along with him. Trance music was not really my thing, so I watched him from a safe distance, sitting in one of the booths while he ground it out on the brightly lit floor.

Sitting there, I realized that Scott, Landry's brother, was uncomfortable and so was his date. After a second, I realized it was because the people in the booth behind them were bumping against it. I got up and Scott reached for my arm to stop me, but I gave his hand a pat and moved by. There were two couples there drinking, and when the one guy slammed down an empty beer glass, he threw himself back hard.

"Hey," I said, smiling down at them all before my eyes landed on the rambunctious guy. "Can you knock it off?"

"What? Who the fuck are you?"

"I'm the guy on the other side of you, so if you could not slam backward, we'd appreciate it."

"See, Brad," the other guy said and squinted at him. "Just chill out already. You're drunk, and this shit is annoying not just to us."

"Oh, fuck you," he told his friend, and then he looked up at me. "And fuck you, man. What kind of pussy comes over here and—"

I grabbed his shoulder hard, my fingers digging, and leaned down so that we were close, almost nose to nose. "I'm asking you nicely, Brad. You're being a dick, and if I have to drag your ass outta here I will, because really, who's gonna give a shit if I do?"

He looked at me, and I stared back.

"Whatever. You guys are all a buzzkill."

"Thanks," I said, straightening up and turning away. When I did, I saw a guy get pushed back from another booth. I wouldn't have cared, would never have even given it a second thought, but he was one and they were many, and Benji Matthews was still weighing heavily on my heart.

"You little fuck, get out of here," I heard as I got closer.

"Mr. Beale," the guy began, "you just don't—you owe me the juice."

"It was a tie, you dumb fuck." He laughed, and his table laughed with him. "Get out of here before me and my friends throw you out."

"I—"

"Run, rabbit," the guy barked at him, and there was laughter again.

All heads lifted to me as I stepped up beside the guy, my hand sliding gently over his shoulder.

"You the gambler?" I asked the guy sitting dead center of the booth, even though I knew he was Mr. Beale already.

"Yeah, who the fuck are you?"

"I'm his collector," I said flatly. "And a tie, as we told you when you started, is different at each house. At ours, it's a push, but you still have to pay the juice. So pay up or you lose your line and your winnings. Your fuckin' choice."

"You think you can—"

"Yeah, I can," I assured him.

"Listen, asshole," he barked at me. "My friends and I will fuck you up if you don't—"

"Oh, shit," I cut him off with a chuckle, "did you think it was just us? Him and me?"

He looked confused.

"'Cause it ain't. It ain't just us. You don't owe Rabbit," I said, using the name he'd given the runner, "you owe the house. We ain't shit, but them? The house?"

The first flicker of concern crossed his face.

"We're talking about guys who know what your car looks like, where you work, and who you know. It's them knowing that you wouldn't want everyone to know your business. I mean, what would your boss think if he knew? What would your family think? Maybe nothing, maybe they don't give a shit about gambling—unless they do."

His eyes were locked on my face.

"Do whatever you want, we'll go, but just so you don't think it's just us—'cause we ain't shit, right?"

I had no idea who he was, but looking at his clothes, the girl sitting on his left, and his friends and what they were wearing, I got the frat boy vibe off them. They were young; they smelled like trust fund assholes to me, so I tailored my conversation to meet the needs of the moment. And then I waited. And stared.

The way he was looking at me, right into my eyes, I got the idea that the gaze was supposed to be intimidating. I wanted to tell him that I was from Detroit. I knew third graders scarier than him.

After another minute, he went into the breast pocket of his suit jacket and pulled out cash. He passed ten hundred-dollar bills to my nervous friend and then looked up at me.

"I've never seen you before."

I shrugged. "You've never given Rabbit trouble before."

There was a quick nod of agreement.

"Thanks," I said, and I left and would have made it back to my booth, but the hand on my arm stopped me.

"Hey." Rabbit was smiling at me, hand raking through his thick black hair, a wicked smile that showed dimples on full display. "Thank you. You saved my ass, here and back at the house."

I crossed my arms. "You need muscle to go with you. I mean, yeah, you get the whole ten to twenty percent of whatever you collect if you don't, but you're—what?— five ten, one forty, one fifty. Man, you need somebody backing your play."

His eyes got huge and excited.

"No, I'm a runner too, and even I have backup, so really, think about it."

He nodded, offering me his hand. "Rush Howard."

I took his hand in mine. "Trevan Bean."

He was taking me all in, his eyes everywhere. "Thank you so much," he told me again, not letting my hand go, lifting the wad of bills toward me. "I want you to—"

"Oh fuck, no." I scowled at him, dropping his hand. "You never, ever, use your collection for anything. All of it gets back to the house, and then and only then do they take your money out of it. How long have you been doing this?"

"Three months."

"Okay," I said with an exasperated sigh. "You need a separate clutch or something with a zipper to keep your money in. Do you keep your totals on your phone or—"

"No, just on a piece of paper."

I growled at him, and he laughed.

"Baby, you need an electronic spreadsheet so you can just punch in a number and it adds and subtracts for you. Gimme your e-mail address and I'll send it to you now," I said as I pulled my iPhone from my pocket.

He took a shuddering breath. "You called me baby."

My eyes flicked back to him from the screen of my phone. "Sorry," I said, withdrawing, moving around him.

"No no." He stopped me, both hands around my bicep. "I didn't mean…." He swallowed hard, licking his lips. "I liked it—you don't wanna be my collector, fine, but you wanna come back to my place with me and fuck my brains out? You'll like it: I bottom good."

If I were single, I would have been all over that offer. He was so pretty with his full lips and dimples and shiny black eyes. His head would notch right under mine, and he was lean and sinewy, with a rakish grin and chiseled features. "Appealing" didn't do the man justice.

"I have no doubt." I smiled at him, pleased that he was not a homophobic asshole. "And I am sorry about the 'baby', but what're you? Sixteen?"

"Oh no." He smiled at me, moving closer, one hand tightening on my bicep, the other flat on my chest. "I'm twenty-one, just turned."

I nodded. "And school?"

He squinted at me. "School?"

"What's your big picture plan?" The confused look I got was funny. "You need to have a goal in mind or the money, and maybe the drugs, the sex, it's gonna go to your head. Don't just flush your cash down the toilet."

He nodded. "What's your plan?"

I moved his hand gently from my chest and smiled at him. "I'm gonna open a restaurant. I've always wanted to. I have a cousin who can cook like a dream, and she and I will do well."

"No bullshit."

I shook my head. "You have to have a goal. Promise me."

"I promise," he agreed, nodding, and he wasn't smiling, which was good, because maybe his brain was actually working.

"So you want the Excel sheet or not?"

"I don't know what Excel is."

"It's a spreadsheet program. Gimme your e-mail."

He gave it to me, had me put his name and number into my phone, and I gave him mine.

"So gimme a call before you leave."

"Sure."

"And gimme a call if you change your mind about anything, anything at all."

I nodded.

When I got back to the booth, only Scott's date was there.

"Where'd he go?" I asked her.

She was resting her cheek on her elbow as she looked at me. "He went to get me another drink."

I looked around and saw Landry still gyrating out on the dance floor. He was having a good time—his flushed face and sparkling eyes told me as much.

"That was impressive."

I looked back at her. "What was?"

"You just got up and handled it, no second thoughts, just took care of things."

I had no idea why any of that was cause for interest, but I heard that comment a lot. My father had once stood up in a movie theater, turned, and asked the man behind him to please stop talking. The guy rose up, bigger than him, and said no. My father then quietly asked him to step outside away from his children so they could talk about things. The man, who was really very big, looked at my dad, the intent on his face, the solid set of his eyes, and the stillness, and sat back down. My father thanked him and that was it. I had always been taught to just take care of whatever the problem was right then.

"What's your name?"

"Trevan," I told her.

She nodded, appraising me as she lifted up off the table, uncoiling. "I didn't really see you before."

I gave her a slight smile.

"Would you like to dance?"

"Here we go," Scott said as he reached the table, putting some sort of blue frou-frou drink in a martini glass down in front of her and a Heineken down in front of me. "I wasn't sure what to get, but I figured it was a safe bet."

"Thanks," I told him, taking a sip before Landry came charging up to the table, falling down into the booth, more on me than next to me. "Hey," I greeted him, passing him the beer. "Thirsty?"

"Yeah, but not for that." He shook his head. "I think I want a margarita or something."

"Okay, lemme out and I'll get it."

"I'll go with you," Scott's date offered.

"No, I'll go with you," Landry told me, sliding back out, grabbing my hand and pulling me up beside him. His eyes were hooded, and the smile he gave me was just a curl of his lip. I couldn't resist.

I slid my hand over his jaw, tipped his head up, and bent and kissed him. It was soft, just barely a press of my lips to his, but it was enough, I saw when I pulled back, to make the man glow.

"I might be ready to just go home," he whispered, staring at me.

"Let's get your drink and you can roll the dice, since you love that; then we'll get a cab and go home."

He nodded and I took his hand, turned and grabbed my suit jacket, thanked Scott for the beer, and tugged Landry after me.

"That girl wanted to fuck you."

"You think everyone wants to fuck me," I corrected him, leading him to the bar. "And it's not true."

He cleared his throat. "I saw you talking to that guy too, and I watched you move his hand off you."

"You know how I am about my personal space."

"Yeah, I know," he said thoughtfully. "And you know how I am about your personal space."

"Yes, I do," I answered as I leaned on the bar and ordered his drink.

It was fun watching Landry roll the dice. He did it for an hour, and the look on his face, like he really thought he'd win, the expectation, was a joy to see. And the pout when he didn't made my heart flip over. As we crossed the floor to the exit, a man stepped in front of me, bringing me up fast. Instantly, without even a thought, I moved in front of Landry.

"What the fuck, man?"

He put up both hands. "Sorry. I yelled but you didn't hear me. You're Trevan, right?"

I squinted at him. "Who're you?"

Big smile as two other men stepped around us, close. "I'm José Cruz, and this is Armando and Che. We all work for the same people."

I nodded, not really understanding, but in my line of work I met new people all the time and in stranger ways than this. When he offered me his hand, I took it, shaking first his and then the others. "Who are you, José?"

He gripped my shoulder as he studied my face. "I'm Rush's boss."

"Oh." I nodded, figuring something like that. "He's a good guy."

"He's young, but he's learning. I liked that spreadsheet you sent him that he showed me. You make that yourself?"

"I did, yeah."

"I like it; I figure with the changes, we'll all be using it."

I was lost.

He cuffed my shoulder. "What I meant before, when I said we all work for the same people, I meant us and you, kid."

"No." I shook my head. "I'm from Detroit. I work for Adrian Eramo."

"You used to work for Adrian Eramo, but now you work for Gabriel Pike."

"No, I've always worked for Gabriel, and he works for Adrian."

He smiled at me. "You need to call home. Eramo's dead."

"Oh God," Landry gasped beside me, clutching my arm.

"Who's this?" José asked me.

"My boyfriend, Landry."

"Nice to meet you, Landry," he said, offering him his hand, the smile genuine, his warm coffee-colored eyes glinting in the light. "It's a pleasure."

"And you," Landry returned, smiling, shaking the offered hand, squeezing mine tighter.

"I'd love for you both to have a nightcap with me."

"Absolutely," Landry agreed fast.

José led us out of the casino, around the corner, and down a hall to a very elegant restaurant. We walked in; the maître d' saw us and immediately led us to a small booth near the back. It was quiet, but the jazz in the background was sultry and rich, and the feel in the room, like you could just relax, was soothing. It smelled vaguely like fire and hazelnut.

"Is this your place?" I asked him, inhaling.

"It's one of my investments, yes. You like it?"

"I love it," I told him.

"You want your own," he said, smiling at the server who came to our table. "Cognac or scotch?" he asked Landry.

"Cognac, please."

He looked back at the server. "Bring a bottle of the Hennessy Ellipse, please," he ordered before turning to me. "You do, right? Want your own place? Rush told me that was your dream."

"I just told him that a little while ago."

"And he told me. Were you telling the truth?"

"Yeah."

He shrugged, leaning back in the booth between Che and Armando. "You can be an owner or you can be an investor, but you're in this business now, just like I am. It's not about just being a runner anymore, Trevan. I mean, I know your name and I'm all the way here in Vegas. You have to think about that."

I leaned forward. "I've only been gone a day."

He nodded as the waiter returned and poured five glasses of cognac, just a small portion in each snifter, putting one down in front of each of us. He then lifted a box from the tray he had brought the glasses and cognac on and put it down in the center of the table, along with a lighter and a cigar cutter.

"Would either of you like one? They're Maduro, which I enjoy."

I shook my head, and Landry politely declined even as he shifted closer to me, his hand on my back.

We both watched José lift the lid of the box and offer cigars to Che and Armando, who both declined, before he took one out and began the long process of smelling it, clipping the end, and getting ready to smoke it.

"So, Eramo's dead," José told me as he took a sip of his cognac and told Landry to try it.

"Oh, it's very good," he complimented José after he took a sip.

"Good." He smiled at him. "I'm glad you like it."

"How do you know?" I broke in because he was talking so civilly, and I was ready to lose my mind. "About Adrian, I mean. How do you know?"

"I work for the Masada family," he told me, "and now so do you. Eramo's dead because the Masada family moved in on him, and he decided to fight instead of either work for them or sell. And I understood; he thought it was a battle he could win, but there's no winning against our resources, which stretch across continents. So now Eramo's dead and Zahir, that's my boss—yours too, now—he doesn't like how Kady handled things with Eramo. He thinks maybe if Kady had taken our offer to Eramo without the bloodshed, without killing his runners, then maybe Eramo would have been more open to negotiation." He shrugged. "I don't know. All I do know is that killing fucks with business and brings cops and attention where none is needed."

"I agree." I nodded.

"See, so you understand."

"What do I understand?"

"Kady hurt your people; Zahir didn't like that, so now Kady's gone too."

Jesus.

"The Masada family doesn't get involved in personal bullshit. Kady fucked up your runners, killed men that Zahir thought would be working for Rigel, his cousin. He counted on those men, and now they're dead. That's a waste. So Rigel, because he's smart, he goes to see Gabriel Pike. Gabriel, unlike Eramo, he's smart too. He sees into the future, not just right now."

"Yes, he does. He can look at someone and see what they could be."

He snapped his fingers, his smile big as he pointed at me. "Yes. Eisa, that's my boss, he said that Rigel liked Gabriel right off, said he could tell a man who could see the big picture. He said Pike is that man. So now your old boss is the new big boss in Detroit."

One day. I had only been gone one day. I could only imagine if I'd been gone two.

"So Eisa, he asked Gabriel for names, and three guesses whose came up." He grinned evilly, waggling his eyebrows at me.

"Okay."

"You get Gabriel's job when you get home. You're number four man. I'm number four man here. When Rush said he ran into Trevan, who was a runner from Detroit—I mean, how many fuckin' guys could that be?"

"Sure."

"I work for Eisa, who works for Donovan, who reports to Zahir. You work for Gabriel, who works for Rigel, who reports to Zahir. Are you following this?"

"Yeah."

He tipped his head at me. "Ask."

"So," I said and cleared my throat. "Your boss never wanted the runners killed. That was all on Kady?"

"Yeah." He shrugged. "I mean, come on, that makes no fuckin' sense. Why would you kill the guys that everybody knows bring in the money? From what Eisa told me, Rigel had a fuckin' fit. I think he cut shit off Kady before they buried his stupid ass."

I nodded. "He deserved it."

"Fuck yeah, plus he owed you guys a ton of cash."

"He did."

"Well, everything he owned belongs to Gabriel now, so… whatever the hell you guys want to do with it."

I took a breath. "I… the Masada family, they're what?"

"How do you mean?"

"Their ethnic background."

"Oh, Arabic."

"Muslim, then."

"Yeah, so?" He bristled. "You got a problem with that?"

I coughed. "No, but… I'm gay. Here's Landry with me, so you understand what I'm asking."

He scowled at me. "It ain't shit, man; we're not the fuckin' mob, you know? This is modern times."

"Not really," I told him.

He gave me a head tip. "Yeah, maybe not, but Zahir, he's got a wife, right, and he's got his half brother, and we know but we don't say and he don't say, and so…. Gabriel told Rigel about you already, and he don't care, so nobody else does neither."

I just looked at him.

"Things will change when you get home."

It sounded like it.

He leaned forward again, studying my face. "Ask you a question?"

"Sure."

"Is Conrad Harris really your guardian angel?"

I smiled. So even José Cruz knew Conrad. "He's my friend."

His eyes flicked to Landry. "Because your boy's here I don't wanna say, but I've seen Conrad do some seriously fucked-up shit." His voice dropped to a whisper. "You should be careful."

I shrugged. "I'll say it again—he's my friend."

Palms up to show me he meant no harm. "Whatever, man, all I'm saying is that ain't nobody gonna fuck with you whether you're in or out, 'cause no one wants to see Conrad Harris up close, you know?"

"I know."

"So I guess it ain't as done as everybody thinks. It's your choice, I guess, and you get to make it because you're friends with the fuckin' angel of death."

All of them were scared of the man who would come and sit with me at the hospital and drive me to my mother's house. It was so weird. A chance meeting that could grant me freedom if that was what I wanted.

"It's not romantic to kill people," I told José. "Or do any of the things your family does."

"No," he agreed. "But people get rich off illegal shit every day. Ours is just easier to see."

"It's still a rationalization."

"Of course it is. So what?"

I finally took a sip of my cognac. "God, that's good."

"That's the difference between the shit you drink and five grand."

A five thousand-dollar bottle of liquor…. Christ.

"That's gonna be you, man."

In for a penny, in for a pound. "Okay."

He grinned suddenly. "Come on, have a fuckin' cigar."

"Pass it over."

His smile was huge and lit his face. "Atta boy."

"SO WHAT do you think?" I asked Landry as I lay in bed beside him hours later. We had both showered and changed and were lying in the darkness side by side. José had put us in his own car with his driver to take us home, which was very nice of him and saved us a small fortune.

"I dunno," he said, rolling over against me, pressing into my side, his arm sliding across my chest. "What do you think?"

"I don't want to ever hurt people."

"Not on purpose without provocation, no," he agreed. "But it's stupid to think that it won't happen. The business you're in, c'mon, Trev, your hands will get dirty."

"Yeah."

"And if it's ever between you and someone else... you better come home to me, you understand?"

"No, I know, I just, I'm not gonna shoot someone because of money," I said, my hand on his ass, rubbing gently and then sliding up to the small of his back.

He moved, groin against my thigh, his leg draped between mine, his head on my chest, under my chin. I wanted him really close, tight around me so I was feeling his presence, the beat of his heart. There were times, like this, when it was hard to tell who the needy one really was.

"I would kill anyone that tried to hurt you or my mother or—"

"I know," he interrupted me gently. "But that's not what we're talking about."

"This is a big deal. I have to figure out how deep into this I'm gonna be. And you, I mean, you have a legitimate business that maybe shouldn't be tainted with 'oh, that's the guy with the thug boyfriend'."

He started giggling.

"I'm serious."

"I'll be a gangster's moll."

"Listen, wise guy—"

"Oh! A pun."

I groaned so he'd know how annoying he was, but when I tried to shove him away, he just tightened his hold on me.

"Gimme a kiss."

"I'm being serious here; I don't ever want to taint your success with who I am."

"Don't worry about that. Let me handle my business, all right?"

"Lan—"

"If anything, it will make me seem more romantic."

"Crime is not romantic."

"Did you see *The Godfather*? It is romantic."

"Did you see *Donnie Brasco*? It's not."

He started laughing again.

"You need to listen to me. I—"

"Just," he said with a sigh, squeezing me tight, "you'll talk to Gabriel when you get back and you'll tell him what you're scared of and you'll see what's what. You don't even know what he really wants until you get home."

And he was right. "Yeah, I guess."

"We're not breaking up because you want to do the noble thing for me," he said, his voice dropping low in warning, the edge there, dark and twisted. "You will never get away from me; you should resign yourself to that now."

"Lan—"

"I'll kill you and then myself, that's a promise."

The way he said it, so matter-of-fact, I really should have worried.

"Trevan?"

"Idiot," I grunted, kissing the whorl of his ear. "Never want to leave you. I'm just worried."

He exhaled out his worry.

"I'm concerned about what's going on with Gabe."

"We should go home, then." He sounded so hopeful. "We could go tomorrow."

"You need to talk to your folks, and then we can."

"Tomorrow at brunch I'll talk to them, and then we can leave tomorrow night."

"Unless something changes, that's a plan." He yawned loudly, and I chuckled. "You're really cute."

"I am not," he barely got out since he yawned again. "And thank you."

"For what?"

"For explaining to José who I was." He sighed happily, his lips brushing over my jaw. "You always tell people that I'm with you, and I love it."

"What're you talking about?"

"Just take the damn compliment."

"Yessir," I said, moving my hands, sliding them into his hair, pushing it out of his eyes so I could see his face, however faintly, in the darkness. "Hey."

The sound he made was almost a purr.

"Kiss me."

He lifted, and his soft, wet lips slid over mine. He tasted like toothpaste and a hint of cognac and like himself, like Landry.

I trembled under him, and he smiled against my mouth. I whimpered just a little when he pulled back.

"Scott's date, she wanted you to fuck her," he said as he kissed me again.

I groaned because it didn't matter, she didn't matter, but he was stuck on her for whatever reason.

His hand slid across my abdomen and made my stomach flutter.

"You know—" I kissed him and nibbled gently on his succulent lips, then sucked on his tongue, the kissing becoming hard and aching the way I liked it. I loved that he never said it was too much or complained that I was rough. "—I only fuck you, you know that."

"I know that," he said, shoving me down under him. "Hey, what are the odds if I keep kissing you you'll end up tearing my clothes off?"

"It's a safe bet."

His evil chuckle made me smile.

Chapter
SEVEN

I WAS surprised the next morning when we came up for brunch, around ten, that the family was there with two men I didn't know. The way Landry fisted his hand in the back of my hoodie made me instantly wary, and the only thing I could think was that the two men were the problem.

"Good morning," Cece greeted us.

"Good morning," I said back, taking a seat at the table one away from Jocelyn, having Landry take the seat between us. I was uncomfortable, and when I was, normally I put Landry beside a wall and me on the other side of him. The closest I could come to safety here was his sister. I put my arm around the back of his chair as the older of the two men took a seat on the other side of Jocelyn with the other man next to him.

"Landry, you remember Dr. Armstrong."

He nodded.

"And this is his new partner, Dr. Kellum."

"What's going on?" I asked, leaning forward, looking at Cece.

"Well," she began, clearing her throat, "I was surprised to hear that Landry had never been medicated or seen a psychiatrist or gone into a treatment center for his bipolar condition once he left home. Since Dr. Armstrong is the one who diagnosed him all those years ago, I just wanted him to see Landry now and tell us what he thought."

"For what purpose?" I asked her. Apparently "friends for brunch," as we had been told to expect the day before, meant Landry's old shrink. "Why are they here?"

She looked confused, like that had actually never occurred to her.

"Trevan."

I looked at Mr. Carter.

"We just wanted Landry to speak to Dr. Armstrong, if he would."

I looked around the table and realized that Hugh was missing, as well as William, but everyone else was there from the morning before, including both Landry's brothers. I turned my head, my eyes flicking to Landry's face.

"You have to believe me and not them, okay?" he asked me.

"Of course," I assured him.

Landry turned his head and Jocelyn leaned back at the same time, giving my boyfriend a clear view of the man. "Yes?"

The doctor was smiling hesitantly. He was an older man, maybe late fifties, early sixties, handsome, tall. He reminded me of a high school principal; he had that look.

"So tell me about yourself, Landry."

He cleared his throat. "We need to clear some things up first."

"Like?"

"Well, for starters, I never did drugs." He sighed heavily. "I mean, I did them, but mostly just to have something to do. I've never been addicted to anything." He tipped his head back and forth. "Well, nothing pharmaceutical."

The table went wild, and he started laughing and then turned in his seat to face me.

"Fuck them," I told him. "Just look at me and tell me."

Noise raged around us, and he opened his mouth to try to speak, but I couldn't hear him. He could barely hear himself.

"Shut up!" I roared, standing up fast and overturning my chair, which brought the room to a sudden hush. "If you all can't give him the courtesy of letting him speak, we're leaving right fuckin' now."

No one said a word.

Slowly, I gazed at each of them, one after another. I finally returned my full attention to Landry as I picked up my cushioned chair and sat back down beside him. "Go ahead."

He released a deep breath. "Okay, see, I hated this place. I hated them." He gestured at his parents. "I hated the rules and the restrictions, and so I tested and pushed to see what would happen, how far I could go."

"And?"

"And nothing. Nothing worked." He shrugged. "I mean, Trev, I stole and I left vials of coke in my gym bag and left joints in my dad's Jag and nothing. No one said a fuckin' word to me."

I nodded. Limits I understood. Landry needed a very tight leash or he didn't feel loved.

"I was a rich spoiled brat, and I know that now, but still...." He shrugged. "No one gave a shit what I did, where I went, who I saw; no one. So I escalated it. I stole and I had raging parties and I got drunk and crashed the cars and still... nothing."

"May I please interject," his father barked at him.

We both turned to him.

"We cared, Landry. We tried to get you help and—"

"But you never said stop. You never said, 'I'm gonna beat the shit outta you if you don't cut this crap out.' You never cared, Dad. You only cared when I got caught with Will in the stables, and you and his dad found us because I made sure you would."

His father's mouth hung open.

"Please," Landry scoffed. "Do you have any idea how long I had sex with Will, Dad? All junior year, all summer, all senior year... we fucked like bunnies."

I didn't have to make everyone silent; they were all staring at him, completely dumbfounded, even Jocelyn. He had them all floored.

"But after that, after you saw us, after you had to apologize to his father, explain it to his mother, people at the country club—then it was different. Then I was crazy. Then I was addicted to drugs. Jesus, that shit was hysterical. I barely did any drugs. I mean, sure, some for recreation, but Trevan can tell you: I haven't done any since he's known me."

All eyes on me.

"He hasn't," I assured them. "I don't do them, he doesn't do them. We're too busy."

He gestured at me as if to say "of course" and continued, "Yeah, exactly. Trev works, I work. I have a business. Drugs are too expensive and way too time-consuming."

"But—"

"Dr. Armstrong," he said, getting up, walking over to the man, standing over him. "Why did you think I was bipolar?"

He coughed. "You were manic, Landry."

"Or I was just bored out of my mind." He shrugged. "I mean, Trevan has cousins, you know, who sit and play video games, and they are just angsty, moody pieces of crap."

"Agreed." I nodded.

"And you ask, you know, 'What's wrong? Why are you sad? What's going on?' And it's nothing. They can't tell you. They can't articulate it. They're just teenagers. When Trev gives them money, when we take them to a concert, do anything out of the ordinary for them, they brighten for, like, a second and a half, and then they go right back to reading their manga and posting on their blogs and snarling. Maybe, and I'm just throwing it out there, maybe that was me. It's just a thought."

Dr. Armstrong was studying Landry's face.

"I mean, who died and made it necessary for me to be happy and smiling every hour of every day?"

"Landry," he said gently, "I understand what you're saying, but son, you had such inflated highs and terrible lows. You went into a rage once that took your father and I both holding you down and my nurse giving you a sedative to calm you. That is not my imagination."

"Sure. And maybe I can still flip out a little sometimes, but so can all of you."

"Landry—"

"I live with him." He pointed at me. "Day in, day out, I wake up in bed with him in the morning and I go to bed with him at night. I have quirks, I need specific, what?" he asked me. "What would you say?"

"Structure," I told him. "You need your routine. As long as there's that, you're fine."

He shrugged and smiled at Dr. Armstrong. "I don't like change. I don't like people I don't know around me, or close to me, and I definitely don't like anyone around Trevan."

Everyone was back to looking at me.

"I know I'm a little messed up. I know that he does a lot to keep things smooth and calm, and I do stupid things like buy boots." His voice went out on him.

"It doesn't matter," I assured him.

The tears were there suddenly. "I was such a brat."

"Yeah, so, who cares?" I grinned at him. "Come here."

He charged back to me, flung himself down into my arms, and buried his face in my shoulder. "I love you."

"Yes, I know," I soothed him, rubbing his back, releasing a deep breath and squeezing him tight as he squirmed around in my lap. "Stop fidgeting."

"I told you I didn't do drugs."

"And I believed you."

"I know you did, but I thought if you knew what a fuckin' brat I used to be, then you'd know it wasn't gonna change and then you for sure wouldn't want me."

"Oh for crissakes, Lan, I love you no matter what, no matter what stupid-ass shit you do. I'm not going anywhere, and one of these days you'll stop testing me and you'll just know."

He shook his head. "I don't test you. I just do stupid crap. I know you love me. You've shown me, and when you make me do what you want—that's the best."

I grunted.

"Remember that time you locked me in the bathroom at Tim's party because I was dancing on the coffee table and I was gonna strip?"

"I remember."

"And when I screamed myself hoarse, you used his bungee cords to tie me up and then carried me out over your back?"

I nodded, mortified that he had just related that story, but what could I do?

"Yeah." He shivered hard. "That was awesome."

I squinted at him.

"And when we got home you tied me to the bed and—"

"Hello," I cut him off. "TMI, baby, okay? Seriously?"

"Oh." He looked around, smiling sheepishly at the looks of absolute horror on everyone's face. "Sorry."

"But you know," I said into the sudden awkward silence, "maybe me manhandling you and being rough with you isn't such a good thing. I've been thinking that maybe I should start seeing someone about that. I don't wanna ever hurt you."

"You could never hurt me." He was adamant.

"Yeah, but Margo, you know, Adele's friend that works with her at the clinic, she said that she's got a really great therapist, and I was thinking, when we got back, that I'd go and see this guy."

He squinted at me before he got up off my lap, took hold of my bicep, and walked me over to the edge of the room. When he turned to face me, his eyes were narrowed with worry. "You don't need to see anybody. There's nothing wrong with you."

"Maybe not, but I should check it out."

He was agitated, shaking his head, biting his bottom lip.

"Baby?"

His hands went to my chest, and he leaned close. "I don't want you to go see some stranger by yourself. I wanna be there with you, okay?"

"If that's what you want. But this guy might want to talk to me alone."

He pressed his lips tight together. "Yeah, but I live with you, so he'll probably wanna talk to me too."

I shrugged. "Could be. You know more about that than me."

His eyes flicked to mine. "You already talked to Adele?"

"Yeah, and you remember Margo; you liked her."

He nodded.

"Yeah, so I figured when I got back, I'd call this guy up."

"After you talk to Gabriel."

"Yeah, that comes first," I said, chuckling a little. "Obviously."

"Okay," he agreed and nodded, hands clutching at my sweater. "We'll go together and talk to this guy 'cause I don't know him, and you know I don't like anyone I don't know being around you."

I knew that. I was counting on it. "Good, all settled," I told him, leaning forward and kissing his forehead. "Now let's go back and finish this."

We returned, and all eyes were on Landry as I took my seat.

"So," he went on, "after you guys"—he gestured at his parents—"were sure I was nuts and wanted to check me into that clinic in New York, I told you I was fine. I told you that being gay didn't mean I was crazy. I might be crazy, but I'm a gay crazy man, not a crazy man because I'm gay. Does that make sense? You thought if you got me sane that I wouldn't be gay anymore, and that's ridiculous. So I left to save us all a lot of heartache. The fact that it took you getting sick, Mom, for you guys to want to talk to me pretty much tells me I was right."

"No, Landry, you—"

"I can't be fixed, Mom; my sexual orientation is homosexual, plain and simple. Maybe if you had come at me without saying that if I was sane, I wouldn't be gay... maybe things between us would have been different."

"But it doesn't matter," she told him.

"Now it doesn't," he replied. "But that wasn't the case eight years ago."

"Ohmygod," Chris groaned, looking back and forth between his parents and Landry. "He was right. All this time and he was *right*? You cut him off because he was gay, not because of anything else."

"It's not that simple," Neil told his son.

But it was.

"Christ," Landry sighed, glancing at me. "Are you hungry? 'Cause I'm starving." His smile was beautiful, making his blue-green eyes sparkle.

"Yeah."

"Come on, let's get some food."

Breakfast was a buffet, so Landry and I went to pile our plates full of food. He left first, walking back to the table, promising me coffee.

"Trevan, is it?"

I turned and Dr. Armstrong was there. "Yes."

He sighed deeply. "I appreciate what you did there, and I'm sure the Carters do as well."

"I'm sorry?"

"Landry needs help, and you're making sure he gets it by using yourself as the patient when we all know it should be him."

"I have no idea what you're talking about."

"You handle him very well. I don't remember him ever being so contained, so calm."

He would not get me to incriminate my boy on any level. The fact that he was even there felt like an ambush to me.

"I see that the Carters were misguided," he said and coughed. "But that does not mean that Landry does not need help."

"Not him, me. I'm the one who needs a shrink. If he decides down the road that he wants one as well, then he will."

"Trevan—"

"I have problems; you heard what he said."

"I heard him say that he was out of control and you took care of him. That's what I heard."

I shrugged. "He agreed to go with me when I talk to someone, that's all I know."

"He'll go with you because he thinks he's doing it for you."

"Or he won't think he's doing it for me, but he'll do it for me anyway because he doesn't actually wanna hurt me, and maybe he worries about that."

He grunted. "That's hardly fair, you denying things and then suddenly telling me that whatever I think, you know already."

I shrugged.

"So Landry gets to pretend he's doing it for you, seeing a therapist, and he gets to keep his pride intact, is that it?"

"That's it."

He stood there just staring at me.

"Doc?"

"That's very selfless," he said softly, his eyes locked on mine. "He has the potential to be very dangerous, you know."

"Or not."

"Or not," he agreed.

I shrugged. "Don't worry. If I die, no one will sue you for not committing him."

"I couldn't commit him if I wanted to. He's not a danger to himself, and there's no evidence that he's a danger to others."

"Nope."

"This is fire you're playing with."

"Lucky I'm an earth sign, huh? So he can't hurt me one bit."

He was confused.

"Astrology. I'm a Capricorn." I shrugged. "Supposed to be hot in bed, but I dunno, it's probably a load of crap."

He grunted. "He's very fortunate to have you."

"Thank you." I smiled at him. "It goes both ways."

I left him at the buffet table and walked back to the table and sat down. As promised, there was coffee, and, fortified, I turned my attention to Cece.

"I want to talk about your remission."

"Oh." She was surprised. "Yes, what about it?"

"Hit me with the specifics. Me and Landry need to know."

She looked back and forth between us. "What would you like to know?"

"Everything."

"Yes, but—"

"He's good," I told her, my hand on her son's chest. "I've got him. We need to know about you because he and I hafta go home tomorrow, and we need to know what's happening with you, when we can come back, and if you're up to flying out to Detroit to meet my family."

She was stunned. "You want me to meet your family?"

"Yes, ma'am, of course I do."

She looked at me, waiting, then at Landry, who was also waiting, both of us ready for her to tell us the plan.

"I...." She stammered, looked at her husband. "Neil?"

He looked at Landry and me. "Boys, we... Trevan...."

"Sir?"

"Do you understand how wildly inappropriate this is to ask? I mean, we don't want Landry in a homosexual relationship. We don't want him in the business he's in, consorting with people below his station. You understand that we want him to stay here with us and for you to leave."

"You do?" I smiled at him. "I thought you liked me."

"I—we—"

"I know I surprised you, both of us did probably. Landry's different."

"Yes he is," his father agreed with me. "But Trevan, the path Landry's on is not the one we want him to follow."

"Maybe," I assented, "but what you want or think isn't gonna change anything. You get that, right? He loves me, he loves my family—my mother especially—he loves his business, and he loves Detroit, his friends, all of it. So you have, like, zero chance of screwing up my life by taking him away from me."

"I—"

My hand went up to shut him up. "So let's get beyond all that. Forget it. I figured maybe you'd want to take a shot at knowing Landry, getting your family back together and all. Do you?"

He stared at me.

"Sir?"

"You are just the strangest man I've ever met."

I grunted. "Yeah, well, I've had a weird few days."

"Trevan—"

"Thanksgiving's in like two weeks. Whaddya say?"

"I say yes," Cece chimed in, nodding. "I want everyone together."

I turned to look at Jocelyn. "You and Hugh? Yeah or no?"

She shook her head.

"Okay, so, maybe you bring someone new, huh?"

Her eyes were leaking tears as she looked at me. "You would… that would… yeah?"

"'Course. You're the one we give a shit about; bring whoever the hell you want. We're a warm welcome just waiting to happen."

"Yeah," Landry told her, taking her hand. "You can come see my shop, and if you want, maybe you can stay. I would love it, and what's keeping you here?"

She nodded, her voice gone.

"It would be nice," I told her.

"I would love it," she said.

Landry beamed at her, kissing her hand, leaning his cheek on it. Of all of them, I could tell she was the one he liked best. They actually had a chance at the brother/sister bonding thing if she visited and played her cards right.

Scott looked incensed. "What the hell is—"

"Me," Chris said suddenly. "For Thanksgiving? Lan?"

"I gave you a bracelet, didn't I?"

He sucked in his breath.

"Even though you thought I was a drug addict and a crazy person, I forgive you." He smiled at his brother. "I'll even let you sleep on my couch if Scott doesn't want it."

"I'm not going to Detroit for—" Scott started, but his mother cut him off.

"Suit yourself," Cece told him. "The rest of us will be in Detroit for Thanksgiving."

"Mother, have you lost your mind? You can't go to Detroit!" he yelled, getting up, beginning to pace. "Dad!"

"Your mother never wants to go anywhere," Neil Carter told his son. "She's been too scared to leave her doctor. But now she wants to take a trip, which I hope will be the first of many." He sighed deeply. "Oh yes, Scott, we are most definitely going to Detroit."

Whatever Neil Carter thought about me didn't matter in the least. His wife wanting to travel he took as a very good sign. Landry being willing to reconnect, give them a chance, was more than he could have asked for, and now he finally saw it. He was not going to miss the opportunity to be with either one of them.

"I look forward to us having an adventure together," he told his wife.

Cece put her hand on his face, and he covered it with his own, the love in his eyes easy to see. Watching his wife want to do something, want to travel, to live, that was gutting him.

"Me too," she told him. "Maybe afterwards we could go to New York. I haven't been to Broadway in a hundred years."

"I would love that," he said breathlessly.

"Good," she said before turning to smile at me. "It's settled. We'll be there, and if there's a change and I can't, you'll come back to see me, won't you, Trevan?"

"Yes," I promised her.

She reached for me and took my hand. "Thank you, for everything."

"You're welcome."

When she let me go, I turned back to my boyfriend. He was looking at me.

"What?"

"It won't ever be like yours, Trev. You get that, don't you?"

His family was not like mine—yeah, I knew that.

"It's cold in Detroit," Scott muttered a second later.

We all looked at him.

"It is, right?"

"You can borrow a coat," I promised him.

He shot me a look and I laughed, which turned the grin he was working hard at not allowing into a full-blown smile.

Landry was stunned.

Jocelyn burst into giggles.

Chris obviously had no idea that Scott's face could do that, smile.

It was nice.

"Trevan."

I looked back at Cece.

"It's you, you did this. You gave me my family back."

"No," I corrected her, tipping my head at Landry. "It's him. My dad always said if your family is together, everything will be all right. Your family wasn't together, but now it is."

"Now it is," she agreed, tears welling up in her eyes.

"Dr. Armstrong, are you all right?" Landry asked him.

"Yes, Landry," he said and cleared his throat. "I am."

My boyfriend turned and smiled at me. "You're right, weird couple of days."

Truly.

MR. CARTER, who I'd thought didn't love his son, mauled Landry at the breakfast table, hugging him so tight he couldn't breathe. I liked it; breathing was overrated anyway. And after that, the light came from heaven just like it did on Paul on the road from Damascus, and the man apologized to me. Gay or not, poor or not, ethnic or not, I seemed to be an excellent influence on Landry, and his wife liked me. He actually hugged me, which freaked Landry out a little and his brother Scott a lot. It was funny.

Jocelyn explained about Hugh after Dr. Armstrong and Dr. Kellum left, about how she had been cheating on her husband and how great Hugh was being about it, how he just wanted an amicable divorce and for them to split everything fifty-fifty. She thought that they might even still be able to be friends and really hoped so. He was her best friend, and not being able to talk to him about the affair was the part that had hurt.

I didn't understand about being friends with exes unless no one had done anything wrong and you just got sick of looking at each other. It was beyond me. But more power to Hugh if he could let it go, his wife's betrayal, and not be bitter. He was a better man than I was.

While I enjoyed sitting there listening to everyone talk, watching Landry, I realized that he was still not engaged. At home, at family dinners, holidays, barbecues, whatever, Landry sat and argued and laughed and was loud. He was asked his opinion and gave it, sometimes harshly, sometimes gently, but never shyly, never like he was being now. It was not in him to sit back and simply observe. That he was doing so pained me.

"Quit," he said softly.

My eyes met his.

"It's not the same." He spoke the words under his breath. "I know your family. I don't know mine."

My heart hurt for him even as he pressed into my side.

Later, as I stood looking out at the enormous grounds, the man-made lake, and the edge of the stables, Mr. Carter walked up beside me.

"I hadn't counted on Landry returning home," he said to me. "I never thought he'd come. It makes everything so much easier."

I wasn't sure what he was talking about, but I let it go.

"Thank you," he said, tipping his head at his wife and children sitting at the table. "We're a family too. We might not be one you understand, but we are one."

I turned to look at him. "I only make judgments if he gets hurt, Mr. Carter, not for any other reason."

"Your own pride, your own comfort, doesn't factor into things?"

"No, sir, not if you love someone."

"We agree on that," he said even as he caught his breath. Something was wrong, but I didn't know the man well enough to pry.

LANDRY surprised the hell out of me, and even though I was worried, I was glad to see him trusting us to be apart.

I had to go home; his father had asked him to stay through the weekend. Landry had agreed and planned to fly back Sunday morning because he needed to be back at work on Monday. He had inventory and ordering to do, and billing and all sorts of assorted paperwork hell. So I was leaving that night, Thursday, and I'd see him in two days. The fact that he felt good enough to let me get on a plane without him made me happier than I could express. And I hoped that time alone with his family would bring closeness. Maybe it was me. Maybe without my presence, they would all rebond. I was hopeful. I had a twinge of worry, but he had shown them, and me, how strong he was, how in control. I left that afternoon, and he was bouncing up and down in the back seat of the limousine as Chris told him that they were all going hot air ballooning the next morning.

Outside departures, I kissed him and told him I loved him.

"I know." He smiled wide. "Take care of things at home and let me know exactly what's going on tonight when you call me."

"I will," I told him, leaning in and kissing his cheek. I waved from the curb afterward.

My phone rang when I was in line to get coffee. "Yes, dear?" I teased him.

"I just, uhm, had this horrible revelation."

"What's that?"

"You're happy I'm staying here because you're worried that you're gonna go home and somebody's gonna kill you, huh?"

"Actually, that thought had not crossed my mind." I chuckled. God, his brain. "I was just happy that your father asked and you said yes is all."

"Oh. Who's picking you up at the airport?"

"Javier and Dave."

"Okay, tell them I said hi."

"I will. I love you."

"I love you too," he said, but he sounded wilted before he hung up.

The plane ride home was nice. I sat beside a mother with an infant in her lap and a toddler in the seat between us. He was cute and wanted to talk, and I gave him my phone to play games on.

"Ohmygod, thank you," his mother said, gripping my arm.

"It's fine," I assured her.

When I changed planes in Dallas, I was sitting next to two guys who were wannabe gangsters. Ever since I was a child, my father used to smile and say that his son did not suffer fools. Nothing had changed. I leaned against the window, closed my eyes, and went to sleep.

In the terminal, I saw Javier and Dave. Hard to miss them in their suits and trench coats and scarves.

"Why are you guys dressed up?"

"I came from work." Javier chuckled, his hand on my shoulder. "And Dave is dressed like an adult because, lo and behold, he had a job interview today."

I looked at my friend. "And?"

"I dunno." He shrugged. "He took me for drinks after."

"That's gotta be good," I said, looking back at Javier.

"God, I hope so. Being the breadwinner in this family sucks."

At which point my friend Dave, whom I had known since the fifth grade, smacked his boyfriend of four years really hard.

"Crap," Javier groaned, squeezing my shoulder.

They were good together, and even though Dave had been looking for a job going on six months, they were still doing fine and had not,

Javier assured me, had to dip into their savings. Tall, tan, beautiful Javier Gomez and short, bald, round David Schroeder made love look effortless and sweet. Sometimes guys looked at Dave and thought they could take Javier from him, and then Javier himself would quickly, easily, and effectively shut them down. No, Dave was not a super model, but God, Javier worshipped the ground the man walked on and vice versa. They were what I wanted for me and Landry.

"Where's your boy?" Dave asked me suddenly, squinting.

"He stayed with his parents in Vegas until Saturday. He'll be back Sunday night."

"Oh." Javier looked at Dave, who lifted his eyebrows and then turned back to me. "Was that a good idea, darling?"

I shrugged. "Sure, he's fine there."

He nodded slowly. "Okay."

I looked at Dave; he forced a smile and nodded too.

"Will you two knock it off? Landry's not broken; he can handle a lot of shit by himself."

"Yes," Javier agreed, "but not as much as you think. C'mon, let's get you some food."

The drive was nice, as was the company and the banter and dinner at one of my favorite places. I got treated, too, which was the best part. Once they dumped me at home, I staggered into my bedroom and passed out.

I thought I had been asleep for hours, but when I opened my eyes, it had been maybe twenty minutes. The reason I was up was that my phone had rung, and after a minute of fumbling around, I answered it even though it was not a number I knew.

"Hello?"

"Trevan?"

"Yep." I was barely awake.

"This is Jo."

"Oh, hey, how's Landry?"

"Well, after all that this morning—" She paused and sucked in her breath. "As of right now, Landry's having a meltdown."

"Define 'meltdown'."

"He's bouncing off the walls."

I grunted. "Did he eat?"

"What?"

"Feed him. When he's hungry, he gets antsy and sort of frantic. Feed him, preferably like a big hamburger or something heavy so he'll sleep."

"You're serious."

"Yeah, go ask him if he wants to eat. I'll stay on the phone."

The sound was muffled, and I started to drift.

"Ohmygod, Trevan."

"Yes, I'm awake."

"That—he's hungry."

"Yeah, I know, gotta go, falling asleep," I cut her off. "Put him on the phone."

"Are you—"

"Please."

Again there was muted noise, and then, "Trev?"

The voice I loved. "Hi, baby."

"Are you okay? I worried that you weren't okay, and then I thought who can I call, what can I do this far away, and I started thinking that maybe your sister would—"

"Love," I said, my voice deep and husky, "deep breath. I'm fine. You need to eat something, yeah?"

There was a catch of breath. "Maybe."

"I think yeah."

"Okay."

"So go eat and call me tomorrow."

"Why?"

"'Cause I'm going to bed."

"You're going to bed?"

"It's late here."

"Oh."

"But I'll talk to you tomorrow, okay?"

"Okay. In the morning."

"First thing you wake up, you call me."

"Okay." He sounded happy.

"Okay, baby."

"I love you."

"I love you back."

And he was humming when he hung up.

Chapter EIGHT

I CALLED Gabriel as I was getting coffee in the morning.

"I said *days*, kid." He drew out the word. "Not *a* day."

"I know, but with everything… I figured it was okay."

He sighed deeply. "It is. Where are you?"

"At your favorite coffee place," I said with a chuckle. "And I got yours already."

"I'll be right there to get you."

"I'll be waiting," I said, hanging up. I was sitting on the bench outside the coffee shop we both loved. The coffee was so strong my friend Stacy said just smelling it gave her a bladder infection. She was funny.

When Gabriel rolled up to the curb, I was surprised to see that Adrian's driver was now his. I couldn't have kept my eyebrow from arching if I tried.

"Don't say a word," he said as the door was closed behind me.

"Why would I?"

He cleared his throat. "So, we have to talk."

"I agree. Nice suit," I added; the Hugo Boss looked good on him.

"Fuck you."

"Hostile."

As the car pulled away from the curb, he sighed deeply. The rain, which had been a steady drizzle all night and into the early morning, decided to become a monsoon.

"So Adrian's dead," he said, turning to me.

"Yeah, I got that."

"I have a new boss, Rigel. Seems okay."

I nodded.

"I told him what I wanted for you, that I wanted you out, and he asked me a lot of questions that I didn't understand."

"Like what?"

He turned from looking at the rain to looking at me, and I was struck, as I always was, by how handsome, and not, the man was.

Gabriel had light-brown hair, pale-blue eyes, blunt features, a long straight nose, and thin lips. His hair fell forward across his forehead and slipped down the back of his nape in thick waves. He looked like everybody; there was nothing about him that made the face memorable—until he smiled. And then you saw the glint in his eyes, the curl of his lip, and saw that he was handsome. Still not traffic-stopping, still not able to inspire lust, but his height, six two, and his build, lean and muscular, made him above average. Because he was the guy who had made it rain for me, had given me a hand up when there was no one else, I had always seen him with my rose-colored glasses on.

"Rigel asked a lot of questions about the kind of man you were, what your temper was like, how long it took you to get mad and how many people you'd killed."

"And?" I asked him.

"I told him the truth, and he was thrilled. Seems a guy with no sins and no skeletons in the closet is just what he's looking for. I told him you wanted your own restaurant, and he said that Kady's is yours to do with as you see fit; make it whatever the hell kind of restaurant you want."

I couldn't breathe. "And the catch?"

"The catch is you're in, and really, you're in whether you wanna be or not, so I would take the damn restaurant and set up your life and be the guy Rigel Masada wants you to be."

But what did I want?

"This guy I met in Vegas, he said that because of Conrad, I had choices."

He shook his head. "I told Rigel about Conrad. He told me he doesn't care. He's not afraid of one man; he has an entire family backing him. You'll like him. He's in Miami now. When he gets back, he wants to meet you, and Landry."

"You like him?"

"He's not erratic. He doesn't want to do everything, he just wants to concentrate on what makes him money. And he was merciless with Kady. I liked that."

I nodded.

"He wants you to be the guy the cops talk to, the guy everyone talks to. It can't be me; I've done too much, am way too dirty—but you, you're squeaky clean."

"I'm a runner," I disagreed with a laugh. "I'm not that clean."

"Oh come on, you don't even own a gun."

I held his gaze.

"From where?"

"Connie."

He nodded. "That makes sense. Give it back to him, all right? You'll have muscle from now on. Gino and Pavel will—"

I shook my head. "I'll ask Conrad."

"You can't afford to pay him day in and day out."

I shrugged. "I think I can, and he likes the idea of the restaurant too."

He exhaled sharply. "You're gonna be in charge of the house, the runners. It's your place now, Trev, you get that, yeah?"

"Yeah."

"I mean, I'm stepping up to do the parts we don't wanna talk about, and Rigel, he's doing the heavy lifting."

I understood. "Drugs?"

He squinted at me. "Fuck no. No drugs, no whores; those were my rules, and that's where I think Adrian fucked up, trying to get in there. Guys bigger than us have been doing that shit for way too long. You don't even want to start that fight."

"You're preaching to the choir. I agree. What'd Rigel say?"

"Rigel's into moving hardware."

I nodded. "Guns."

"And cars and black market shit."

"But no drugs? Are you being naïve, or he said?"

"His father said. No drugs, no prostitution, and no alcohol."

"Oh." I laughed. "No booze. That's funny."

He shrugged. "It's still illegal, the shit we do trade in. We can all still get killed, busted; any numbers of tragedies could befall us."

"Or we just fly under the police radar 'cause they care more about drugs and whores and alcohol."

"Make no mistake; guns are a big fuckin' deal."

"Bigger than drugs?"

"Yeah, I dunno," he sighed. "Maybe."

"Whatever. Sounds like I got the easy job compared to the rest of you guys."

"You'll be the respectable one, and that's necessary. You're the guy who gets to go to grand openings and to campaign dinners and make donations. You're the honey that'll draw the flies that get caught in the web."

"That's quite the sinister metaphor there."

He grunted. "Yeah, well. It'll be shit to be you sometimes too. When some dirty politician realizes that you're not as benign as you seem, there will be trouble. That's why you're gonna move. House, cars, Landry will have people watching his place, keeping him safe. The step you're gonna take is for life. There's no turning back."

"Landry can't ever be in danger, or my family, Gabe."

"I know. Everybody knows. There are rules. The target will be on your back, Trev—just like mine, just like Rigel's—but if they squeeze the trigger, it gets squeezed back, right? And who's gonna fuck with the man who has Conrad Harris for muscle?"

The thing was, I wasn't scared. I was at the shallow end of the pool; Gabe was the one navigating the shark-infested waters.

I studied his face. "I'm sorry it can't be you."

"What do you mean?"

"I'm sorry you don't get to be the mostly legitimate guy."

"I should have thought of that before I did my three-year stretch. And once I was out, I should have gone straight instead of letting Adrian Eramo talk me into being his muscle and his man. The first time you pull the trigger, it's over."

"I wouldn't know."

"And that's how I plan to keep you." He smiled, leaning forward to squeeze my shoulder.

I took a deep breath. "What if Rigel gets killed, and then you, and I'm left alone without any backing? Then what?"

"Then you roll the dice and hope for the best. I'll be dead. I won't give a fuck."

"Nice."

"Just tellin' it like it is," he said and shrugged. "If I get hit, you'll have to step up and be me, and then you won't even be able to pretend you're legit for the cops; they'll know you're dirty. And I'm sorry about that. But since we're bein' honest, I need to know that you have my back so I only have to worry about what's in front of me."

I understood that.

He put his hand on my cheek. "I know that you will never walk away from me. I knew that day in the hospital; I knew before that. Adrian was always a little jealous. I know he wished there was one guy who he could point to and say, 'That's my guy, and I trust him with my life.'"

"He trusted you."

"Yeah, but he shouldn't have."

And I heard what he was telling me, that he had been the one who killed him. "Did it hurt?"

"No, it was fast. That was their concession to me."

"If you ever have to do me, make mine the same."

The slap was fast and sharp. I was startled as my hand went to my cheek.

"Fuck you, Trevan," he snarled at me. "I brought you in, I just raised you up—you're mine. What do you need me to do to prove it to you?"

My eyes narrowed as I looked at him. "You take me home with you and you introduce me to your wife and your kids. Today."

Not what he had expected. "What? Are you fucking with me?"

"No. Your wife knows my face, and your kids, and if you ever have to do the whole Michael and Fredo scene in the boat, then you gotta tell Landry and your wife and your kids."

"Jesus," he gasped, taken aback. "My family is completely separate from my—"

"Yep. Nope. Not after today, not with us, not anymore. We're gonna be family or I'll walk away and Conrad fucks over anyone that tries to stop me."

"Oh you cocky little bitch; you think Conrad Harris will—"

"Yeah, I do, and you know he will. For whatever reason, that works, it's there, and it ain't changing," I told him. "So, what? Are we going?"

He shook his head.

"No?"

"Fuck."

I grabbed him suddenly, putting my hands on his face as I had never done, holding tight, eyes locked on his. "I will never leave your side, do you understand? Never. I'm loyal, and that still has to count for something, or the rest doesn't mean shit."

He grabbed my wrists tight and stared back at me.

Neither of us moved for long minutes until he finally closed his eyes and exhaled. I let him go because I knew I had him.

"Your sense of loyalty is all fucked up, Trev."

"Yeah, I know, that's why I'm gonna go see a shrink."

"What?" he asked, leaning back, releasing a deep breath as well.

"For Landry, you know. 'Cause he goes a little nuts sometimes."

"Between the two of you, Landry's the normal one, you know that, right?"

I nodded as he shifted forward and told the driver to take us downtown.

"So you can see Kady's restaurant that now belongs to you."

I smiled as I looked out the window, listening to him as he made a call. He let his wife know that he was bringing home a friend for dinner that night. I liked hearing it.

I GOT home late, stuffed full of Gabriel's wife Pam's peach cobbler as the final act of the evening. She was amazing, his kids were cute, and his housekeeper, his two bodyguards, and the nanny were all pleased to meet me. I had stayed with them, the Pike family, from seven on, having spent the day with Gabriel looking at the space that had been Kady's restaurant and would be re-opening under new management with a new name. After that, we took a tour of the rest of what Gabe now ran. He took me to meet the new runners who had been hired into the fold, and all of them looked at me the way I looked at Gabriel. I understood. He had introduced me as their boss, and that was what they saw. Now that I was Gabriel's right hand, he shared everything with me, and I found that I liked that more than I would have imagined. To be trusted implicitly, his faith absolute, had made me mute for a while in the car, the emotion welling up within me.

"You've wanted this," he concluded.

"Of course I have."

And he liked that I confessed to it so he didn't have to wonder.

"Do you have a nice girl, Trevan?" his wife Pam had asked me.

"I have a nice boy," I told her.

"Oh." She made a face like *how adorable is that?* "Will you bring him next Sunday for dinner?"

"I would love to."

She was very pleased, and Gabriel just rolled his eyes.

"So," I said when I caught him in the kitchen, "me being gay is cool with you and your beautiful wife. How 'bout Rigel?"

His eyes flicked to me. "His stepbrother lives with him."

I waited.

"His wife lives in Paris."

"Okay."

"And he can't say, but I'm not stupid. I know how my eyes follow my wife when she walks into a room. His eyes do the same when he's looking at his stepbrother, Omar."

Well all right then.

"No more talk about gay or straight. Nobody cares. Besides, it will probably make you seem even less threatening."

I chuckled. "That makes no sense."

He shrugged and told me to get the hell out of his house. I went to kiss his wife goodbye before his driver took me home.

I felt good by the time I walked into my apartment and my phone rang.

"Hello?"

"Trevan?"

The sniffle I got made me wary because I already knew her voice. "Jocelyn?"

"Oh God," she moaned.

That fast, my heart was in my throat. I had been so consumed with Gabriel all day, with my new place in the hierarchy, with what I would have to give up and with what I would reap, that I had forgotten about my boy and the fact that I never got a call from him when he got up that morning. It seemed small—he was with his family, he was safe—but now Jocelyn was crying.

"What's wrong?"

"Ohmygod, Trevan, he's gone."

"Who's gone? Landry's gone?"

"Yes."

"Gone how?"

"Taken. Kidnapped. We're waiting to hear about a ransom, but it's been hours and—ohmygod!"

"I'll be right there," I said and hung up.

I called Conrad because I was certain he'd know what to do. I apologized for not calling when I got home, wanting to explain everything to him, and asked him to meet me in Vegas.

"No," he told me. "I'm coming. I'll pick you up. Wait for me."

"I gotta go to the airport and get a ticket and—"

"Just stay there, I'm on my way. Don't move."

I waited and paced and called Jocelyn back and asked her to tell me everything from the beginning, very slowly since I was not absorbing words as easily as I normally did. It was hard to retain facts when you were no longer breathing.

Chapter
NINE

I SAT in first class the next morning nearly climbing out of my skin. The only thing that kept me grounded at all was Conrad's presence beside me. Of course, after the first hour, I attacked him because he was geographically accessible.

"Why do you care?" I asked him, wanting the fight, picking it.

His head rolled sideways so he could see me.

"I've never done anything for you."

The look in his eyes was hard to read.

"You don't wanna talk?"

Still nothing, just the stare from his lime-and-gold cat eyes.

"Fine, forget it," I said, turning away, looking out the window at the black night sky.

"Look at me."

My head snapped back, my eyes returning to his face.

"Friendship means shit to you?"

"Of course not."

"But that's what you're saying."

"No," I told him. "I just—"

"Everyone wants something," he said softly, leaning closer to me, "except my friends. I have very few, and you're one of them."

"Con—"

"You never expect anything without paying. You never ask for favors, you never take us, this, me and you, for granted. Do you know what that makes you?"

I shook my head.

"It makes you one of ten people in the world who give a crap if I live or die."

His eyes, with the flecks of gold in them, were really the most extraordinary color.

"And then there was Andrade's."

I took a deep breath. "That was nothing, and you always bring it up like it was."

He shrugged. "Because it wasn't nothing; it was a helluva lot more than that."

But for me it had never been the extraordinary happening that he thought it was.

IT HAD been a routine collection. Walking into Tajo Andrade's club to pick up the money he owed me, we had no idea that we were interrupting a robbery. When we walked down the stairs into the main room, the man turned and, with him, the shotgun he was holding. I didn't even think. I stepped in front of Conrad on instinct, shielding him with my body. Our diversion allowed Tajo the moment he needed to pull his Glock and drop the robber with a shot to the head. The second guy took a bullet from Conrad's gun, the silencer muffling the sound only a little. In the aftermath, as Tajo passed me an envelope and thanked me for being punctual, then ordered his guys to get rid of the bodies, Conrad turned me around and looked at me like he'd never seen me before.

"You okay?" I asked him.

And he nodded slowly, his eyes staring holes into me.

"IT WAS no big deal," I told him, back in the present, for what felt like the hundredth time. I patted his thigh before I let my head fall back against the seat. "Any of your friends would have done it."

"That's what you're missing," he told me. "There aren't too many of you."

But I refused to believe that; the man was much too constant not to be beloved by many.

"So you have a new job, huh?" he asked me.

He was trying to divert my mind, keep me from shattering into a million pieces. "Yeah."

"And who's gonna watch your back?"

"I was gonna ask you, but maybe there's not enough money in it, huh? Gabe doesn't think there is."

"I have enough money."

"I can pay you something, just not whatever you get for taking out drug lords in third world countries."

His laugh was throaty and low. "Whatever is fine. If I need more, I'll take a contract and kill a dictator."

"Yeah?" I croaked out, my voice succumbing to the emotion twisting through me.

"Of course," he assured me. "Tell them all that I'm your shadow."

"Please, they think you are now. It's why Kady didn't fuck with me—too scared."

His sinister smile, the one that reminded you that he was lethal, was there, curling his lip. "Good."

"Ask you a question?"

"'Course."

"That day I met you, what were you doing there?"

"I was supposed to take Hawkins that day."

"No shit?"

He made a noise in the back of his throat.

"And you didn't?"

"Nope."

"Why?"

"You were more interesting."

I sighed. "You didn't get in trouble?"

"I don't get in trouble."

"But people pay you. Don't they want a refund?"

The long exasperated sigh let me know that I was annoying.

"Tell me how it works."

"No."

"Is Hawkins still alive?"

"No."

"Why?"

"Really?"

"Come on," I pleaded.

He turned his head to me. "Money gets wired, and I either make the transfer when I finish the job or I don't."

"Oh." That answered one question. "And Hawkins?"

"Someone else did that."

"Okay."

We were silent.

"We will get Landry back," he promised me.

I pushed air through my lungs. "How do you know?"

"I just do."

I tried to let his certainty comfort me.

"What are you thinking?"

"That none of this makes any sense, you know?"

"Yeah, I know."

"Why Landry?"

"We'll figure it out."

I looked back out the window, unable to talk anymore.

When we landed at McCarran International, I texted Gabriel to tell him I had landed fine and that I would give him an update as soon as I knew anything. I had called him the night before after Conrad picked me up and explained what had happened. He was furious for me and made me promise to let him know if I needed anything at all.

"Thanks Gabe," I had replied softly.

"You'll get him back Trev," he promised me. "Make sure you call me."

"I will," I sighed and hung up.

After Conrad and I separated, me to duck into the bathroom and him to go get a rental car, I went to wait for him on the curb outside in front of arrivals. Ten minutes later, he rolled up to collect me.

"That's amazing," I told him as I opened the back door and threw my duffel in.

"What is?" he asked when I got in the passenger seat and buckled in.

"I've never gotten a car that fast."

He squinted at me. "You reserve it online, they come pick you up, take you to the rental car place, you sign, they give you keys, and you drive away. What's to wait for?"

"You must be, like, a gold member or something."

"Try platinum."

"I guess you rent a lot of cars, huh?"

"Contract killer, comes with the job."

"You don't say hitman?"

"We don't say contract killer either. For fuck's sake, Trev."

"I've never, you know," I said, looking at his profile, the dark aviator glasses, the chiseled features, his dark smooth skin, "told anyone what you do."

"I know that," he said, checking the rearview mirror, distracted.

"Just so we're clear."

"We're clear," he murmured, but he wasn't really paying attention to me.

"What're you doing?"

"Is your seatbelt on?"

"Yeah."

"Okay."

I looked at him again—his black leather jacket, the cashmere turtleneck underneath, the scarf the same color—and thought that he looked like he was ready to go sightseeing or something.

"Do me a favor."

"What?"

"Reach under the seat and pass me the gun."

"You just rented this car and there's a gun under the seat?"

"Yeah."

"How?"

"That's not that big a deal right now. Could you get the gun?"

When the handgun with the silencer was in my grip, I straightened up. At the same moment, he began to slow. Another car flew by us, several others having passed, but when this one did, we were suddenly in pursuit. He had the Lexus up over ninety before the car in front of us missed a turn, skidded, slid, and hit the concrete barrier. When the car stopped, we did too, in the middle of the freeway, and got onto the median. He reversed fast before spinning around and driving the wrong way back to the car. It was early, so we were mostly alone, but still there were lots of blaring horns before we stopped.

I reached for my door as Conrad threw his open and grabbed the gun from me.

"Do not get out!" he barked at me even as he did.

"I—"

"Do not get out!" he roared a second time, standing outside the car before sprinting toward the other.

I couldn't see—not from my angle or the other car's—and I wanted to go, but the man had given me a direct order, and it was more about trust than anything else. Did I trust him enough to stay put?

When I saw him loping back, I turned and waited for him.

He got in, shoved the gun at me, threw the car into drive, and peeled out, fishtailing back onto the freeway as we drove away.

"Jesus Christ, Conrad, what the fuck?"

"There should be a holster under your seat. Can you get that for me?"

"Conrad!"

He growled at me. "Okay, so those guys were supposed to kill us."

"Kill us?"

"Well, you. I wasn't on the menu since no one knew I was coming."

"Are you kidding? What the hell is going on?"

"Someone is really sloppy, because this plan is bad."

"What…? This doesn't make any sense," I said, leaning over, reaching for the holster, feeling around until I found it, pulling it out and showing it to him.

"Unscrew the silencer, holster the gun, and then pass me the silencer and then the gun."

It was hot. I turned to him. "You fired the gun?"

"Of course. You don't let people live who are trying to kill you. That's, like, the number one rule of survival."

"But we could have turned them over to the police. Maybe they could have led us to Landry." My voice quavered.

"They had no idea where Landry is; all they were supposed to do was keep you from making it to the house. Period."

I took a breath. "They weren't very good."

"No," he agreed. "Which tells me a lot."

"It does?"

He nodded. "This, combined with your earlier point that none of this makes any fuckin' sense, because why?"

"I dunno, why?"

"Landry's been gone—what'd you tell me when we were talking about this a while back— like, nine years?"

"Eight years."

"Okay, so eight years he's been out of the picture, and the second he's back he's a ransom target? Yeah? Does that make any sense?"

No. None at all.

"Think, Trevan. What could it be?"

"I don't wanna learn anything here, Connie; just fuckin' tell me what you think."

"Well, logically, it can only be family bullshit or friend bullshit. Whoever took Landry knows him or knows of him. There's no way someone waited all this time. This has crime of opportunity written all over it."

"How do you know?"

"Like I said, nothing else makes sense, and those idiots back there, they were guys that somebody knows and asked for a favor or threw money at."

"And you killed them."

"Yes, I did, because *a*, that's what I do, and *b*, they were trying to kill you. You stay safe because people know if they come for you, they die. If people ever find out that someone tried to kill you and lived through it—that's my reputation."

"You would kill people for your reputation."

"It's my name, Trevan. You don't know. My name is all I have."

"No one would have known if you let them go."

"I would have known, and believe me, those assholes would have talked. People know that I'm your shadow; all they have to say is, 'We tried to kill Trevan Bean and lived.'" He shook his head. "There's no way."

"Jesus."

"Get the fuck over it, it's done."

I nodded because I didn't have a choice.

"Think now," he said as he drove, slowing to a pace that would not alert highway patrol. "Who would want to hurt Landry?"

I had no idea.

"Are you thinking?"

"I am, but I don't… I don't know."

"Okay," he breathed. "What does Landry have?"

"He has nothing worth a ransom. He has a jewelry business, and he rents an apartment with me, for crissakes. He doesn't have shit."

"Yeah, but you said his family does."

"Sure, and that's who they want the ransom from, but—"

"But why would Landry factor in? How does he factor in?"

"I don't—"

"You're not thinking."

I wasn't, I was barely breathing.

"Trevan."

"What, fuck, how the hell should I know?"

"C'mon, Trevan, use your brain. When Landry left, was there a trust fund? Did he have one? Was there money that got moved around? How many kids are there?"

"Four."

"And did that become three and now it's back to four?"

"Are you serious? I have no—"

"That's motive, do you understand? Money is motive, the biggest one, always."

"Money." I had to wrap my brain around it. I had none; I grew up lower middle class, dipping into poor after my father died. There had never been enough. I didn't know about money.

"You have to think; how much is enough to fuck someone over for?"

"That can't be."

"It's the only thing it can be."

I shook my head.

"Yes."

"No," I insisted. "It can't be his family. You weren't there, you didn't see them. They all want him to love them so bad."

"You're wrong. Somebody doesn't give a crap."

I never argued with him, but this time I could because I knew what I saw and I knew love when it looked me in the face.

"Listen to me."

"I am."

"I think Landry was out of the will and now he's back in and somebody's pissed about that. Or someone used up their trust fund or borrowed against it and now it's gone because Landry's back. I dunno, but it has to be about cash either being gone or being smaller. Any way you slice this, it's money."

I just stared at him.

"What?"

"That's a lot of fuckin' scenarios."

"And I've been the deal breaker on the end of all of them at one time or another."

"Everything you just said—you've actually lived all those. Those all really happened."

"Yeah. I've killed people because of all those things."

"Jesus."

"You don't get it, but Landry's been gone a long time. Eight years is long enough for things to have been changed, and now that he's back, money will get redistributed. And probably his folks haven't even thought about moving things around yet, but it follows that they will. Whoever did this is counting on it. Landry's parents would want everything to be equitable between the four children."

"You're telling me that either one of his brothers or his sister arranged this."

"Yes, that's what I'm telling you."

"That's crazy."

"That's money. You have to think. What is some prodigal son when weighed against millions?"

"I just can't believe it. I mean, I saw them with him."

"Which is why seeing is bullshit, hearing is worse, just like the saying goes."

"Then how do you know what to believe?"

"You follow your heart and listen to your goddamn friends."

I took a deep breath. "I want him back. I need him back."

"I know you do."

I worked hard not to hyperventilate.

There were police cars in the driveway of the house when we reached it half an hour later. Conrad and I were allowed through the barricade, both of us given admittance without question. Someone had made sure my name was on the list, along with anyone who was with me. As the front door was opened by a uniformed policeman, I heard my name yelled from the opposite end of the room. I turned and Jocelyn ran fast to fill my arms.

"Oh, Trevan, I'm so sorry. You bring him to us after all this time and this happens," she cried, hands on my chest. "I'm so sorry."

I wrapped her in my arms and saw the looks of a pain and sadness on all the other faces in the room.

Except one.

Except the person I would have never suspected.

Neil, Landry's father.

I had counted on Scott. Scott was the perfect choice. Scott was hard to like. He wasn't warm like the others, and I had thought he wasn't crazy about Landry. But the surface was one thing, and what was underneath was something completely different.

The look Scott was giving me was one of begrudging concern. He was sorry for me and worried about Landry; it was all over his face. What was on Neil's face was surprise. He was absolutely stunned to see me.

"I gave the cops your name so you could come right in," he told me.

Because he never thought I'd make it there.

My eyes locked on his face. He shivered hard.

"Folks," a man said, walking over, looking at Neil and Cece, "it seems we have a development and something we all need to discuss."

They looked at the man as he pointed to me.

"Are we free to talk in front of these men?"

"Oh God, yes," Cece told him. "Detective Baylor, this is my son's domestic partner, Trevan Bean, whom we told you about, and his... friend?"

"Yes, ma'am," Conrad told her. "And Landry's as well. I'm Terrence Moss."

I turned to look at him, confused for a minute until it hit me. This was a police detective that he and I were being introduced to. It had never even crossed my mind, how close Conrad himself was standing to danger. And he was doing it for me, there for no other reason.

"Thank you for being here, Terrence," she told him. "We appreciate you coming all the way from Detroit with Trevan."

"Yes, we do," Jocelyn nodded, tears leaking from her eyes as she clutched at me.

"So, what?" Scott demanded, annoyed. "Jesus, do you have news? We need to do something... he could be really hurt and... what?" he barked at the detective.

He turned to Neil. "Two men, Joshua Beatty and Topher Jones, were just found dead on Highway 15." And because he was looking at Neil, I knew he was already aware that Neil knew them. His fixed regard, the squint of his eyes, was not good.

"Joshua and Topher." Scott said the names, trying to think of something, trying to dredge something from his mind. "Joshua and…. How do I…? Oh, I know. Dad, aren't those friends of Brendon?"

"Who's Brendon?" I asked.

Scott turned to me. "He's our maid Christine's son."

I looked back at Neil. "The maid's son. Does he live here?"

"Yeah," Scott answered for his father. "He lives in one of the larger cabanas down by the lake, close to the one you and Landry were sharing. His mother used to live there, too, before she passed away."

"Who is Brendon's father?" Conrad asked.

I turned to look at him. Everyone did.

"Why is that important?" Scott asked him.

He turned to look at the detective. "I think it's very important."

"As do I," Detective Baylor agreed. "So we checked. No father on record."

"How did they die?" Neil asked the detective, his voice sounding almost robotic. "The two boys."

"They weren't boys, Mr. Carter, but to answer your question, they were both shot in the head with a small caliber handgun."

He nodded and dropped down hard on the chair beside him, like he had just been drained of life—boneless, soulless, just empty.

"Mr. Carter?" The detective said his name sharply.

"He promised me no one would get hurt."

The hair on the back of my neck stood up.

"Who promised what, Mr. Carter?"

He just started shaking his head.

"Mr. Carter?"

"My son."

"Which son?" Detective Baylor asked him, and we were all silent.

Conrad put his hands on my shoulders, squeezing tight.

"Daddy?" Jocelyn said.

He looked up at his daughter. "Brendan."

"Brendan?" She squinted. "What are you—"

"Oh God," Scott groaned, sounding like he was going to be sick.

"Brendan is your son?" Cece Carter asked her husband. The look on her face went from horrified to furious in a matter of seconds. "You told me I was seeing things! You told me—ohmygod!" she shrieked.

Once she started screaming, it quickly became a howl that wouldn't stop. Scott went to her; Jocelyn got on her cell phone and called the doctor even as the wail went on and on. It was horrible to hear, and I watched Neil Carter's life end right there in front of me.

"Mr. Carter!" Detective Baylor yelled, ordering the officers to take Mrs. Carter away. Jocelyn went with her, squeezing my hand before she left, making me promise to come to her mother's room the minute I heard anything, the minute I knew the whole story.

"I promise," I said without turning to look at her, my eyes locked on her father.

"Mr. Carter," Detective Baylor barked again. "Tell me what happened now."

"This wasn't supposed to happen."

"Where's Landry?" I roared at him.

"I don't know." He looked up at me with broken eyes. "He took him, and he was supposed to give him back the minute the ransom got paid."

"But there's been no ransom demand," the detective reminded him.

He turned his head to the policeman. "I know, and that's troubling."

Troubling?

I started to shake, the desire to tear the man to shreds coursing through my body.

Troubling, he said.

Detective Baylor grabbed a chair and put it down in front of Mr. Carter. "Explain this to me: you had your one son kidnap his brother?"

"Half brother," Scott almost snarled. "Jesus Christ, Dad, what the fuck did you do?"

"I—"

"Please," Detective Baylor almost yelled, hand up. "Any more outbursts from anyone and I will clear this room. Do you understand? If you can't contain yourself, Scott, we will have you removed." He turned and glared at me. "That goes for you as well, boyfriend, do you understand? Everybody shut the hell up."

I nodded furiously and Scott seethed beside me, arms crossed, the energy just sparking off him.

"Now," the detective began again, facing Mr. Carter. "Sir, what did you do?"

"I didn't do anything." He shook his head, and I saw his chin quiver with the control it was taking for him not to cry. "And that's my crime." His eyes lifted to Baylor. "He told me. My son told me what he was going to do, and I told him to wait. I didn't want him to touch Scott or Christian because I was scared, but when Landry came home...."

I almost went down; my legs barely held me up. He wasn't about to feed either of his good sons to the beast, but the prodigal, the prodigal could be led to the slaughter.

"Breathe," Conrad ordered me, his voice cold and hard and quiet.

"When Landry came home, I thought he was the answer to my prayers because he probably wouldn't get hurt, but this way—" He lifted his head to meet Scott's gaze. "I couldn't take the chance on you or Chris. I would have had to stop him. I would have had to tell."

Landry was expendable.

"When he called me yesterday and said that he had Landry," he said, eyes returning to Detective Baylor, "I was terrified, but I told him what to do. I told him to call for the ransom. He just needed the money I promised him, that's all."

We all waited as he took a shuddering breath.

"When Landry left, I changed the trust," he explained. "I thought he was gone forever and didn't want anything to do with us, so I went to Brendan and I told him that the money that I had set aside for Landry, his trust fund, now belonged to him."

I heard Scott take a breath beside me, and I reached out and grabbed his bicep hard. I didn't want him to interrupt again, but I also didn't want him to get us all thrown out of the room.

Amazingly, his hand covered mine and he squeezed tight. Like we were in it together. When he stayed quiet, because no one interrupted, Mr. Carter continued.

"But when I went to change the trust this year"—he turned his head and looked at Scott again—"I found out that you had changed the terms."

Scott was taking no chances of being removed, so even with his father staring at him, he stayed quiet.

"What did you do, Mr. Carter?" Baylor asked Landry's older brother.

He took a breath. "When I became CEO of Carter Limited last year," Scott told us all, letting my hand go, looking at his father, "I saw that Landry's trust was up for review. And I thought about breaking it at that point and dispersing the money, but no matter what, he's a Carter, and that trust was set up by my grandfather when he was born. I had to think of Melvin Carter's wishes, and I realized that he'd want Landry to have what was his. So I changed the terms and locked it until he turns thirty. I figured if nothing changed by then, if he was still a no-show in our lives, if the silence continued, then the money could be allocated to wherever it was most needed or even given to a charity in his name. We could distribute it if Landry wasn't home before he turned thirty, but no way was it getting touched before that."

"I had no idea," Neil whispered. "And when I found out, I said nothing. I figured that I could get Brendan the money from some other source, and I had time because he knew that the trust couldn't be opened for a while, but then... then...."

"Then he needed the money," Baylor offered.

"Yes."

"And Brendan, who had been content to wait, not knowing that the trust was locked anyway, asked you for the whole sum."

"Yes."

"But you couldn't get it."

He shook his head.

"So Brendan decided that kidnapping one of your sons was the way to get it," he said.

"Yes."

"And you were in the process of stalling him when Landry came home."

He nodded.

"Did Brendan also believe that because Landry showed up, the money automatically reverted to him?" Baylor asked.

"Yes."

"Even though that was never the case because the money had never left Landry's trust to begin with, you let Brendan believe it was."

"Yes."

"Did you tell Brendan Arnold how much was in Landry's trust?"

"Yes."

"Did you tell Brendan to take Landry instead of either Scott or Christian?"

"Yes, I did."

Yes, he did. It was why he asked Landry to stay.

My stomach lurched hard.

"Mr. Carter, where is your son, Landry?"

"I have no idea." He shook his head. "I don't. Brendan took him somewhere, but he was supposed to call yesterday, and now... something must have gone wrong."

"Tell me, when Brendan took Landry, what was his plan?"

"To ask for the amount of the trust in ransom."

"And so because it was for Landry, to get Landry back, the trust could be opened and the money released."

"No," Scott interjected, shaking his head. "It doesn't work like that. The trust is sealed until Landry either dies or turns thirty. There's no way to get that money out. To pay off a kidnapper, we would have had to dig into the company assets."

"Which Brendan Arnold didn't know," Baylor told Neil, "because you never told him that Landry's trust couldn't be transferred to him."

"Jesus," Chris yelled, startling us all, especially since I had basically forgotten he was still there. "For fuck's sake, Dad, call your fuckin' bastard son and tell him to bring my brother back right fucking now!"

And even though it had been an outburst, Baylor didn't even chastise him. The story was out by that time; we all knew what was going on, now it was simply getting Landry home.

Baylor turned back to look at Neil. "Do you have a number to reach him?"

"I've been calling it. He doesn't answer."

"Is that his cell number?"

"It's one of those disposable ones."

"Tell me what it is."

As he gave the detective the digits, the rest of us just stood there silently.

"Okay," Baylor said after he called in the number to someone, told them to try and start a trace. "It's been close to forty-eight hours; Landry needs water and food. Try and think of anywhere that you think he might be, something Brendan said or did."

"I just don't know."

"His mother, maybe," Baylor suggested.

"As I said earlier, his mother died two years ago," Scott told him. "There was a skiing accident, but my father let Brendan live here rent free even after his mother didn't work for us anymore."

"And now we know why," Chris told his brother.

Scott nodded. "Yes, we do."

"Please," my voice cracked, because I was barely hanging on. When all eyes turned to me as I moved to stand beside the sitting detective, having freed myself from Conrad's supportive grasp, I didn't care. "I need Landry back. I need you to think of where the hell he could be."

"Right now it's not murder," Detective Baylor told Neil. "You and Brendan will still face serious charges, but there are mitigating circumstances here. If Landry dies, though.... You need to think, Mr. Carter."

"I don't know!" he yelled, getting up, crossing the room to the edge where it opened out onto the porch. "He didn't tell me anything; he—"

"Somewhere you two have gone," Baylor cut him off. "Someplace where no one would see you and question what you were doing with the maid's son."

"I don't... there's nowhere. I gave him scraps of my time and he had to watch my children receive all my attention and never get any. He... he hated Landry so much because he left and Brendan thought he had everything because he had me, he had a father."

"Oh shit, I know," Chris said suddenly.

We all turned to look at him, and I was praying, *please God, let him know what he's talking about. I lost my father too soon, don't let me lose Landry.*

"The hunting cabin," he said, staring at his father. "I hate hunting, so does Scott, but you keep that damn thing and I always wondered why. Your friends don't hunt. There's no one for you to go with. But I bet your son who only wanted to please you, I bet he was down with the cabin, huh?"

"How far is it?" Baylor asked, standing and getting back on his cell phone at the same time.

"Up by Lee Canyon."

"That's probably why you can't get a hold of him," he told Neil. Then he spoke into his cell phone, directing people on the other end to call the Forest Service, Fish and Wildlife, getting as many people mobilized for the hunt as he could.

"But what if he's not there?" Neil asked.

"It's the best lead we have, and with you not being able to contact him and him needing someplace out of the way to stash Landry, I think it's a safe bet."

"Brilliant," Scott told Chris, gently patting his face.

He nodded, and I could tell that he was not used to being on the receiving end of praise from his eldest brother.

"You all have to be ready for whatever we find," Baylor cautioned us.

I had to grab for the wall because my heart stopped.

"Go get him," Conrad barked at the detective.

"I wanna go," I told them.

Everyone yelled "no" at the same time, even Conrad. "We're gonna sit here with Landry's family and wait."

I flopped down onto the couch and watched Detective Baylor start to pace as he got back on the phone, and then saw him gesture at the plainclothes officers to take Mr. Carter into custody. They put handcuffs on him and led him from the house.

"I'm gonna go talk to Mom and Jo, bring them up here," Scott told us. "I'll be right back."

But it took him longer than that. The entire house was like a resort. Even Neil and Cece's bedroom was in another building attached to the huge area we were all sitting in. I couldn't wait to leave it and never come back.

Scott returned with his sister but not his mother. The doctor had called and told Jocelyn to give Cece a sleeping pill and that he would be there soon to check on her.

"She's resting," she told us all before turning to Detective Baylor. "You'll let the doctor in when he gets here, won't you?"

"Of course."

She nodded and sat down beside me.

Scott got on the phone to call a lawyer because he had to go to the police station and be there when his father was arraigned, and post whatever bail was needed. He was the man of the house now.

"Call me with news as soon as you have it," he told Chris, who was still standing beside him.

He nodded, squeezed Scott's arm, and then let him go. I was surprised when Scott took hold of my shoulder as he walked by. And I understood. He loved Landry, he did, but he also loved his family, and his father was still part of it. He needed to handle all the business, both legal and otherwise. I understood all of that and held no resentment toward Scott for doing his duty to his father. I just wanted Landry.

I trembled hard, but there was no sound and no tears.

"You'll get him back," Conrad promised me for the second time that day.

I prayed he was right.

I SAT still and silent, listening as things whirled around me. I heard the detective give exact directions to Mr. Carter's hunting cabin as Chris gave them to him. He gave them longitude and latitude, and I sat. I heard the radio and hard-soled shoes slapping over marble and wood and saw people moving out of the corner of my eye. There was the blast of a siren, the calming voice of the lead detective, and Jocelyn squeezing my hand at different intervals. She sat shivering beside me until I took pity on her and put an arm around her shoulders. Another half hour passed, and Conrad sat down and put an arm around me, hand on the side of my head as I tried to breathe. His presence, the strength in the man, how solid he was—I would never be able to thank him enough.

No one said anything; what would we have said?

The detective walked in after what felt like days, and we were all on our feet.

"He's secured; he's en route to the hospital."

"Is he speaking?" Conrad asked.

"He's screaming. They can't get him to stop."

Oh God.

"Brendan Arnold is dead. Once the cabin was breached, he was shot twice before he could shoot Landry."

Like I cared about some faceless guy I had never met.

"Landry's lost some blood, but he's conscious, and that's amazing."

But he was screaming.

"We need to get you"—he turned to me—"on a helicopter *now*."

"Why?" Chris asked him.

"Because Landry is screaming Trevan's name."

Chapter TEN

HE WASN'T conscious when I got to the hospital. He still wasn't conscious when everyone else made it. Five hours after that, he was still out. The doctor said we just had to wait.

Landry had sustained a blow to the head that had caused a minor concussion. He was also banged up and bruised and suffering from mild hypothermia and dehydration. His physical injuries, all in all, were not bad; they would heal. What had gone on in the cabin, the psychological trauma, was harder to gauge.

"He's going to hate me," I told Conrad. "He's going to think I should have fought him and made him go home with me. He'll never forgive me."

Conrad looked at me like I was insane. "There's no way."

But he didn't know Landry.

The nurse told me that he had been yelling and screaming *at* me, not *for* me. He had been enraged that I was not the one to find him. It confirmed my very worst fears. My life, on the cusp of beginning, had just ended, because the man I loved hated me.

As I stood outside his room, I let my head hit the wall hard.

"Don't to that," Conrad growled at me, his hand sliding around the nape of my neck so he could look into my face. "You don't know shit about anything yet. Now if you go in there once he wakes up and he's pissed at you and he hates you, then we'll know that he actually is all kinds of crazy and there's nothing, really, for you to hold onto anyway."

My eyes flicked to his face.

"I like Landry, I do, but he is volatile, and sometimes I worry. But you're not going to listen to me about what I think he needs and—"

"There's nothing wrong with him."

"Maybe not, but when he's with you, it doesn't matter. When you two are together, he's different. Now, if he's given up on that, if his anger is misdirected, you have to get used to him being gone. I will not allow you to go crazy trying to win him back. There are people beyond Landry Carter who are counting on you and who need you. And maybe right now you think he's the only one that matters, but bigger picture, he's not."

I took a shuddering breath.

"When Landry wakes up, you'll see what he says and we'll go from there. Do not stand out in this hall and try and figure out your whole life when you don't even know what the fuck is going on with it yet."

It was good advice.

At the eight-hour mark, after Conrad made me eat a granola bar and Jocelyn watched me drink water, after Scott showed up at the hospital and said that his father had broken down sobbing, and after Chris went out and got us all burgers, finally, Landry woke up.

I heard him scream from the hall where I had gone to stretch my legs. Staring at his face, seeing the marks, the bruises, the yellow that his eye would turn as it healed, had made my stomach roll, and I had needed to move.

I bolted back into the room and stood still at the doorway, terrified and hopeful all at the same time.

For once, I prayed, *let me be wrong about Landry Carter.*

I swallowed hard, frozen there, and my stomach twisted into a knot with sharp edges and thorns.

"Trevan!" He shrieked my name, high and wailing as he flung his arms out to me, for me.

I ran.

"Ohmygod, I knew you'd come." He sucked in his breath as I grabbed him and hugged him and kissed his face, his eyes, his nose, his cheeks, and then his mouth. I slanted my mouth down over his, the kiss demanding and deep, tasting him, devouring him. He was shivering in my arms when I stopped sucking on his bottom lip and leaned back to look at his face.

"Baby." My voice broke as I choked on the words. "I know you blame me, but please don't send me away. I'm so—"

"Blame you?" he almost shrieked at me, hands on my hoodie, holding tight, not letting me go. "Why in the hell would I blame you? I wanted to stay, and even if it hadn't been today or now, that crazy fuck Brendan was going to get me."

I took his beautiful face in my hands and stared into the eyes I adored, that were everything when he looked at me. "You still want me? You're not sending me away?"

"What the fuck?" He scowled at me. "You came right back the second you knew I was gone, and I'll bet that somehow you saved me. I don't know how yet, but I know that's true. I know if you hadn't come, I'd be dead."

My knees almost buckled at his faith as doctors and nurses streamed into the room.

"I love you. I will always love you. Don't ever fuckin' leave me."

"No," I promised him, holding his hand tight even as medical staff tried to move me away, push me back. "Never."

And he took a breath as the deluge began.

"THOSE two guys getting shot," Detective Baylor said after the second hour of us all being in Landry's room. "That's what broke this case. Mr. Carter lost it when he heard about that. I shudder to think what might have happened had they not been killed."

My eyes flicked to Conrad's.

"And it's such a waste that they had to die, but when you involve yourself in crime, eventually you will pay for it."

Conrad grunted.

"You disagree, Mr. Moss?" Baylor asked him.

"I do, detective. I think if people were as choosy with their friends as they were about their cars, a lot less criminals would ever be caught. You have to be smart."

"Are you speaking from experience?"

"I'm speaking common sense," Conrad told him. "How many cases like this one have you seen cracked because someone was stupid?"

He shrugged before turning to me. "You know, Trevan, you and Mr. Moss would have passed right by those two men on your way to the Carter home. Are you sure you don't remember spotting anything out of the ordinary, seeing a car stopped on the side of the freeway?"

"I wasn't looking," I assured him. "The only thing I was thinking about was getting to Landry."

He nodded. "Understandable."

"You told Mr. Carter they were killed by a small caliber bullet."

"Yes. Putting it all together now from e-mails and phone records, we know that those two were friends of Brendan's from school. After Mr. Carter told Brendan that you were returning, Trevan, Brendan sent them to intercept you, but the information from Mr. Carter must have been faulty, since they never even saw you."

"So my father had talked to Brendan earlier today?" Scott asked him.

"Probably sometime last night before he left for the cabin with Landry, but that's why, we think, he was so horrified when he heard that they had been killed. Mr. Carter felt that he sent them into the path of whoever killed them by notifying Brendan. He felt responsible."

"And who do you think killed them?" Chris asked him.

"Right now we have no suspects, but whoever did it, it was a clean, professional hit. Someone was very precise, and that just doesn't happen for no good reason. They were dirty beyond trying to intercept you two," he said to Conrad and me. "We just don't know from what yet or who they pissed off."

I nodded.

"It's very lucky that whoever got them took them out before they got a hold of you two," Baylor told us. "We could have had a very different outcome here today."

Landry tugged on my hand, and I leaned close so he could press into my chest and inhale me but also whisper. "Who's Mr. Moss?"

"Conrad." I replied under my breath even though with the detective still talking no one was paying any attention to us.

"Because of…" He trailed off, knowing I would understand him.

"Yeah."

"First name?" Landry asked me, as in Conrad's alias.

"Terrence."

He took a breath and said, "Terrence."

"Yes?" Conrad answered, looking at Landry.

"Thank you for taking care of Trev for me and for being his guardian angel."

"You're welcome. I promise to always do it."

"That will help me sleep for the rest of my life." He exhaled.

"Good," Conrad told him, and then I felt his hand on the back of my neck, squeezing gently. "So, I have shit to do. You think you can manage to get him home without me?"

I squinted at him, and his smile was huge.

"I guess that answered my question," he said, and then he turned and walked out the door.

"Is he just leaving?" Jocelyn asked.

Yes, he was, and I was torn, because our relationship was based on specific parameters that I was not supposed to violate. Like when the man wanted to leave, let him. But there had to be more.

"I'll be right back," I told Landry and ran after him.

He was almost to the stairwell, and why he was going to walk down sixteen flights, I had no idea.

"Do you need to be away from me?" I asked instead of hailing him.

He turned and looked at me. "Not yet."

"So can I hug you, or is that too much contact for you?"

"No," he acceded. "It's okay."

I shot forward into his arms and hit him hard and hugged him so he could really feel it, using more force than was necessary.

"Okay," he muttered under his breath. "I get it, I'm important, now lemme go."

I stepped back fast because it had been an order.

"I'm going to your place when I get home to take back the gun. You don't need it, not anymore. My reputation, your new status, it'll be enough."

I nodded. I didn't ask if he knew where the spare key was to get into our apartment; the man had never needed it before. He got in and out all the time without it.

"I was thinking, at least you don't have to worry about Kady getting what was coming to him anymore. Benji was avenged. You new boss took care of that."

"Yes he did," I agreed.

"Going forward, you don't get to think about that kind of stuff anymore. That's my department alone."

I nodded.

"Call me when you're home so I can walk beside you when you go in places."

"I will."

Quick nod and he was gone, the door to the stairs closing behind him.

The thing about Conrad Harris was that he knew his limits. Knew them like most people didn't. He could tell the exact moment when you needing him became cloying, when you wanting to show your respect for him became unnecessary, when love tipped to hate and he just had to kill you because he needed the quiet. And he didn't scare me because I absolutely respected his boundaries, and even though his patience with me seemed boundless, I knew it was not. But still, whenever I needed him, he was there. So who was to say what I could and could not ask of him? The thing was, he was important enough to me not to push, and I think most people did. It was important to actually listen to your friends as well as love them.

When I got back to the room, Landry was talking. And I understood, as I listened, as I took my place back beside the bed and he reached for me, that yes, the man sounded manic. But it was just him hyped up, and really, what had he eaten?

His doctor loved his chatter, liked seeing him animated and alert. The nurses were charmed, and the detective, when he stepped up, just wanted my boyfriend to hit the highlights for him if he could.

It was, in the end, anticlimactic. After dinner, Landry had been walking back to the guest house he had shared with me and been jumped and hit on the back of the head. One minute Landry was awake, the next minute he was knocked out. Detective Baylor filled in the blanks with chloroform—they had found it in Brendan's car, and he had used it to keep Landry under during the long car ride—and a bed with chains soldered to it and rations that had been stored at the hunting cabin.

"When can I go home?" Landry wanted to know, and I could see the panic start to settle in. He needed quiet; he needed all of it—his family, the lights, the hospital, the questions, the fear, and the movement—to just stop. He needed to be in bed with me staring at the ceiling in our bedroom. It was all that would give him peace.

"Not for at least a couple of days," his doctor informed him. "We need to be sure of the concussion, make sure you have enough fluids, check to make sure—"

"Fine," Landry almost whimpered, the tremor in his voice hard for me to hear.

I squeezed the hand that I was holding before I lifted it, brushing my lips over his knuckles. He turned, and I put my arm around him as he pressed his face into my throat, trembling hard. My eyes flicked to the doctor.

"Maybe just overnight," he recanted.

"Overnight he can do," I said with a smile. Sometimes medical science had nothing on going home and getting under the covers in your own bed.

Once everyone was gone and we were alone, Landry begged me to get up on the bed with him.

"Babe, I can't fit up there."

But his face, his eyes, the need welling up in them, I had to make it work. Off came my shoes and sweater, and in just jeans and a T-shirt, I climbed in beside him.

"Oh God." His moan was soft and hoarse. "If you weren't here.... I mean, I'm fine when you're around, I am."

I kissed his temple gently, careful of the golf ball-sized lump there.

"I just fray some when you're not."

"Me too," I told him as he moved until I was basically under him and he was lying on top of me.

"Start talking; tell me everything. Start at the beginning."

"I think you should sleep," I suggested.

"Did you call Gabriel?" he asked me, licking the side of my neck, nuzzling before I finally felt his teeth.

"Yeah, a little while ago," I told him.

"Was he glad I wasn't dead?"

"When you're well, I will beat you for that remark."

"Promise?" He sounded way too excited.

"Go to sleep or I'm getting up."

"Oh?" He chuckled, hands sliding up under my T-shirt, smoothing over my abdomen. "You think you can do that considering that your eyes aren't even open?"

The man was like a drug. I was warm, and his kisses, his mouth slipping over my skin, felt so good. I just wanted to be wrapped in him.

"What about my new job?" I offered. "I should sit up and tell you all about it."

"You can tell me about it later."

"But I need to get up so you can sleep."

"Shhh," he hushed me, kissing over my jaw. "Just give yourself to me, baby."

I didn't remember drifting off.

I WAS jostled, and when I opened my eyes, Landry was pulling a blanket up around us.

"What're you doing?" I asked, not really awake.

"Nothing," he said, moving half on and half off me. "Go back to sleep."

"I need to get out of your bed," I told him, my eyes refusing to stay open.

"Nuh-uh," he muttered, nestling into my side, his leg between mine, head down on my shoulder. "I won't feel safe if you move."

"Bullshit, I'll be right there in the chair, and the nurses are gonna make me get up when they come in anyway."

"They've already been in. They didn't care. They both said how pretty you were and how much better I looked."

"Lan—"

"I need you right here, Trev. Once we get home, you can sleep without a Landry blanket, okay? But for now... I need you."

I wrapped my arms around him, nuzzled my face against his neck, and kissed the smooth, warm skin. "I love you."

Small whimper from him as I felt him shiver. "I love you too."

"Go to sleep."

"Okay."

And there was silence for at least three whole seconds.

"Am I bugging you?" Landry whispered.

I squeezed him tighter and smiled into his hair.

Chapter ELEVEN

THE first thing Landry said the following morning was that he wanted out of the hospital. He wanted to go home, he needed to go home, and when he demanded that I leave immediately and go get all of his things from his parents' house, I thought he was kidding.

"Do I look like I'm kidding?" he snapped at me.

The needy, clingy Landry was gone. Landry on a tear because he wanted the hell out of the hospital, that guy was the one driving. I bailed, and as I passed the nurse's station, I suggested that they get a doctor in there and get the man released before he made a king-sized pain out of himself. They had not seen a snit like the one Landry could throw.

Since Conrad had taken the rental car, I took a cab out to the Carter house. I called Chris and woke him up and told him I was on my way over. He was only halfway coherent, but still, he was there at the front door when I pulled up.

"Why're you awake?" he asked me.

"Because Landry's awake," I said, trying to widen my eyes because I needed coffee badly. "And he wants his stuff because I'm pretty sure he's going from the hospital to the airport. So if you want to see him before we go, if your mother does, she should—"

"My mother—" He yawned. "My mother's gone."

"What?" I was surprised. "Gone where?"

"On extended holiday," he replied, moving aside so I could walk past him. Once he closed the door, he turned to me. "You want some coffee?"

"No, I…. What do you mean she's gone?"

"Oh man, she's not gonna stay here and have her friends look at her and think shit about her because my dad cheated with the maid. She left.

She's meeting one of her sisters in New York, and then the two of them are flying to Paris to stay with my other aunt, her other sister."

"When will she be back?"

"I have no idea."

"She just left without saying goodbye to Landry? I mean, she just got him back and now, what, she just takes off on him?"

He was squinting at me. "I dunno what you're all upset about. My mom's the one dealing with gossip and innuendo and everything else. She had to go."

I was utterly gobsmacked.

"I'm sure she'll be in touch with him."

"But how does she know if he's okay?"

"I'm sure Scott told her he was fine." He was smiling at me. "It's more of a 'no news is good news' kind of thing."

"Don't you care?" I was stunned.

"About what?"

"She left you too!"

"Yeah, but that's because she's cancer free, so I'm thrilled, and she's been wanting to spend time with my aunts, and now she is, and so I'm doubly happy. So are Jo and Scott. And me and Jo are coming to see you and Lan for Thanksgiving and Christmas, right? I mean, that's still on, isn't it?"

"Yeah, of course, but—"

"What's wrong?"

"What's wrong is that your mother just left without saying goodbye to Landry!" I shouted, upset for my boy and the rest of them. What the hell? "She didn't go say goodbye to him or hug him or tell him she loved him! She just left! I can't believe she just left!"

"Why?"

"Because she didn't even see him after he was kidnapped! She didn't squeeze the crap out of him and gush all over him and kiss and tell him she loved him!" I railed at him.

"But she's been sick."

"So the fuck what? If my mother was sick, it would not keep her from coming to the hospital and sitting at my bedside and holding my hand and being the second face after your brother's that I saw when I woke up!"

"Why are you comparing your mother with mine? I don't get that."

I just stared at him.

"She is how she is, Trevan. You're not gonna turn her into June Cleaver, you know? It's not her. She loves us, and for now she's gonna love us from Paris. Nothing's stopping us from going to her, and we probably will at some point, maybe after New Year's, but seriously, the whole hold your hand when you're sick bit, that's never been her. We had the nanny for that."

I left him then, walked downstairs, stalked through the gardens, and finally came to the guest house I had shared with Landry. I packed all his things, checked everywhere, missed nothing, moving fast in my anger-spurred frenzy, and then slammed out through the door.

When I returned to the living room, having walked back up the same long stairs to the immense panoramic-view patio, I found Scott there as well. He was dressed for work, I assumed from his tailored suit.

"Are you coming to the hospital to say goodbye to Landry?"

"I am." He smiled, taking the duffel bag from me, leaving me with Landry's garment bag. "And I'll drive. I paid for your cab."

"Thank you, you didn't have to do—"

"I know," he assured me. "I have to pick up my father this morning. He stayed at a hotel last night while my mother was still here, but he can come home now that she's gone."

I nodded. "Are they going to charge him?"

"Yes. They're charging him with obstruction and being an accessory either before the fact or after, I don't remember. I mean, I don't expect him to do any jail time. I expect many hours of community service."

I didn't doubt it. He was a pillar of the community. How did you put a pillar in jail?

"So I'll see you at Thanksgiving, okay?"

My eyes flicked to his. "That would be great."

He smiled suddenly. "I'll be sure not to bring any women that want to sleep with you along. I know Landry found that annoying."

I sighed deeply. "I'm sure that—"

"No excuses, let's just forget it."

But he had brought it up.

"And you won't bring your father," I said flatly.

"No Trevan, you'll never see my father again."

"That's how it has to be. He and Landry, that's not gonna happen."

He nodded."Agreed. Shall we go?"

I reached for Chris, and he stepped in close and hugged me tight.

"Thanks for everything, Trevan. I know it doesn't feel like it, but it was for the best. We were all living a lie, we just didn't know it. The truth was gonna come out sooner or later, and if it hadn't been Landry, it would have been one of the rest of us."

He was right. Brendan Arnold wanted money. It had been promised to him, and his father would have made good on his word eventually, but not in the timeframe that his illegitimate son was counting on. He had been holding out for something that was never coming, and had Landry never shown up, then it would have been Scott or Christian. Why Jocelyn wasn't ever a consideration had come out the night before. She, apparently, had been the only one ever to give Brendan the time of day. He liked her, so he wasn't ever going to kidnap her. It was amazing.

The whole thing had come to a head because of the money, yes, but also, it was simply too much to bear after a lifetime of being kept a secret. Brendan Arnold had needed to be recognized as Neil Carter's son. I could only imagine what it must have been like to see your father right there in front of you but never be able to just run up to him and hug him without permission. It had to have been like a knife in his heart.

"Trev?"

I realized my mind had been drifting, and came back to the present, where Chris was standing there looking at me. "Sorry."

"No, it's okay. I'm gonna call Landry now, but I'm sorry, I just don't think I can go back to the hospital. Are you pissed?"

"No," I assured him. "You were there last night, all night, until the hospital staff kicked you out, just like Jo. You were there, I know you love him."

He nodded. "I do, and I'll see you at Thanksgiving, okay?"

"I'm looking forward to it."

His smile was bright as I turned to Scott, who was standing with the front door open, ready to leave.

"I'm surprised," I said as I walked beside him toward his black Jaguar, "that there weren't reporters at the end of your drive when I got here."

He grunted. "My father has friends in the district attorney's office—he's a generous campaign supporter—so the report of his arrest and arraignment wasn't released until this morning. I suspect they're going to start converging soon, and I have men meeting me at his hotel, and my assistant is taking care of security for the house and grounds as we speak. It's probably best you and Landry are leaving today. It's going to be a circus around here."

"I'm sorry."

He shrugged. "Did you fuck the maid?"

I looked at his profile, saw the muscles in his jaw cord; he was more upset than he sounded. "No, but I'm still sorry."

"I'm sorry Landry's name will be included in the media dump."

"It's okay. If we see any reporters when we get home, I'm sure Landry will use it to his benefit from a marketing standpoint. Buy the kidnapped guy's jewelry, you know?"

He chuckled and ended with a sigh. "I'm so sorry for all this," he told me.

"Did you fuck the maid?" I threw back at him.

There was a snort of laughter and then a rare smile. "No, I didn't either."

"So see, neither of us is to blame."

"No, we're not," he said as he turned at the end of the drive. We passed three news vans on the road.

"Excuse me while I make a call," he said.

I listened as he spoke to his assistant, Candace, on speakerphone in his car and explained that they needed the security now. She assured him that they were on their way and she had already called Chris and told him that and advised him not to open the front door.

"Thank you," he told her.

"Of course," she said softly. "I'm at your father's hotel in the lobby. I'll see you soon."

When he hung up, I told him that Candace sounded hot on the phone.

"She's even better in person," he informed me.

"And?"

He scowled. "She's my assistant, and I, unlike my father, actually respect the people who work for me."

I couldn't argue with his logic.

At the hospital, I was happy to find Jocelyn already there, and, surprisingly, Hugh. Landry was talking to them, and when Scott came in, he lifted his arms for his brother. Up to that point, I had not thought that Landry and Scott were close, but the hug they shared said different. They spoke softly together, and I moved away, giving them their privacy as I faced Jocelyn.

"So." She nodded, her eyes glistening with tears. "Thanksgiving."

"Absolutely," I said, reaching for her.

She hugged me tight, leaning heavily.

"Thank you for being here for Landry. Now that he and his father are done and with your mom basically bailing on him, you and Chris and Scott are all he has."

"My mom didn't bail on Landry, she left her life here. She'll be back."

They were all making excuses for her. "Its fine, like I said, he has you guys. It's more than enough."

"He doesn't give a damn about us," she told me.

"That's not—"

"Yes it is." She was adamant. "And you know it is. He cares about you, he loves you, I can see the difference, I'm not stupid. But if we work on him, if Chris and Scott and I show him that we're constant, I think we can eventually change his mind. Don't you?"

"I do."

Her smile was huge.

After Scott left and Landry went into the bathroom to shower and change, Hugh went to get him and Jocelyn some coffee.

"So what's with that?" I asked her, tipping my head after her husband.

"You know, I'm not sure," she told me. "I called him last night when I got home just to warn him that he might have reporters skulking around his brother's place where he's been staying, and he just showed up back at our condo and we talked all night."

"You did?"

"Yeah." She smiled at me. "I thought that we were done, you know? I mean, we've never been…. I've always loved him, but I've never been in love with him like you are with Landry and he obviously is with you. We've always been buddies, but not—"

"Not honest."

"Yeah," she agreed, nodding.

"But now?"

"I don't know. We talked two years' worth in one night and then—" She paused and shrugged, blushing. "You know."

"Oh." I arched an eyebrow for her. "You guys worked it out, huh?"

"Oh God," she moaned, face in her hands. "I mean, my mother's life is falling apart and everything that happened and Landry and the kidnapping and this whole thing where I know we're gonna be dragged through the mud, but… I mean…." She looked up at me. "He wants to trudge through it with me. How the hell do I deserve that?"

"Maybe you were looking for something Hugh wasn't providing, with Marc?"

"But there's no excuse for cheating."

"No, but there's reasons for cheating. You're just supposed to tell the person you're with before you act on them."

She sighed deeply.

"Unless, you know, you're a sex addict or something and need to seek professional help."

She swatted my arm. "I am not a sex addict!"

"Well then, yeah, you fucked up, but maybe with some counseling, some forgiveness, some great make-up sex, you guys can get through this. If that's what you want."

"Ohmygod, I want," she said, suddenly breathless. "I was so dispassionate at brunch that day, but the reality, once Hugh left, of him being gone—Jesus, Trevan, I didn't know it was going to feel like that. I'm such an idiot."

"Only if you don't recognize the truth and only if you do nothing about it."

She nodded furiously, and Hugh reappeared with coffee for the three of us.

"Awww, shit man, you're a fuckin' saint."

He waggled his eyebrows at me before he put an arm around Jocelyn's shoulders and drew her close to his side. "So, Thanksgiving, Jo says?"

"Yeah." I nodded, watching her eyes fill. "Thanksgiving."

WHEN it was just me and Landry again, later that afternoon, waiting for the doctor to release him, he put his hands on my face and looked into my eyes.

"What?"

"You know, I don't need my family to love me; I have you and your family for that."

"Yeah, but your mother—"

"You are the only one who loves me unconditionally; you're it, and you can never stop."

"Of course not," I assured him, my voice bottoming out.

His smile made my stomach hurt.

I didn't understand Cece Carter running away, taking a vacation like her family had not come apart at the seams, but Landry reminded me that as nice as she was, as warm, as kind, she was also the woman who had let him walk out of her life for eight years. She was not as emotionally invested in her children as my mother was in me or my sister.

"But that doesn't make her a bad person," he told me. "It just makes her different. You can't judge her based on your mother."

"This isn't what you said when this all began," I reminded him. "You said she didn't care about you, didn't love you, and that's why you didn't want to even come."

"And I was wrong," he confessed. "I forgot what she was like, and I blamed her and my father for the separation, but the truth was it was just as much my fault as it was theirs. You can't get blood from a stone, you know? All my life, I was searching for more. I needed more, and I wasn't even sure what that was before I met you. But now I know that what I needed was to feel love, to hear it, taste it."

"What do you mean?"

"I mean your family—Jesus, Trevan, I get mauled every time there's a get-together at your mom's place. Your uncles make me sit by them, your aunts drag me into the kitchen and make me taste food, your cousins make me play baseball in the street or show me their new videogames or try and shock me with what they posted on their blogs. Your mother makes me play Escoba with them, and I'm still lost most of the time."

I chuckled, my hands closing around his wrists, and stared into the gorgeous blue-green eyes that I loved.

"At your grandparents' place, your aunts ask me to help in the kitchen, your grandmother sits and shows me her photo albums, and everyone includes me, and they're loud about it, and they grab me and hug me… it's amazing."

I nodded. My family, on both sides, they all loved Landry Carter.

"I'm accepted and loved and no one gives a shit that I'm gay. The only thing they see when they look at me is Trevan's partner. I'm the same as a wife or a husband. I'm just a part of the family to be loved and pushed around and told to get ice because no one else remembered to get it and we were the last ones there."

I nodded, too choked up to speak. He loved me, he loved my family… what the hell else could I ask for?

"God!" he yelled suddenly, letting me go, hopping off the bed, starting to pace again. "Seriously! I want to go home!"

I went to the nurses' station to find out if anyone knew when the doctor would be in. Landry was very close to just leaving. They promised they would page Dr. Han again.

He was fuming when I returned. "I have a life to get back to."

And he did. He was overdue to be leaving. He had wanted to be out of Vegas that morning, Sunday morning. In his original timeline, he was supposed to be on a plane instead of sitting in a hospital room. What was worse was that he was being kept from going, and Landry caged was never a good thing. Since Detective Baylor had given us the okay to leave town, he wanted to bail.

When the doctor finally came in twenty minutes later, I thanked him profusely.

There were a few quick questions for Landry, and then, finally, he was discharged. He was walking out the door as I thanked the doctor, grabbed his garment bag—he had grabbed his duffel—and ran to catch up with him at the elevator.

Downstairs, I put him in a cab and we were on our way to McCarran Airport.

"You okay?" he asked me, worried, like I was the guy who had been kidnapped and not him. "You don't seem like yourself."

But I couldn't talk, so I grabbed him instead and held him close, kissing his cheek as I shivered beside him. "I just wanna go home."

"We're going," he assured me. "Everything's okay. But we might be there a long time depending on what flight we can get on."

"It's fine."

"You just want to hang out at the airport?"

"Yeah," I nodded. "I just wanna be right there, ready to go."

"Okay, baby. I like that plan too."

I would be better once we were on the plane and gone. If I never got back to Vegas it would be too soon.

WE ENDED up spending the entire day at the airport, walking around, eating, but mostly just talking which was nice. Landry and I never ran out of things to say to each other, and I told him about Gabriel and his family and he told me about Koa wood that he was thinking about having shipped from Hawaii. We bought magazines and made out in a bathroom stall, and shared ice-cream. It was a great day of hanging out. Getting on the plane was sort of anticlimactic.

LANDRY was very concerned with the smell emanating from the refrigerator when we got home early Monday morning, just after nine.

I went to make sure the radiator was on because you could hang meat in our apartment.

"Gross," he mumbled from the kitchen. "I think the oranges are moldy."

He was fine. He had been on the phone with both the women who worked for him, waking them up, I was sure, but they were both so happy to hear his voice that it didn't matter. He was asking about sales and how some new piece was selling and how the fall promotion was going. The man had been kidnapped, his life had been turned upside down and inside out, and he was perfectly fine. He was actually very interested in going out for breakfast with me as well as others, having called Javier and Dave, Jeff and Tim, and Russell and whoever the flavor of the month was.

"They might not be able to, babe," I told him. "It's Monday morning, after all. Everyone has to work."

This was not a consideration, and I was certain once I explained to everyone, they would change their plans to be there for him.

"I'm dying to see the restaurant Gabriel's setting you up in," he said happily, dumping what was dirty into the hamper and hanging up what was clean. "Is April excited? I bet she's excited. I bet she can't wait to quit working at the bank and start training her staff and thinking up menu items. Oh honey, I'm so psyched for you. Your restaurant dream is finally coming true! We have to celebrate and have a huge party as soon as your mother gets back from visiting your aunt." He sucked in his breath. "Oh my God, did you call your mother and tell her the good news? Does she know that her—"

"Jesus, Landry, could you shut the fuck up?"

"What?"

His brain and his mouth were going a hundred miles an hour.

"Trev?"

I took his face in my hands, staring at him, studying him.

He was looking at me like I was nuts. "Baby, are you okay?"

"I am, but how can you be?"

"Why wouldn't I be?"

"Landry." I choked on a breath.

He started laughing, and I shoved him down onto the couch. "You're not—"

"Love," he said with a giggle, sitting up, "I understand that to you this is weird. I mean, I was kidnapped and held for ransom, and I had a SWAT guy on top of me when I heard them fire the shots into Brendan, and I should be freaking out, right?"

"Yeah."

"I should be a puddle on the floor."

I nodded.

"Because I'm fragile, I break easy, and I break a lot, right?"

What was I supposed to say? "I'm just worried that—"

"I'm gonna fly apart."

"Yeah."

He nodded and bit his bottom lip before he made a face at me like he'd bitten a lemon. "Yeah, I'm not gonna do that."

I flopped down into the overstuffed chair beside the coffee table, just staring at him.

"Listen, I know your life has been a little surreal over the past week, but really, my life used to be like that all the time. Everything changed constantly. I mean, my father traveled for work every week, my mother had so many social engagements I never saw her, and us kids, we were so heavily scheduled that we never even saw each other. I saw our housekeeper, our nanny, our chauffeur, but between school and sports and activities and friends... I didn't have the kind of life you had. Once I left, once I left that life and came here for college, between working all the jobs I needed and friends and then parties and guys and everything else I was into—it was the same. It was a big blur. So what you have to understand is that only within the past two years, only since I've been with you, has there ever been a routine in my life. You are the only constant I've ever had. Do you understand that?"

I didn't, not really.

"So we're fine? I have my routine back, and I'll go to work tomorrow. I'll come home after that and make you dinner. When you get home, you'll tell me about your day, I'll tell you about mine, and it's all good. I'm good. All that crazy that we just went through, all that shit, I can shake that off easy as long as this, this right here, doesn't change. This, us, can never, ever, change. Do you understand?"

I stared at him.

"Do you?" he asked again.

"Yes."

He smiled at me. "Good."

I watched him get up and walk to the bedroom. After a minute, he poked his head out.

"I was thinking that when I see Dr. Chang tomorrow, when I go have her check me out like Dr. Han said I'm supposed to, maybe I'll have her recommend a therapist for us to see and maybe make an appointment. I prefer going to somebody's office instead of going to a clinic, and I know that's sort of elitist of me, but that's how I feel, okay? I mean, you just got a promotion; I actually have health insurance… let's get somebody good to tell our problems to, okay? Or, you know, my problems."

I just stared at him.

He giggled.

"Lan—"

"Oh c'mon, I'm not stupid." He grinned at me, his voice low and husky. "There really isn't anything wrong with you, but I am a little too fucked-up possessive sometimes. I can own that now."

"What brought this on?"

"When I was lying on the cot in that hunting cabin, I got really scared that I wasn't going to see you again."

I got up and was across the room fast, grabbing him tight, crushing him against me, holding him so I'd know he was really there with me.

"And I thought," he said softly, "that if I did get to see you again, I would commit myself to being the guy you really deserve."

"Landry, you're better than I deserve."

"You've got that backward," he assured me, snuggling against me, taking a deep breath. "But as long as you think so, I'm happy. The thing is, I know I can be a handful, but you just press on like it's normal, and you never freak out like everybody else in my whole life has. It makes you different, and so because I want you to stay, I want to change some so you will."

"No matter what, I'll never leave you, you know that."

"But you might if I scare you bad enough or do something really stupid, so before that happens, before I lose it, I wanna talk to somebody."

I bent my head forward, and we stood there, foreheads pressed together, noses touching, quiet and just breathing each other's air.

"I'm never gonna take pills or shit like that, I just won't, but maybe I can learn to get myself unfixated when I do that or realize that you being a nice guy and people wanting to touch you really has nothing at all to do with me."

I smiled, so content with him there.

"I know you, I trust you, and so I need to stop being such a spaz."

"I don't love the jealousy, but I love you enough to overlook it."

"Yeah, I know, but you shouldn't have to. I mean, what the fuck?"

I chuckled, kissing his nose before letting him go.

"And you're gonna go with me? To the therapist?"

"Of course," I assured him. "You know I will."

"And tomorrow at lunch, will you take me to see Kady's old restaurant?"

"I will."

"And can I go with you when you tell April the good news?"

"Yes, you can." I smiled at him because he was getting so excited and lighting up, just glowing he was so happy.

"You know I'm sorry for everything that happened, right? I mean, I'm sorry about Benji and Adrian, but that guy Kady, he was bad news, so I'm glad he's not around to try and hurt you."

I nodded.

"I just, out of all this shit, I feel like we're still us, you know? We're Trev and Landry, and we'll always be okay because we always have each other."

"Yes, we will," I told him.

"Yes, we will," he repeated before he released a deep breath. "Now seriously, I need to eat. I'm frickin' starving. Get in the shower; you reek. I'll start making calls."

"What?"

He nodded, wincing. "You smell, but you've gone almost two days without a shower, it's really not that surprising."

"Nice."

He shrugged as I turned toward the bathroom.

"I'll hurry."

But he wasn't listening; he was already on the phone.

BREAKFAST was nice. Our friends all gushed over Landry, kissed the boo-boos on his face, and told him how brave he'd been and how strong. They were all in awe of him, and he ate it up—the looks on their faces, the way they all had to touch him, and of course, the hugs and the petting. Landry loved to be smothered in open displays of affection. He was basically floating on cloud nine.

Back home, I told him to go take a nap, but he didn't want to. I told him if he did that I would watch his shows instead of mine that evening. Since his were all frou-frou girl shows and I watched the History Channel, he was cackling as he went to lie down. I was sure the snickering was what it sounded like when you made a deal with the devil.

I was right, though, he needed to sleep. I didn't want to leave in case he woke up, so I called for deep-dish spinach pizza, his favorite, and had it delivered. He woke up yelling for me, which he did sometimes.

"Hey," I soothed him as I walked into the room. He looked so good with soft eyes, bedhead, and his face flushed with heat from being under the down comforter. He was just staring at me, mouth open, like a fish. "You okay, baby?"

There was no change, no signal that he heard me, no sign of life, and I started to get a little worried. "Love?"

"I had a dream about Robbie Stone's party."

"Robbie Stone." I took a breath of relief. "What made you think of him?"

"You guys used to be friends."

"Yeah."

"But you stopped being friends because of me."

"No," I assured him, even knowing it was a lie. Robbie and I had absolutely parted ways over Landry Carter.

"Yeah, ya did."

"We didn't, but who cares." I wanted to move on. "Tell me why you were dreaming about him."

"Not about him, about that party we went to."

"Okay. Why?"

"I dunno."

But I had an idea. It was the last time the man had felt powerless, and being kidnapped had reminded him. "That was right after we started dating."

He nodded.

WE WENT together, like our fifth time out as a couple, and Kent Jeffries, a guy I had never liked, came up to us as we were standing with Robbie and his date for the evening, some underwear model who was walking around in leather chaps and nothing else.

"Did you know that your boyfriend gave me a blowjob?" Kent said to me instead of hello or kiss my ass or anything else.

And it wasn't that I couldn't handle people saying crass, lewd, crude, or obnoxious things to me, it was more that he said it to purposely embarrass me and make Landry feel cheap. I was instantly furious, and I had that sinking feeling in the pit of my stomach.

Kent smirked at me. "And he wasn't even that good."

"Oh yeah?" Robbie scoffed. "When was this, stud?"

"I dunno, like, what, a month ago at that party at Drake's."

The same infamous party where I had seen my boyfriend on his knees as well.

"Oh." Robbie laughed, slapping Kent's face gently. "That's where you were." He looked at Landry. "I knew you were in the back givin' head."

I grabbed Landry's arm and walked him away, through the lounge, and out onto the patio of the club. There were tiki torches everywhere and those portable heaters, because it was October in Detroit and it was cold outside. I didn't stop until I got to a dark corner. I pushed him up against the wall and stood in front of him. He wouldn't meet my gaze, so I tipped his head up with my fingers under his chin. I was surprised at how wary he looked, his fox eyes, wild and bright and angry, staring at me.

"Look," he started defensively. "If you're pissed that—"

"Shut up," I cut him off, and those eyes of his got huge. "I don't give a shit what you did before I took you home." My voice was low, and there was a chill to it that I didn't want him to think was directed in any way at him. "It has nothing to do with me."

He nodded slowly.

"All right?"

His eyes searched my face. "Are you sure?"

"Yes."

"You sound like maybe you're not." His voice was cautious and hopeful at the same time.

"Because I'm so fuckin' pissed at Kent that—" I couldn't even think straight. "—that I just wanna walk back in there and break his fuckin' face!"

"You promise you don't care?" he asked me, and I could hear the catch in his breath, the crack in his voice that let me know he was terrified.

"Yes, baby." I took a deep breath, trying to make my voice soft as I put my hands on his face and looked into the dark blue-green eyes. "Never doubt it."

"'Cause it's gonna keep happening." His voice rose, getting more guarded and more defensive with each syllable he uttered. "I mean, I've slept with so many guys that there's no way that we won't keep running into—"

I pinned him to the wall when I leaned in and kissed him. It was one of those moments where I just knew I could lose him right there if I screwed up. There was no recovering if he felt for even a second that I thought he was trash. He had to know that to me, he was everything I could have ever hoped for.

His hands were like claws on my zippered roll-neck sweater, he was holding on so tight.

My body pressed to his, my knee wedged between his thighs, I broke the kiss and bent to the side of his neck at the same time my hand went up under the skintight silk shirt he was wearing to the button of the low-rise jeans. I didn't work it open, just ran my fingers over his flat, smooth stomach, teasing, letting him anticipate what I wanted.

He shuddered against me. "Trevan, please," he moaned.

I leaned back and looked into his eyes, which were swimming with tears. "You're mine," I told him, kissing each of his eyes before I looked at him. "No one gets you anymore; no one touches you anymore. Right?"

He nodded, and I felt his heated breath fan over my face. "Put me up against this wall."

"No." I shook my head. "No one sees you but me. No one hears you but me. All of you, your skin, your smell, your cum, all of it is mine, and especially your voice when you scream my name."

He looked indignant all of a sudden, and I almost broke down right there. If the man was annoyed, he was good. "I don't scream."

I just stared at him. "You're kidding."

"I don't."

"Oh, okay."

"I don't," he insisted even as his head bumped against my shoulder, his face buried there as his arms wrapped around me tight.

"Fine, you don't. I love you."

"I know you do, and I'm so thankful."

"Don't have to be thankful, it just is."

"I could thank you in the car," he said evilly, and I could hear the smile in his voice. "If you park, I'll blow you."

"How 'bout I blow you in the car," I offered, both hands taking hold of his tight firm ass.

"Oh God, Trev, stop teasing me. Just take me home and fuck me."

"Are you sure we can leave?" I pretended to be uncertain, biting my lip for effect. "I mean, coming to this party was your idea. I didn't even want to show up and you gotta work early in the morning, but you were like, he's your friend, we should go."

He laughed at me. "Yeah, we can bail."

We walked back through the lounge together, me leading, Landry behind me with a hand fisted in the back of my sweater. I sent him to get our coats, and when I turned to look for Robbie to say goodbye, Kent stepped in front of me, laughing, barring my way.

"You know, Trevan, you—"

My anger came roaring back. "Fuck you, Kent," I spat at him, instantly furious all over again.

His jaw clenched as he put a finger in my face. "Listen, Trevan—"

"Just stay the fuck away from me and don't even look at Landry," I cut him off.

I got the two-finger poke in the chest then. "Fuck you, Trevan. I—"

"How come all you got was a blowjob, Kent? You weren't good enough for him to fuck?"

"You conceited prick." His face was starting to splotch red.

"You don't get fucked much, do ya, Kent?"

He shoved me.

"Oh sorry, I forgot about the rent boys. You gotta pay to play, huh?"

Second shove, harder this time.

"I bet you gotta pay a lot."

"Fuck. You."

I laughed at him.

"You sonofabitch!" he roared and hit me.

I let him because my father always said the other guy had to be allowed to throw the first punch. You got in trouble if you started it, just like you did when you were in the fourth grade. The cops always questioned witnesses and asked the same question, "Who hit who first?" So he caught me under my ear, half on my jaw and half on nothing. With my adrenaline pumping, I didn't feel anything. I heard my father's voice in my head, instructing, and I raised my left hand to protect my face, dropped my right shoulder, and came straight up. I got him under the jaw, which was more luck than anything else, and he went down hard. People don't sink slowly to the floor like they do in the movies, they just drop instantly. I had to step back as his face landed on the toe of my hiking boot.

"Oh shit," I heard Robbie swear behind me.

"What the hell happened?" Landry asked, coming up behind me, his arm wrapping around my neck.

"I dunno," I said with as much astonishment as I could manage. "He just came at me."

"What?" Robbie yelled, crouching down beside Kent, who was already stirring. "You're so fulla shit, Trevan." He looked up at me. "What'd you do?"

As I shrugged, the bartender vouched for me, as did three women crowded around the bar, Robbie's friend Dan, and some other guy I didn't know. They had all seen it; Kent had thrown the first punch, attacking me without provocation. When the manager and the bouncer showed up, they told Robbie that Kent would have to leave the club. Attacking me would not be tolerated. They asked if I wanted them to call the cops. I said that getting him out was good enough. They seemed very relieved.

Kent was surly when they got him to his feet, and he shouted at me as he was escorted from the club. I waved just to be a dick. He lunged like he was coming after me, but the bouncers were big. There was no way he was getting anywhere near me.

Landry put an arm around my abdomen, breathed against my ear. "What'd you do?"

"Me?" I was the picture of innocence.

"Trev."

"I dunno what you mean."

He chuckled low and kissed the side of my neck. "It was over; why would you bait him?"

"I didn't."

"Of course you did. Why?"

I took a quick breath so I wouldn't yell. "He shouldn't have said a fuckin' word about you."

"You're very protective."

"You're mine."

"And I love that, I do, but you cannot go around defending my honor."

"The fuck I can't."

Robbie, who had followed Kent and the bouncers outside, reappeared, grabbed my arm, and walked me over to the couches. He shoved me down on one of them and waited.

I sat there and looked up at him as Landry took a seat beside me. "What?"

"You're going to have a bruise on your face."

"Probably."

"Christ," he grumbled, shaking his head. He was staring at me like he had something to say, stalling for whatever reason.

"I'm gonna go get some ice," Landry said, quickly so I had no time to argue with him before he was gone.

Robbie watched him leave, and then his eyes were instantly back on me. "You're so stupid," he snapped at me, his voice changing to a sharp whisper as he gestured after Landry. "He's pretty, Trev, I'll give you that, but to move him in like I heard you did, what the fuck, man?" His face said even more than his words about how distasteful he found the whole idea.

"He belongs to me," I told him.

"Are you fuckin' kidding?"

"Do I look like I'm kidding?"

"Oh for fuck's sake," he groaned loudly. "The man is a piece of fluff; there's no substance there at all. And for you to waste your time and energy on him is just so fuckin' ridiculous I don't—God! You're such an idiot!"

"Are you done?"

"He's not good enough for you," he half shouted at me. "You deserve someone better!"

"There's no one better, and if you're my friend then you accept him just like everybody else has." I smiled at him. "C'mon, man, my mom's crazy about him, you will be too."

"I can't," he said seriously. "I can't watch you throw your life away on trash."

"Okay," I told him flatly, because I knew right then, at that moment, that we had ceased being friends, because he obviously didn't know me at all.

"I'm back," Landry announced before he sank to his knees on the couch. He slid into my lap, his long legs folded on either side of me as he straddled my hips. "I got some ice, baby."

I smiled up at him as he put the sealed Ziploc bag on the side of my face, his other hand on my cheek, his fingers stroking my skin.

The way he was looking at me—his eyes so soft, the gentle, careful way he was touching me, the caressing sound of his voice—was all a little much, as my adrenaline had died down. I shivered hard.

"You all right?" He shifted in closer to me, his legs tightening.

I slid my hands over his thighs, loving the feel of him. I forgot all about Robbie, and when I looked up for him, he was gone. But that was okay. It didn't matter. I was in love with Landry Carter, and my real friends, the ones who shared my life with me, they understood, they got us together, and even if it had started out as something they were unsure of, they trusted me and my judgment.

"Let's go home," I told him, hands on his face, his beautiful face, as I bent him toward me and kissed him.

"Whatever you want."

So I pulled Landry along after me and then put my hands on his shoulders and steered and pushed him all the way out of the club. Outside on the street, I draped an arm back over his shoulder before I eased him in against me.

"Ask you a question?" He smiled at me as we walked.

"Sure."

"You love me, huh?"

I grunted because it was a stupid question.

"Did you love anybody before me?"

"No."

"And if I die, will you love anybody after?"

"You won't die," I said flatly.

"But if I did."

"Only you, Lan."

He nodded, pleased with the answer. "You promised, right, the night we met. You're gonna love me forever."

"Yes. I promised."

We were silent then before I realized he was humming softly, and I turned to look at him.

"So, what're we gonna do when we get home?"

I just looked at him.

He blushed and it was so cute, and other people might have thought he was sweet and innocent, but between the bedroom eyes and the hint of a smile, I got that he understood me and where my brain had gone.

"If you're lucky, I'll let you out of our bed before the weekend," I told him.

"Who says I wanna be?" He chuckled and the sound made me sigh.

I was so in love with him. I told him.

"I know," he said smugly. "I love you too, Trev."

"TREVAN?"

I looked back at Landry in the present. "Sorry, I was thinking about that party, since you brought it up."

"No one ever fought for me before you."

"I know," I said, reaching for him, putting my hand on his cheek. "I got pizza. Go wash your face, wake up a little, and come out and eat."

"I don't wanna eat," he said with a sigh, staring at me, at my mouth.

"Yeah, but you need to, come on." I got off the bed and started for the door.

"You always think you know what's best."

"'Cause I do," I assured him.

He grunted, but he did as I told him.

I had set the table and put a piece of pizza on each plate and poured some Chianti because he liked it. As I moved around the kitchen, I heard him behind me. Turning, I saw immediately that the slumberous look in his eyes had been replaced by something purely predatory.

"I like those brown jeans," he told me.

"Thanks." I smiled at him. "What're you doing?"

He was standing there, leaning against the counter, just watching me.

"Just admiring my stuff," he replied casually; the mischievous grin was very sexy.

"So I'm your stuff, am I?"

"Yessir."

"Come sit down." I chuckled because God, he was cute, and if I didn't know that he had to be hurting from all the bumps and bruises and scrapes, I would have attacked him.

I was turning off the light over the sink when he walked up behind me and put his hands on my hips.

"You need to eat," I breathed out.

"Oh, you took that breath."

"I did not." I swallowed hard, trying to get myself under control. He had been taken from me and I wanted to feel that he was well and whole, and if I could bury myself in him, hear him cry out my name, I'd know he was as okay as he said he was. Without the physical joining, I wasn't sure.

"You did," he insisted, hands sliding up under my T-shirt as I closed my eyes against the onslaught of desire that swept through me. I would not attack my boy; he was too fragile.

"God, Trev, I love the feel of your skin, warm and silky under my hands," he whispered, "and I love it when you shiver."

"Lan," I rasped.

"Yes, love?" he asked as he tugged the T-shirt up over my head, balled it up, and tossed it onto the counter.

"It's late," I said without much conviction. "You're exhausted, and you need to eat."

He kissed down the side of my neck to my shoulder, then back to my ear, nibbling the lobe as he popped the top button of my jeans and moved to the zipper. "We can eat later."

My head fell forward as I leaned over the sink. "Jesus, how does this happen so fast?"

"What's that?"

"You just put your hands on me… it's amazing."

"Is it?" he teased me.

"Landry," I said, trembling under his touch.

He slid his hand under the waistband of my briefs and down around me, drawing my hard, already leaking cock out so he could stroke me gently, firmly, as he kissed between my shoulder blades. "Maybe you like me a little."

"Landry," I moaned, pushing in and out of his hand, loving the feel of his fingers, the tug, the slide.

"Take these off," he asked, pushing on my jeans.

I followed directions, shucking them off, kicking them away from me.

"Spread your legs."

I heard the snap of the bottle right before cold, slick gel slid between my cheeks. He had brought it with him, intent on this seduction. I moaned as I felt the hand pushing me down, and I leaned farther forward, widening my stance to give him what he wanted and what I suddenly craved.

His finger breached me, sliding easily, and I moaned loudly as he touched my gland.

"You don't get to always say what I need," he told me, his breath in my ear, hot and wet. "I know what I need, Trev, and I need to show you that I'm okay. I need to feel you around me, holding me... I need you."

I gasped as he added a second finger, pushing, stroking, scissoring even as his left hand fisted around my cock.

"God, your ass is so beautiful," he told me, and I felt his cock rub over my crease. "Tell me it's mine."

"Yours," I managed to get out, lifting up even as I felt the head slide between my cheeks.

"Oh God." The husky moan was torn from his throat as he pushed into me. He instantly gave up stroking my shaft, instead grabbing hold of my hips and pulling out only to drive back in deeper and harder, the pain exquisite with the sharp edge of pleasure before the heat spread and became a throbbing heartbeat of want.

I tried to lift up, but his hand shoved me back down, and I knew from the grunts that accompanied the thrusts, the groans that followed the retreat, that he was watching his dick slide in and out of my ass.

"Is it good?" I asked, so close to coming, teetering on the edge of it as I milked my cock, rougher with my body than Landry ever was.

"Oh fuck yeah," he growled, clasping my left ass cheek hard, his nails digging into my skin before he abandoned his hold on my right hip and grabbed the other cheek, pushing them roughly apart. "You're so tight, Trev, you should see your hole suck me in. God, I'm gonna come just looking at you."

I felt my balls tighten, and I knew I would give anything if he could just not stop what he was doing. I pushed back into him, bracing my hands on the edge of the sink, letting my head drop down between my arms.

The sound that came from him was like a cry and a moan and like crowing all together, my submission totally doing it for him. He pounded into me, harder, deeper, and I lost myself as I came, splattering the cabinets and the floor as I called his name.

"Oh fuck, Trevan," he hissed out, my muscles—I knew because I could feel it—fisting around him tight, clasping hard, my orgasm making me want to hold him still as my release sent chills through my body.

He bucked forward, jolting me as I shuddered with aftershocks. When he suddenly froze, I felt him come, pumping me full of hot, thick liquid until it was running down the insides of my thighs.

"Trevan," he said, collapsing over me, giving me his weight, knowing I could hold us both up.

It took long minutes before the shuddering stopped, before I could lift up, before he eased out of my body and I sagged forward against the counter.

"Baby," he whispered, and I felt a gentle hand on my shoulder.

Straightening up, I turned to him and he lunged, his arms going around my neck as he clung to me, his face pressed into my throat.

I hugged him tight, petting his hair, my other hand locked around his back.

"I didn't hurt you."

"You never hurt me," I assured him.

"I used to."

"But not in so long."

"You promise?"

I nodded.

"I just wanted you to see that I'm okay. You know that now."

I did.

"And I needed you."

"I hope you always will."

"Jesus, Trev—" He took a halting breath. "Of course I will. You're the one. You're the one who's not fucked up. You're the one who's gotta keep loving me and never stop."

"I'll never stop. I promise."

He nodded fast and we separated, just staring at each other.

"You're covered in cum," he said.

"You're all sweaty." I grinned.

"We should take a shower."

"The pizza's cold already."

"It's okay, baby." He sighed, taking my hand, tugging me after him, leading me out of the kitchen. "That's what the microwave is for. It'll be fine. Everything will be fine."

"Oh yeah?" I asked. "Everything? You're so sure?"

"I'm sure. As long as I'm looking at you, I'm sure."

And really, I was exactly the same.

MARY CALMES currently lives in Honolulu, Hawaii, with her husband and two children and hopes to eventually move off the rock to a place where her children can experience fall and even winter. She graduated from the University of the Pacific (ironic) in Stockton, California, with a bachelor's degree in English literature. Due to the fact that it is English lit and not English grammar, do not ask her to point out a clause for you, as it will so not happen. She loves writing, becoming immersed in the process, and falling into the work. She can even tell you what her characters smell like. She also buys way too many books on Amazon.

Also from MARY CALMES

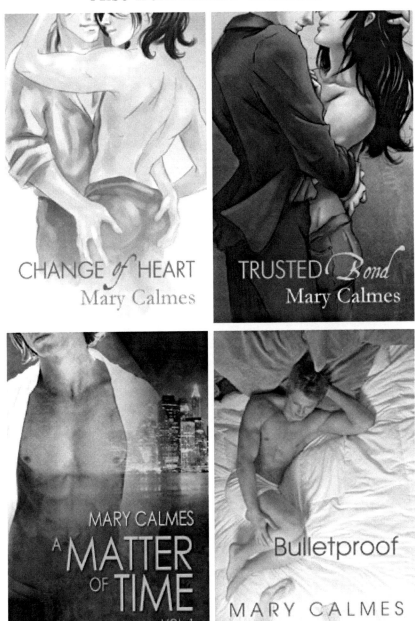

CHANGE *of* HEART
Mary Calmes

TRUSTED *Bond*
Mary Calmes

MARY CALMES
A MATTER
OF TIME
VOL. 1

Bulletproof
MARY CALMES

http://www.dreamspinnerpress.com

Romance from MARY CALMES

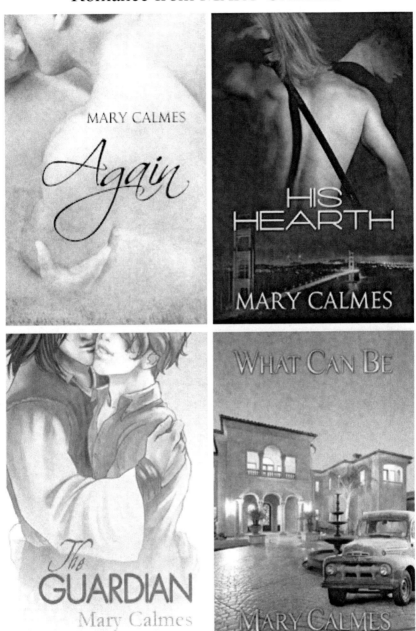

http://www.dreamspinnerpress.com